BUMPED OFF

A HELPING HANDS DETECTIVES NOVEL

JEFFREY MESSINEO

By Jeffrey Messineo

REAPING INDEPENDENCE

CALIFORNIA HUSTLE

BUMPED OFF

BUMPED OFF

ISBN: 979-8-9871924-4-3

Swift Media

Laguna Hills, California

All of us could use

a little help from our friends.

Chapter One

The Office Scene

On this day, Los Angeles City Hall, the towering white obelisk famous for contrasting perfectly with the azure sky, was obscured by low clouds and their outburst.

Further downtown with his view of the intersection of Broadway and 3rd, bare feet crossed on the windowsill, Edward Macondo intermittently counted raindrops and swiped his phone. Outside his window a dilapidated Million Dollar Theater marquee veiled a short glimpse of a meticulously dressed woman walking boldly through the puddled gutters toward his building.

The side stairs creaked. Solid footsteps echoed up the checkerboard hallway and approached his dark wood door cut in half by frosted glass.

Perhaps he had a prospect. Mac checked his crisp white shirt and brown pinstriped trousers down to his toes. His wool jacket hung in the corner from a coat tree, his shoes and socks under the desk.

A pause preceded the opening of the stenciled and flaking door of Golden State Detective Agency.

Even after the rainy intersection below she was fresh as a school picture. "I need your help. My father is in trouble."

"Where is he?" Mac said past his phone from behind his desk.

Her prim mint green dress was dry underneath a long stylish black coat above handsome black boots.

She was a certain type. The ones that made her problems your problems. There were times Mac forgot that was the business. Other people's matters becoming his own.

"What seems to be the trouble?" Mac turned to put his feet under the desk. He pointed the woman to a wooden chair, the one that scraped these floors since his grandfather started the place fifty-seven years before. His father's father.

"They ran him out of town."

He let her talk.

"The blame for the bridge collapsing in this storm has been placed directly on his shoulders. There was nothing he could do."

Mac wrote January 31 with a red felt tip pen on the yellow legal pad atop his desk while he said, "And how can I help?"

"I need you to prove his innocence. Get him out of trouble."

"I'm not sure you're in the right place. I'm not a cop, I'm a PI. Says it right there on the door."

"I saw it. I know what you are. And it is you that I need."

"I don't usually get people out of trouble. My business is to get them *into* trouble." He put his pen down and looked her in the eye. "Affairs. Fake insurance claims."

"The same principles apply. You find information. You give it to me."

Looking at her, his gut already told him nothing good would come from this job.

Through his silence she sat and studied Mac's face,

"Have I interrupted something?"

"Why would you say that?"

She shifted and crossed her legs demurely from one leg to the other. "Your curt attitude is unnecessary."

Maybe he was being a little rude. "I apologize. Sometimes I get ahead of myself. Tell me more about your father."

"My father does not deserve this treatment." She pulled a cigarette from a sterling silver holder. "That town has been our home." She lit, dragged and blew. "They have been our neighbors for generations."

That's what was noodling him. He'd never seen an innocent person hire a PI and it wouldn't start with this one. "Where did these people with torches and pitchforks chase dear old dad?"

"Out of town. His accommodations are the hotel across from Pershing Square," she said. "The Biltmore. Do you have an ashtray?"

He proffered his empty coffee mug. Despite his one monthly retainer — that didn't even cover rent — Mac didn't have much cooking. "I'm five hundred a day plus mileage and expenses," he said. Still, his gut told him the whole thing was trouble.

She pulled out a wad and placed it on his desk. "Here is five thousand dollars to get you started. It is a simple job. If you finish before the allotted days, keep the remainder."

Wads of cash. Now, he trusted her even less.

Maybe he should have given her a higher day rate. When clients throw money around, there tends to be a catch. "And if I go over?"

"There is no need for concern. We have the wherewithal, Mr. Macondo."

"Clearly." And smug about it, too. Mac finally got to it, "Who's your father?"

"Chester Mills Filmore."

"Oh." Every breathing person knew this guy. Chester Mills Filmore was a big deal down by San Diego. A little place called Cuyamaca. A Pandora's box of bad land deals, avocados and corruption. And Filmore was smack dab in the middle of it all. A mayor accused of misappropriation of funds. The woman didn't need Mac to tell her this. It was all over the TV, newspapers, internet, social. Hell, it was such a freak show Frankie, his monthly retainer, mentioned that mess the last time they talked.

"What do you need from me that the papers haven't already dug up?"

"The Truth." Yes, she said it with a capital "T".

Boy, that was a loaded statement.

"If Aristotle couldn't find it, I'm not sure I can help you."

"These fake news people. They are smearing our good name, and it is time we put an end to it."

"Meaning me."

"Meaning you."

These people, the Filmores, were the type that obfuscated, sued and lied about everything just to make it harder to tell when they lied for real. The thinking goes: *if you constantly lie, they'll never recognize the truth*. Now she came here looking for truth. Rich. From first blush, Mac didn't want to get tied up.

His answer was a little less caustic. "I don't know that I'm the guy for this job."

"Oh, you are." Her phone lit with a bing. It rattled her focus for a flash, but she resettled. "I understand you have ways of getting information more ethical institutions do not."

"I don't break the law. Not for anyone."

"Do you do what is right? What is right is not always legal." She opened her phone as she said this and checked the reason for the notification then returned her focus to Mac. "Information wants to be free."

"Sure, it does. Like that water flowing in the street out there." He looked out to the intersection and said without looking back. "You may not like what I find. A lot of people don't like what I find."

"With this payment, I expect you will begin

immediately." She indicated the cash, which he hadn't touched, yet.

"As in today."

"Of course." She stood. Straightened her dress.

"Look, you aren't my only client."

Deliberately, she placed her phone in her small clasp purse. "So, you have accepted my offer."

"Don't jump to conclusions."

"Don't you." Reaching into a dark pocket of the clutch, she pulled out a business card. It was square, made of crisp white linen with a classic black serif font. "This card contains all my contact information. You can reach me anytime."

He read the card: Delilah Filmore.

"Sure thing. Let me just —," he opened his laptop. "Get a contract printed up."

"Oh, no. That is unnecessary." She flashed a grin. "The cash is our bond."

She left the money on the desk and the tea tree mint essence from the ghost of her rain damp hair.

Chapter Two

The Lunch Scene

The Filmores. Of course, the old man would hide in that old hotel. The Biltmore hosted presidents and kings in its time. Filmore sought the reflected glory.

And now, would Mac get tangled in that family web for a paycheck? Normally he chased away the ones he didn't really cotton to, but with the mix of Christmas and two straight weeks of rain, business had slowed considerably. Compound spending the years in a pandemic, Mac's rainy-day funds were dry. New Year's was bare, and Three Kings' Day came and went without a hint of a decent payday.

Even so, he didn't like the implication of taking the job. The aura of desperation.

Of course, he dropped the cash in his bottom desk drawer for safe keeping.

To ease his mind, Mac researched. Although the Filmores wasted more virtual feet of newsprint than the Arco Building was tall, Mac had deeper resources.

He fired up the special VPN imagining a nice article would be right there on the government server. But no dice. He couldn't access the network. While Mac's inherent laziness told him a few Herald articles would do, his professional pride knew that wouldn't be good enough. Mac needed to go to the source, start down in the town. Find out why people were so worked up.

He picked up the laptop and prepared to board the San Diego Freeway, I-5 South when the door swung open, and the leaves of his legal pad feathered like a spirit swept through the room.

"Oh. Good you're here," his dad said silhouetted in the doorway. He stepped all the way into the office, in full uniform, of course. "Let's get lunch."

"I was just heading towards San Diego." If Mac was taking the job. Was he really going to work with these people?

"You gotta eat. Besides, even if you're going down for a stiff, they'll still be dead a half-hour later." The elder Mac was LAPD but didn't carry a gun, he taught at the academy just over the hill. Surprising his son for lunch was one of his favorite activities.

"Let's go to Grand Central Market. One of the guys told me an empty stand filled."

Private investigators weren't the only ones who had a brutal pandemic. Sure, business-wise, more than a few closed. Money. Health. Hakim never woke up in the middle of the original scare. Phil, who ran the wok place, caught it and lived, but hasn't walked since. They say he will.

Dad was a government worker, never sweat a paycheck after he took the badge, but he was the son of a small business owner. If a new place opened, Dad wanted to help them get started. They had to earn his patronage with good food but if they did, he told everyone who'd listen. He knew what looking for customers was like. That's why he never worked for his father and why he got into a line of business that had a steady flow of clientele with a never-ending budget. Although he was twenty years past his full pension vesting, Dad wanted to give back all he'd gotten from the department, and they were more than happy to have it.

Grand Central Market was a building over and a bazaar of dozens of vendors in every flavor and style. A mix of locals and tourists, the place bustled under the graphic neon lights advertising each space.

The two Macs sat down amidst the community tables. Dad with a Katsu chicken sandwich, a spring roll on the side and Mac with a vegan ramen from one of the other vendors. Mac knew the ramen place and wasn't as inclined as his father to try new ones.

This brand-new shop was squeezed between the vegan ramen, an Italian joint, and a Brazilian gaucho grill. The smallest available slot. Smart.

Dad dug into the Katsu and tucked the bite in his cheek with a nod and single eyebrow, "Was the bombshell coming out of your office who I thought it was?"

"I thought you missed her."

"I don't miss anything, son."

"Always the detective."

Dad pushed on. "Is she looking for you to clear her crooked father?"

Mac tested a spoonful of scalding soup then emptied the spoon into the bowl. "Something like that."

"The pay better be good."

"Why would you say that?" Because it was.

His dad held Mac with one of those looks only a father can do. "Don't take the job for the money. If you're tight, I can kick a little over, kid. It's no big deal. Happy to help."

"I don't need any help."

"We all need help. We can't do it all alone. None of us."

"C'mon, I'm Superman." Mac wasn't going to be made to feel like a kid again. Except for the superhero thing. "I don't need help."

"Even Superman had Lois."

"A lot of good she did. All he did was rescue her." Mac stretched out a chopstick full of noodles and blew.

"And what would've he done otherwise? Live a life stopping villains and eating canned soup in his apartment alone is what." The elder kept chewing. Through the bite he changed the subject, "I'm heading over to the garden later, you want me to water your plants?"

"In this rain?"

Dad laughed. "You're right. Well, I'm going over to check on things. I'll make sure everything isn't thrashed from the rain, then."

"Don't worry about it. I can do it later."

"You can't do everything yourself, Mac. Everybody needs a helping hand once in a while."

"That's exactly what I have you for, pops." Mac's ramen was finally just right so he could eat, which was what he did. They both took a few bites in companionable silence.

A young man and woman grimly walked by on their way outside, a baby crying in the umbrella stroller.

His dad broke their silence, "You know, there'll come a time when I won't be here."

Mac wasn't having it. "Don't be morbid."

"Eventually you have to trust people. Count on someone other than yourself." It was Mac's turn to hold a look. Senior laughed in acknowledgment and said, "And me." Then he offered a piece of advice Mac should have heeded, "Don't get in too deep."

"I never do." Mac always did.

"Oh, I know." And Senior always did, too.

Dad finished the first half of his Katsu and dug into the spring roll, dipping it in the sweet and sour sauce. "Did she tell you not to go over to see her Daddy?"

"Yep." Dad was right. Asking was his way of encouraging Mac to check on this character before he traipsed the two hours down to the town.

"Are you going over to see her Daddy?"

"Yep. I think so." Mac thought about it. "Well, if I take it."

"That's a fishy lot. I don't know if I'd take the job, kid." Then he offered, "Just take enough to cover the month."

Mac picked a piece of bean sprout off his soup and looked his father in the eye. "And then some."

"Good but don't you get caught up and be their fall guy."

"I haven't taken the job, yet. I see it, too, Dad. There are already too many questions about this case and, to make matters worse, the only question we really have an answer to is the one they're asking me to disprove."

Dad nodded in agreement, "Yep."

Mac got a text, read, rolled his eyes then committed. "Alright. I gotta make a stop and I'm burning daylight." He didn't ever tell his dad he worked for Frankie, either. His dad was government, but her little slice was more secretive than the LAPD. It was easier this way.

He put the top on his ramen and pointed at his dad. "Thanks for lunch."

"Claro." He smiled. "Come over for dinner on Sunday. Stephanie's got a new recipe she wants to try."

Mac agreed despite all the work and everything else. He'd make it work. Mac wasn't going to be able to act like his dad didn't have a new wife. Or that he shouldn't have one. Mac just didn't really want to deal with it.

His dad broke the revelry, "Don't get in trouble."

"Now why would I do that?"

Chapter Three

The Frankie Scene

Mac walked down a smooth-walled, shined concrete hallway. After passing through the initial security check, his steps echoed in unison with the guard who escorted him. This guy walked in perfect pace with Mac. Knowing this agency, the stealth practice was another way for them to hide things.

Shown through a solid black door into a windowless, white-walled conference room, Mac discovered Frankie waiting for him.

Well, her holograph waited for him in the middle of the long table. She wore a standard issue black skirt suit.

"Edward."

"Frankie." The door closed behind him as Mac found a seat. He immediately pushed away from the table a full slide. The holo, of course, was digital, but Mac couldn't get past the feeling that those things invaded his personal space. Too close for comfort, you might say. "What can I do for you that you couldn't tell me about on a video call?" Mac said, then added, "In my office. By the way, my VPN is down."

Frankie looked off camera

"Dianne!" Frankie spoke to her assistant, wherever she was. "Get them to reset his VPN —Mac— the token must've expired. Thank you." She turned back to the camera and Mac, "They'll get you set up." Frankie smiled.

It occurred to Mac that a smile on her face was always a little pained.

"There's a dust-up brewing. A company made illegal dumps off the coast, and I need you to find out about them.

The real dirt."

He didn't have to ask why she didn't use her own people. Independent contractors were held, or more specifically not held, to the same standards as her employees. This project meant a deep dive. The year was already looking up. Little did he know how deep the dive would be.

"The case file will be right behind your new token. Don't hesitate with any questions." She clicked off.

Power play. She had him come over here because she could. Mac knew it. She knew it. She was visceral. Did things because she felt like it. Frankie was not one for self-reflection upon motives. Not her own, at least.

Before he traveled south to look at the town and start his interviews, Mac adjusted the plan. Dad's insinuation filtered in. He wanted to get a handle on what this client was all about. Next stop: Filmore at the Biltmore.

Chapter Four

The Biltmore Scene

The downpour thundered on the roof of his car as he parked around the corner from the hotel entrance.

This storm was one of those arctic California rains. An atmospheric river. The kind Easterners liked to mock while they searched for the cold weather gear they abandoned after they moored here in the West. The stuff the brochures told them they'd never need again. All orange blossoms and sunshine.

California fool's gold. Sunny and comfortable. But when the storms came: floods and mudslides or smashed fenders from oil slick streets. The intersection ahead was filled with run off from gutters and clogged with hamburger wrappers, cigarettes and sycamore leaves.

Cooling a bit until the rain softened, Mac then walked the sidewalk as ficus berries smashed under his feet. Those same berry filled trees were thick and buffered another deluge. Once he emerged from the tree's protection, Mac stepped up the pace. A doorman held open the door under an arch and column facade of the jazz age brick Biltmore Hotel.

Expecting the lobby, he entered a foyer and restaurant. The spacious room projected elegance with an ornate gold and burgundy cathedral ceiling. Polished marble floors surrounded a Spanish fountain but where was the front desk?

Across the long room, he climbed a split staircase surrounded by marble walls and lead banisters detailed with cherubs trapped between wings.

Past two couples awaiting the elevators, he walked into

a high-ceilinged colonnade. The place was a collection of small shops.

Where was the lobby in this place?

A security guard must have recognized the look as he passed Mac and said, "The lobby is across the way."

Mac entered the comparatively small lobby and instead of fighting the front desk, he bee-lined to the concierge.

"How may I assist you?" Brisk and efficient but still warm.

"Thanks." He loved these places, but his nature was not to be waited on. As they say, he worked for a living. "Mr. Filmore." He smiled. "They contracted me as a detective and I need to speak with him."

Her demeanor changed. She picked up the phone, "One moment." The lady closed off. "There's a gentleman—" She looked Mac in the eye.

"Edward Macondo."

"A Mr. Macondo who says he has business with Mr. Filmore." She listened. "I'll tell him." She hung up.

"They said Mr. Filmore isn't taking visitors. You'll have to call another time."

"They just hired me. If you'll give me his room number, I'll hop on up and settle this."

"You and I both know I can't do that."

As if a guy like that would meet with anyone. He smiled at her, "Mind if I take a seat and work this out?"

"Of course not," she said as she indicated, in a practiced motion, the wood and leather craftsman chairs filling the lobby's center.

As he sat well out of anyone's ear shot, he glanced at the concierge, who was already on the phone again. He guessed she was on the phone a lot in that job.

No sooner had Mac settled than he saw Filmore's kid, Junior, heading for the elevators. If you believed the media, the kid was inept. Mac rushed to follow. The kid had to be going to see his daddy.

Mac missed the ride although Junior was alone in the elevator. Patiently, the numbers above the lift lit up until it reached a stop. Seventh Floor. The lift came right back down, the doors opening with a ding.

The interior of the elevator was mirrored all around and a million versions of himself diminished into the distance. He pushed the button and the lift rose.

When the elevator doors split, he looked both ways. No movement. The hall had a white chair-rail and a red patterned carpet. It smelled of ancient cleaning fluid and dust.

One way was as good as the other, so he took a left and as soon as he turned the corner, he spied two lugs posted outside a door.

Very discreet.

No sign of Junior but the genius led Mac to the prize anyway.

As Mac approached the two, one of them spoke up without moving his chin, eyes forward, "Don't. Just keep walking."

Mac hadn't recognized him in the ridiculous mirrored aviators.

"Truman, I didn't recognize you in those things."

Truman was hired security.

"Get outta here, Mac. Filmore ain't talking to anyone."

"I just saw the kid come up."

"That may be the case, but you aren't getting in."

"His daughter hired me."

"Don't matter. It ain't his kid in there. Ain't nobody allowed in there right now. He's busy."

"With his wife?"

Truman lifted his glasses at Mac. "It's similar."

Well, no need to push it. At least the visit wasn't completely in vain. Now Mac knew Filmore was screwing around on his third wife, too. Or did he divorce that one, too. Either way, all information is useful information.

"You be safe, Truman." No need for a dust up.

"Go on. Get outta here, Mac."

Mac got a text from Delilah: Are you here? Come to room 749.

She opened the door as Mac strolled up. She was in a light blue silk and lace flowing type get up, like a Bogart movie or Carver book. Red lipstick, too. "Come in."

He followed her bare feet into the seating area of her suite. "Please, make yourself comfortable." She sat. "Cigarette?"

At this moment, Mac felt as cliché as a used car salesman.

"I don't smoke."

"Suit yourself." She lit up. Didn't ask if he minded and certainly ignored all the "No Smoking" signs in the room. He guessed you can do that when you have money. It's not that they re-write the rules, the rules just don't apply. It was moments like this when Mac figured he should have listened to his dad.

She made a ghost with her smoke, sucked it in and popped three rings. "Why are you here?" she said as she watched the rings float up and dissipate.

"I wanted the info straight from the horse's mouth."

"My father does not talk to strangers." She hit the cigarette long and steady as she gazed out the window and without looking over said, "In any event, I told you not to contact him."

"To do the job, I need information." He shouldn't have to explain this to her. "The best place to start is the source."

"You will upset him."

"He doesn't even know I exist."

"Keep it that way, shall we?" She smashed the half-smoked cigarette in a water glass, "Now go prove his innocence." It was a dismissal.

He got up to leave. *And when he came to the room, he thought she was going to come onto him. She just sits around looking like that. What type of person does that?*

In the hallway Mac waited for the elevator alone but as he entered, the second lug from in front of Filmore's room followed him in the car. He pushed Mac into the corner as the closing doors ding meant he was trapped. The guy turned him around, looked him in the eye and rabbit punched Mac right in the nose. "Jesus, that hurt." Mac's eyes watered, he couldn't see.

"Boss said stay away."

The doors dinged again, and the lug was gone by the time Mac wiped his eyes clear of the tears. He didn't like that word tears, sounded like he was crying. It wasn't that. You had no choice when you took it in the nose. Your eyes water up. That's what happens. He liked the sound of that better. They watered.

As the doors closed, he hit the button for the third floor then checked his nose and the pathetic thousand versions of himself reflected in the mirrors.

Soon, the lift slid open, and he took to the hallway full of doors with the red, repeating pattern carpet. Halfway down a sign broke his line of site for one of those ice machines. Once he entered the little room, he took a hand kerchief, yes, he still carried one, put a couple pieces of ice in and held the wad to his nose. He didn't want this thing to swell and bruise. It looked bad when you looked like that.

Mac found the stairwell that predated the elevators. The stairs were carpeted and surrounded by wrought iron painted white. On the way down, while his shoes softly thumped off the musty stairs, he got a text.

It was Frankie: Sent info and new VPN. You haven't logged in yet. Problems?

As if she, they, were his only client.

So needy.

He texted back: Have a meeting. Will tackle later today. Thanks for checking.

Then Mac exited the hotel. The street shined from the rain and the newly emergent sun. A gaggle of reporters swarmed. TV, print, news organizations, gossip shows. They were definitely here for Filmore.

Boom mics floated above reporters' heads; lights shined. The cameras rolled for three of the TV talent breathlessly delivering live updates that shot to the towers on Mt. Wilson and the satellites for immediate home consumption.

The reporters filled in the public on the movements of Filmore. Two more of them used selfie sticks and their phones. There were two still cameras, one clicked, the other beeped.

Mac ducked his head on the way through and hoped no one would take notice. One lady looked at the pack on his nose as they locked eyes, but she was national. No interest in Mac.

Until he ran into the next guy.

"Mac."

"Brad." There was no love between these two. But Brad was a journalist through and through. Mac was here and that meant there could be a story. There was information nobody else had. Scoops kept the doors open.

"Visiting Filmore I see."

"Who says?"

"What happened to your nose?" Brad smiled at this.

"Nothin'." Mac knew, any pain he felt gave Brad joy. They had history.

"Maybe you can use that medal they gave you to cool it."

That medal was from the LA Sheriffs. Brad was the type who thought if you were too close to the system, you were part of the system. Fight the power and all that.

Nowadays, he was what they call a citizen journalist. Really, mostly, probably, a freelancer. He ran a blog on Downtown LA. He kept an eye over the goings-on with the city government, and more salacious things like Filmore, to keep the clicks coming. There were those who wanted to keep up and the bigger organizations had too much overhead now to support the small numbers who paid attention to local politics. Seemed to be enough to support one man though. He'd found a niche.

Anyway, Mac was proud of that medal. He earned it. Mac kept moving.

Brad said to his back, keeping up, "Do me a favor and keep me in the loop and I'll make it worth your while."

"I don't want your money."

Brad cackled. "Maybe I could get you another medal." Brad stopped following. "Help a guy out."

"Sure, I'll let you know." They didn't like each other but both were sure the other would be useful, somehow, down the road.

"That's all I ask." Brad turned away and then back real quick. "By the way, you got blood on your shirt." He gave a chin and returned to whatever it was about Filmore all those reporters were scrambling about.

When Mac pulled the ice off his face, there was, in fact, a little blood on his kerchief and when he looked down, there was a drop on his shirt. Professional hazard.

As the berries from the Ficus tree stuck to the bottom of his shoes again, he ventured to his car. Mac figured he'd swing by the office before he headed south. There were extra shirts there.

Driving the car, three of those damn berries fell to the floor and Mac had to kick them out from under the accelerator.

He was practically a stone's throw from the office, walking distance, but he could save time driving over instead of walking the quarter hour there and back. He didn't need that time to think, he needed that time to drive.

As he reached the building, Mac stopped his car just before a prime spot with a steel fold-up construction sign, orange and white striped, city stamp. It sat on a plywood sized piece of steel marking the spot as off limits. Mac folded it and dropped it at the center of the spot. Pulled his car over it and went upstairs.

Chapter Five

The DDT Scene

Inside his office, just as Mac opened the big bottom right-side drawer of his desk and laid a finger on his new crisp white shirt, he got a text.

Frankie, again: Let me know when you get in. I want to talk about the package.

Mac took off his dirty shirt while he thought about whether he wanted to answer Frankie. She constantly pushed him. There were times Mac thought if she, herself, worked on the cases as hard as she chased his tail, she'd have solved the issue herself. But we both know, someone else had do the work. The tactics weren't necessarily available to government employees.

He pulled out the bottle of hydrogen peroxide and spilled a little on the blood stain that marred his shirt. It would take the spot out. He balled the shirt up, dropped it in the drawer, then put on the clean one.

Buttoning the shirt, bottom to top, he wondered what could be such a big deal with the dumping off the coast. To be honest, her pushing did make him curious. It had to be pretty dirty. And dirty was interesting.

After Mac booted his laptop, he downloaded the new VPN package. His new token worked fine and the whole dossier on this illegal dumping waited right behind.

From a quick read, the attention intensified after *The Herald* ran a column-one article about the entire debacle.

Frankie didn't mention the dumping was more than simple garbage. The company dropped DDT out there. Dubious but legal, they made matters worse because they didn't go miles out to the designated zone. The sailors, term used loosely, barely exited the harbor before they rolled the fifty-gallon drums off the boat as they chugged along. They were dropping poison all over the Southern California Coast and, for all anyone knew, maybe those schools weren't over-fished like everyone assumed. Maybe those fish and birds and sea lions and whales and dolphins and abalone and every other animal that lived in the great big blue were flat out murdered. And that's just the beginning? This was big.

And Mac needed to work on this Filmore thing.

He texted Frankie: Got the stuff. Looks interesting. On the road but will review and check in tomorrow.

Mac figured this dumping had waited thirty-five years to be discovered, another day wasn't going to change anything.

He headed downstairs, set up his construction sign again and prepared to hop on the 101 to the 5 South.

A text from Frankie. Well, voice memo. He played it. "They're having a press conference on the dumping. Get over there before you go south. You need to see the players up close and personal."

Mac rolled his eyes and knew what kept his doors open: long term clients. Frankie had been around a long time and paid him every month. The Filmores would wait. He flipped around and got himself on the Harbor Freeway and headed south on another one of Southern California's clogged arteries.

Chapter Six

The PR Scene

The place was called Wilmington Chemical, but it was in Torrance. Mac could see both the Torrance and Wilmington oil refineries on the horizon to each side, though miles apart.

The group gathered behind an empty loading bay with rusted roll down gates, and peeling, yellowed, cream paint. The rain dissipated as fast as it came, and the mostly dry asphalt was sun-bleached with what looked like raised veins traversing the parking lot with flowering grass growing out of the splits.

He assumed, and would find he was correct a bit later, that this Wilmington company was defunct. Any mess like this, the dilapidated building and the chemical dumps, meant the company was dissolved. Our government was left holding the bag. Then, inevitably, people got upset because the mess, that wasn't theirs, ours, didn't get cleaned up fast enough.

It's what this press conference was about. Mac figured the EPA would lead the charge but the NOAA, National Oceanic and Atmospheric Administration, had an outfit about Environmental Information. The government was working to at least educate the public about the process. Mac thought it was a nice piece of transparency from the wonks.

The situation didn't seem to bring much interest from the press. There were no video or television cameras. Mac recognized the reporter from the Herald piece, a local beat reporter and a few others most of which looked like environmentalists based on their sandals, demeanor and aroma of patchouli oil. Not counting himself, it seemed the officials outnumbered the interested parties two to one and there was only a dozen of those government officials in gray or blue suits, panted and skirted, shoulder to shoulder, in solidarity.

Mac didn't mingle. He minded his own business. He listened to the press conference and specked out the small attendee clusters of two and three. Maybe one of these people could lead him to a piece of real information instead of the regurgitation of facts every person here had already consumed and assimilated about Wilmington Chemical.

Little did he know there was another person doing the same thing, checking the crowd more than listening.

Until she came right up to him.

"Hey." She was slight and strong with will. Mac could tell. She went on, "Didn't I see you in the video outside the Biltmore earlier?"

"Must've been someone else." It wouldn't work but he'd try.

She pulled up her phone and showed him a picture of himself. "It's you."

"I know what I look like."

"Then why deny it?" She put her phone in her hip pocket and put a thought straight at him with her eyes then said, "You're working with those Filmores, aren't you?"

She turned away with a finger on her chin, "And you don't want anyone to know." She turned back to him, "But is that because they don't want people to know, or you don't want to be associated?"

Mac didn't have a chance to even answer except for a stone stare.

She didn't need it, anyway. "You don't like their type, do you?" Now, she had an idea. "But this is a great story. The Filmores. The DDT is going to take too long. The Filmores are already coming to a head. He got kicked out of town, didn't he? He did."

He couldn't take it anymore. Mac walked away. Never tried to get a word in. Didn't care to.

JEFFREY MESSINEO

The lady watched him go.
Problem was, he somehow knew that he'd see her again.

Chapter Seven

The Cuyamaca Scene

Cuyamaca, a Spanish corruption of Ekwiiyemak. Go ahead, say it out loud. The name bungled by the ones who took it (the mission Spaniards) before it was taken by the next ones (the colonial Americans). The original peoples, the Kumeyaay, called it 'the place where it rains' or 'behind the clouds'.

It was a small town tucked in the San Diego mountains with the big city, well big sprawl, on one side and the high desert on the other. The mountains were forested with pines, juniper, oak and sycamore. The small city itself sprang up after a cattleman and former slave found gold in the 1870's. The gold rush was on, and the city became the second largest in San Diego County pretty quick. When the need for timber, the search for gold and additional mining over the hill all dwindled, the town eventually transitioned into a gas stop with a quaint hotel and diner.

As a result, the town's now famous for avocados, apple picking, apple pie and vacation homes.

Two and a half hours south and east from his departure Mac pulled into town after enough winding, cloud drenched road to be thankful for a stop. The main drag was nestled under an arch of sycamore trees with a small hotel and visitor center as the focus of the manmade structures. At the end of the small street, centered around an ancient sycamore, was a round-about where, leafless from winter, its majestic branches stretched over a crane as it removed from a pedestal the statue of a man on a horse.

On the drive he decided to get his bearings and would pass through town to set eyes on the source of the kerfuffle.

The bridge.

When he double-checked his phone map, it was clear why the town was so pissed off. The bridge was ten minutes out of town on the desert side and with it washed out, nobody could work their way from the desert through town and over the hill to San Diego. Through Cuyamaca was the straight route. Now, the tourists had to take the long way around, which kept them on major highways but added sixty miles to the trip.

In short, the detour meant no pass-through business. For a tourist town, no visitors meant their revenue was gone. All of this after the pandemic everybody suffered through. Nobody could withstand that type of hit to their bottom line.

Filmore was in a heap of trouble, the least of which would be his re-election.

The point of interest, the bridge, was outside the collection of houses and side roads that dappled the highway as Mac worked his way out of town.

Orange striped roadblocks and a blinking mobile Sigalert trailer announced the closed bridge. Mac pulled as near and behind the electric signage as he could then he covered the football field length of highway on foot to gander at the culprit.

Everything smelled of rain and earth, clean pines with a little dust underneath. When he reached the edge and looked down, a man screamed behind him.

It didn't register to Mac what the man said until a second time. "Bridge is closed!"

Mac looked at the screamer then across the chasm where a throw from short to first was missing from the structure, then down into the gully. "I noticed that."

The bridge wasn't much. Not like he was looking at that one up in Big Sur over Bixby Creek, majestic and haunting. This thing looked like it was built during the thirties as a public works project, with the arch and finials of that art deco approach.

"It's best you stay away from the edge, there." The old

guy had a purposeful gait, giving him a carriage much younger than he looked. He was an older guy, maybe his dad's age.

Mac said, "Slow down. You might have a heart attack." Gulp. Mac didn't mean for that to come out.

Luckily, the old guy took it in stride. He laughed but stopped far enough away that he had to say a little loudly, "I'm fine but you might not be." He threw a chin between where Mac stood and the gully. "There isn't much earth under that asphalt. My advice is to back away."

Mac didn't have to be told twice. He leaped three strides toward the man. The earth underneath wasn't what Mac was worried about at the moment but maybe it should've been.

When they reached each other, Mac faced a guy that probably had more white hair coming out of his ears and nose than he had on top of his head. The bunches were certainly longer. But he had a good smile. He wore a Caltrans vest and helmet. The pickup truck, yellow siren and all, parked in the dirt turnout behind him.

"Ya, I'd stay away from those edges if I were you."

Mac nodded along and said, "I was trying to get a look at what happened down there."

"What happened was while the rains came ripping through the creek, that water brought some boulders along for the ride. Did you ever read The Hobbit? Those stone giants? That's what they did to the base of that poor bridge."

"It was boulders?"

"A combination of the water undermining the abutment then the boulders pummeling the same abutment. Mother Nature had plans and the long life of that bridge wasn't part of them."

"So, what do you do now?"

"That's the interesting part." Caltrans enjoyed this. "This little lady was due for a seismic retrofit, so we'll probably utilize those funds and the FEMA, federal emergency, funds to get the bridge rated for higher capacity."

"Does higher capacity mean weight or the amount of traffic?"

"It'd mean both."

"What about what's going on in Cuyamaca?"

"It's out of their hands now. Like I said, Mother Nature took care of that. It's in Caltrans' hands."

Interesting. "Well, good luck with it."

Caltrans stopped him. "You aren't from the papers, are you? If you are, you're supposed to be talking to the P.I.O., Sal. They'd be real pissed if I was spouting off to the press."

"No. Not the press. I'm just the curious type."

"Well, you be careful around here with these rains. The geology tends towards a lot of movement when we get consistent pounding from the storms."

"Are you saying mudslides?"

"At the very least." He gestured to the bridge. "You can see what happened over there."

"Point taken."

"Now get out of here. You got your informational lecture." He waved Mac out of the place. "We've got this area cordoned off for a reason."

"Ya, thanks for that."

"You be careful. There's a lot of stuff going on."

"You have no idea."

"I don't want to know."

Mac got in his car and out of Caltrans' way. It was time to see this town and to obtain a sample of this world-famous apple pie, if he could. After parking in a spot in the middle of main street, Mac walked the block to the greasy spoon.

A smell hit him in the gut before he heard the sound. Below the stark sycamore branches, he laid eyes on a small pen of baaing goats. The enclosure was tucked not too far behind the empty pedestal from which that statue was removed earlier. A sort of tourist petting zoo. They had gum ball machines with pellets and scattered hay around to add to the rustic charm and to soak up the goat pee.

"Interesting spot for goats", Mac said to himself as he pulled the door to the restaurant and entered below a sign that read: "Try the pie!".

Wafting around him was the pleasant aroma of baking apple pie. The cafe was set up with a row of three orange booths and a half dozen other tables.

A young waitress approached as Mac sat and scooched into the pleather booth. She placed a menu, a water and a coffee cup with the carafe poised in her hand. Mac imagined she must have three hands to carry and do all that. She raised her eyebrows in a silent offer of the coffee, which Mac affirmed. Then she spoke as she poured, "Anything else to get you started?"

"Yes, hi," Mac said. "I have a question. I'm allergic to milk and nuts. Does your apple pie have dairy or nuts in it?"

"Nope, we make the dough with vegetable shortening. I'm a vegan and wouldn't eat it either."

"Perfect. Then a piece of apple pie. Warm, please."

"Ice cream?" She caught herself and laughed nervously. "Sorry: habit. No ice cream and I'll be right back with your slice."

He added sugar to his coffee and stirred; tested it.

The coffee was too hot. Mac sat patiently and waited for his world-famous apple pie, spinning his cup absently. No sooner had his warm pie arrived and Mac dug his fork into his piled high apple slice then the lady from the press conference plopped in the booth across from him in a pea coat and a thick red scarf wrapped around her neck which she was already unwrapping. He lay down the fork, the bite still piled on the prongs.

"Fancy meeting you here," she said as she picked up the fork from the napkin on her side and directed it at his pie. "May I?"

"No." He slid the plate a touch away.

She put the fork down, "Oh."

Now Mac felt bad, and it was her who had been too forward. She should feel bad. He slid the plate to her.

"Now I feel bad," she said, smiled, and dug in. Then she charged forward with a different attack. "Look, we could help each other with these Filmores. Why don't we team up?"

"I don't even know your name."

"Zoey." She held out her hand. "Zoey Clayton. Nice to meet you." She took another bite and said, "This pie is terrific."

Mac raised an eyebrow then shook her hand, "Edward Macondo. Mac."

"Hello, Edward Macondo." She swallowed, smiled. "Now we know each other. I say we team up."

"It's not that easy, Zoey. I'm on a job. I have responsibilities, not the least of which to client confidentiality."

"You're no lawyer." She indicated the pie. "Don't you want a bite?"

"No, and, no, I'm not. Which makes it all the more important to be known for discretion." He sipped his coffee. Burnt coffee. Then added sugar, again. "I can't do it."

"C'mon," she said and made a show of twisting her curly hair. When she knew there was no affect, even a smirk, she dropped the play acting, "Mac, many hands make light work."

"My client's dirty laundry can't be broadcast on some podcast."

"Your client's dirty laundry is broadcast on the nightly news, the newspapers, cable television and social media every hour of every day. My podcast doesn't matter."

"But it would with my information."

"Is that supposed to discourage me?"

Mac stopped. She was right, that line of thinking would only make her more interested. Why would she care about keeping secrets? He didn't know her podcast but, by definition, she made a living talking about things other people didn't know about.

"Lady—"

"Zoey."

Mac nodded. "Zoey. I'm not discouraging you. I don't care what you do, simply stay out of my way." Disgusted, he got up, threw his napkin and a ten on the table without another word. Surprisingly, she kept her mouth shut and watched him walk out the door. He didn't think he could get off that easy with her, but you never know. Mac waited for the feeling behind him. That she would appear at his shoulder with more reasons he should help her or let her tag along. But apparently she relented. Good.

Zoey's visit disrupted Mac's plan. He hoped to pump local information from the waitress, but Zoey ticked him off and now he was outside with nothing to show for it.

He surveyed the town and wondered where else he could go to get dirt. With an idea, he turned around and walked behind the building to the back of the restaurant. Luckily, as he reached the kitchen, the busboy carried out two bags of garbage with the cook right behind him.

With a KN-95 mask hanging off his ear, the cook already had a cigarette in his mouth and was feeling all his pockets presumably for a lighter.

Mac pulled a zippo out of his own pocket and offered it to him. He didn't smoke himself, but Mac knew the communal nature of smokers. Having a lighter gave him access to a space where people naturally chatted.

The cook lit up, flicked the zippo closed. Handed it to Mac with a nod and a look. The look said, "What do you want?"

Mac loved cooks, they cut the crap. "So, what's up with these Filmores?"

"Bunch of assholes." The guy scratched his thinning pate.

"Claro. But is this stuff for real?"

"Oh, that. Ya, I don't know," the cook took a hit, let it sink in and blew out slowly. "He's a pendejo but I don't think he'd do that." Correcting himself he said, "He's a crook, but he's not stupid." The cook picked a burnt clump off his white apron.

"You mean stealing city funds?" Mac said encouraging him to share.

The cook ran his index finger and thumb over his mustache, "Oh, that stuff? He'd find a better way."

What was the cook talking about? "You meant something else?"

"Sure," the cook looked directly at Mac now. "I thought you meant that stuff with Olivera's daughter."

"What stuff?" How could there be more than what the national reporters had dug up?

"Everybody talks about the money, but the old bastard knocked up the girl." The cook kicked and ground his toe at the line of weeds between the asphalt and cement pad.

Mac was confused. "Who?"

"I don't know shit, but it looks to me like Olivera started up all this stuff about Filmore because Filmore was screwing around with the girl."

"I don't get it."

"The girl's twenty. Filmore and Olivera hate each other and Filmore knocked up Olivera's kid. And, like I said, I don't know nothing but I sure as shit don't know why a hot little piece of ass like that would bang that old fucker on purpose."

The cook threw down his cig and stomped, "Gotta get back."

He went inside while Mac tried to figure out what the hell the cook was talking about. There's more history than Mac had taken into first account. Of course, there was. Well, he was getting paid to investigate.

Maybe he could gather a little more of the official story as well as native flavor about the past. He clocked that visitor center on the way in. Those places had two types working there: bored retirees and bored teenagers. If Mac was lucky there'd be a geezer bubbling over with stories.

He worked his way to the main drag and headed two doors over to said visitor center and town hall. The building was at a corner and in keeping with the pioneer motif was yellow with brown trim. A half-dozen stairs led to a pair of half-paneled, half-windowed doors also yellow and brown with gold stenciled text: Cuyamaca Town Hall on one, Chamber of Commerce Visitor's Center proudly displayed on the other.

With a pull on a door that didn't want to open, Mac entered the building which smelled of fine dust, old wood and Pine-Sol. Sort of like the crawl space at his grandpa's house. Minus the Pine-Sol. He directly faced an inside wall with his choice of a city worker to the right and visitor center to the left. Seemed like a good a time as any to stick to the plan.

Chapter Eight

The Visitor Center Scene

The visitor center was designed as both a tourist trap and a resource. They had one of those wooden tri-fold displays for all the touristy businesses in the area like horseback rides, a zip line joint, panning for gold, even information about Anza Borrego over the hill in the desert. There were shirts, stickers, buttons and trinkets. Old signs and plastic miner's hats and picks. Gold shaking pans that were really pie tins. A few travel books.

Unfortunately, there was a teenager behind the counter. Mac wouldn't get anything out this kid. The boy was probably a junior in high school and barely looked from his phone when Mac walked in. The kid simply gave a smile.

Mac was here to try, so he did. "Hi."

"Welcome," the kid said. "Can I help you with anything?"

The kid was polite. Mac figured maybe it was worth a shot. "To be honest, I'm looking for gossip on Filmore."

"The cable news has that for you, mister."

"Right. But what I'm looking for is what they don't know."

The kid laughed. "Do you see where I work? I'm not a bumpkin and I know who pays my checks. No offense, but I just show up to work and stay out of the way. Let me know if you want a shirt or something." He went back to his phone.

Mac couldn't fault the employee, but he'd come up with an angle. A book about the founding of the town was at

Mac's fingertips so he flipped through when the kid took a video call. The boy held the phone between his legs as he sat.

"Yo!" the kid said.

"When you get off?"

"'Sup?"

"Let's go to the mines. Beers."

"Can't."

"Why?"

"Doing work up there."

"Oh - What're they doing?"

"No clue but it's the Filmores or some shit. Heard 'em talk about it next door."

"Assholes. How about the river?"

"Bet." Off.

Mac didn't always have to get the answers directly from questioning. It was true, occasionally, he needed to shut up, listen and be a little lucky.

A local map posted on the wall caught Mac's attention, so he went for a closer look. He saw three mines denoted. Two had tour companies attached, the other was clearly marked as private but skirted the county parkland. Deduction, my dear Watson.

Mac would check out the Filmore mines. Good thing he kept that earthquake bag with comfortable shoes and clothes in his trunk. From the looks of that map, he had a hike in front of him.

Chapter Nine

The Mine Scene

The first two miles out the trail was fire road. The walking as easy as walking on the sidewalk except for the occasional rivets and gravel. Mac soon ran alongside an old barb wire fence strewn from old uneven branches. Eventually, a few rusted, bent surveying posts dotted the twisting and ill tended wire which protected one side of the tall dry waist-high cheatgrass, wild oats and the scattered green sprouts from the other grasses. Mac eventually reached an old rancher's gate held closed by a deeply rusted chain and a shiny lock.

He looked both ways then hopped to the middle support of the gate and swung one leg, then the other, over. On the opposite side of the locked gate the trail was much less traveled than the county trail and turned to a single track.

The compact dirt was light colored, almost golden, and had a fine silt layered over, and piled around, the trail. Mac wended his way from the trail head and took a deep nose breath to enjoy the slightly licorice scent of the reawakening brush. Nothing wrong with getting a day out on the trail, even if it was for work. Especially if it was for work. This little trek counted into his day rate.

There was a woodpecker working on one of the barely budding sycamores that created the canopy for this little stretch of path. The knock-knocking was right there but Mac couldn't quite lay his eyes on the red-headed little thing despite the fact the trees were nearly leafless, just sprouting their new batch of foliage. There were a few oaks hidden around, too, but those stayed impenetrable.

On reflection, Mac was surprised by his luck with that

kid at the visitor's center. And what the cook told him. This little job had more twists and turns than an old Dashiell Hammett. And here Mac was sure this case would be like a Dashiell Hammett story with bratty daughters and gambling and hard drinking, maybe even a little bit of risky business.

So far, there wasn't any sex. The money was front and center with an expanding cast of characters. The Filmores and now the Oliveras. Delilah the daughter. Both daughters. What was her name, anyway? The one who was supposed to be knocked up. It all points to a jealous patriarch pissed about his daughter, about the land, the goldmines and whatever else Filmore had planned for this place.

There had to be a plan for construction because Mac soon heard rustling up ahead. Two guys surveying the property. One holding a tall rod, the other pointing a laser and recording the information in a tablet. They weren't forest service because Mac already knew he was trespassing. He waved to the workers.

"What're you surveying?" Mac preferred the direct approach. Ask what you want to know.

"The beginnings of a road. That's only thing we ever survey for," the one with the rod answered. He was closest.

"No kidding." Also, lead a little and if you shut up, a lot of people will just keep going.

"Roads is all we ever do." He itched his nose and gestured up a ways. "But seems to me they want to do something with that mine up there."

"Do you know what?"

"No idea."

"I think I'll go check it out."

"Just don't take any gold!" The guy laughed and Mac went on his way. Everybody knew the beginnings of the town but even at the beginning nobody took that much gold out of these hills.

Were they planning on a full operation for gold? As the price of gold went up, the more difficult mines became more active. That was true of all geological 'products'. If it's worth more, they can spend more to get it. It was true for oil. It will soon be true with lithium and all those batteries coming along for cars and phones. Extraction as they called it. Gold was the original precious ore.

Mac learned a little more about this stuff when he investigated his stocks and mutual funds. He decided a handful of years ago that he'd only invest in companies that were good stewards, as they say. No dirty energy, no mining that blew up whole landscapes, and no sweat shops for elementary school aged children. Mac could make money off other people's work, but he wasn't going to make it while ruining our one and only world.

About half a mile past the surveyors, light gusts of wind worked up the canyon, rustling the trees like hidden forest elves. The ground started to change complexion and gain elevation. More and more rocks surrounded the trail and Mac traversed swaths of quartz with stripes through it. This is more of what he expected. Precious metals show up crushed between other materials. The 49er's dreams of easy money tended to dissipate when they realized their claims went through hard rock. Less panning in a stream and more frustration as miners chipped for the elusive metal spirited in and out of quartz or granite. This difficulty was one of the reasons the most money went to those who sold the tools, not the gold diggers themselves.

When he finally arrived at the mine, Mac was surprised by the size and scope. Imagining a little hand-dug mine, he found one with an opening you could fit a truck through. In the middle was a small gauge track for mining carts. A clearing and work area had been established long ago with one of the shacks still standing, barely, over to the side.

There wasn't much to see if he was honest, but Mac had come up here with the idea that he would have an epiphany about the situation after eying it himself.

Well, he didn't.

The only thing he got was a nice walk and a wasted morning. The place wasn't interesting enough to make a tourist trap. Maybe they would make a run at the gold market. Set up a road, get in and dig up all that fine Au ore. If Filmore even had the rights to it. Mac had a lot of strings to follow and none seemed to have anything to do with Filmore as an innocent. Filmore seemed to be exactly what he was but, Mac had to admit, none of the clues pointed to him stealing city funds. Not yet at least.

His phone blinged. Mac peeked. It was Frankie: Are you making progress?

With her needling, it felt like he worked for her. Mac meant —actually— worked for her. She took ownership of his time in a way no other client dared. She wanted all his time, but she didn't pay Mac enough for all his time. He had to say no to her. Well, at least he had to evade her a little bit.

He texted: Ya, going out on a boat tomorrow. Let you know what I find.

She gave him a thumbs up in response.

With his phone out, Mac realized it'd be worth it to click a few shots. He took a series of photos of the area standing in the same spot, rotating three hundred sixty degrees. A wide shot of the staging area, the falling down shack, the mine, the tracks. A sign with numbers and letters drew his attention. It was a designation. He didn't know what kind, but he'd find out. He zoomed in, clicked.

The decaying leaves rustled down the valley, shuffled their way towards the mine. The dust devil swirled the dirt, silt, sycamore, and oak leaves through the staging area, past the mine and into a silent chill until Mac moved into the clear sun.

After a review of his phone, Mac was disappointed in his uninterested, detached shots. He investigated the sign designation again. Mac needed to do better, if only to earn the day rate. On closer investigation the sign offered nothing new.

Moving on, the rotten shack consisted mostly of wet leaves, mold, fungus and lichen of green, yellow and aqua splayed in the corners.

Mac walked to the mine's opening and heard another wind devil roll through the space behind, like the wind was a wave at the beach in perfect intervals. The only sounds were his shoes in the gravel and a consistent plink, plink of water.

After a dozen steps, Mac plonked into a puddle that sunk his entire shoe, wetting his sock and killing the dripping sound. He thumb-pressed the light on his phone and found he was lucky enough to find the only puddle. The quartz walls were uneven and severe enough to force Mac to avoid the outcroppings.

Another gust ran by and swirled down the tunnel. After it passed, Mac listened to the silence, checked behind then forward with his light. Would a bear hide in here? With the rains and the cold, this would be a good spot. He would certainly consider it for shelter. And it wasn't cold enough in Southern California that they would hibernate. Right?

Gust.

What was he learning in here?

Swoosh.

This cave was spooky. He rationalized it, that peek. But, after all, there was nothing. Mac turned around and marched straight out, step by step emerging into the brightening light of the open air.

He paused. Since he'd taken a bunch of shots, he filed copies away in his cloud folder. You never know what might happen. Besides, there was more to be found by researching the mine than getting muddy in that hole.

Chapter Ten

The Beach Scene

The surf's white noise hissed persistently while delivering the gentle ebb and flow beyond Palos Verdes. Mac sat on the cliffs above the ocean, focused past the black rocks dotting the deep blue, imagining what kind of devastation those barrels of poison reeked upon the sea life.

Mac was early for the noon launch with Skip. They would set out by boat to check the actual DDT barrel spots the scientific researchers recorded.

Two seagulls landed a few arm lengths away and cawed in investigation. One bird hopped towards him. Mac looked the bird in the eye, "Get out of here."

The gull cawed again. The other hopped, wings out.

"I don't have anything. Get." He shooed them again and the two birds spread wings and flew a car's length away. Upon landing they watched him again sure he was holding out.

According to the report in his hands, there were two dumping areas. Area #1 consisted of haphazard dumping spots on the Palos Verdes Sea Shelf in depths 40-150 meters and contained much of the known contamination from a slow burn of leakage from those DDT barrels. And Dump Area #2 half-way to Santa Catalina Island which, said island, was pretty as a picture southwest on the horizon. Oil drilling wastes, chemicals, radioactive wastes, military explosives and plain old garbage were government approved for disposal. It all lived a thousand meters down, in the San Pedro Channel, well past the Palos Verdes Sea Shelf.

Mac turned his attention back to the water. What was the big picture here? As humans we're searching for a reason, aren't we? A way to link a purpose to all the random, selfish decisions people make in the world. It's why we have conspiracy theorists. Conspiracists want to believe there's an responsible party to blame rather than random outcomes and unintended consequences. The start of this situation began with a company ridding itself of the liquid gold they manufactured after it became illegal. They were given permission to dump the poison in the ocean although it had been proved dangerous to humans and birds and small mammals. Did they really think our cousins in the ocean wouldn't suffer? Or all the divers, swimmers, surfers and fisherman?

Now, Mac wanted to know if these guys who dumped the barrels were simply lazy, dumping the 50-gallon drums in succession as soon as they got out of the harbor or if there was more. They were allowed to dump the drums in a particular radius, but these guys practically bated the entire area. Well, to Mac's mind, poisoned the area.

The more he chewed on it, the more he wondered if these barrels killed the fisheries here more than over-fishing had. To be honest, Chicken of the Sea and Star-Kist both had San Pedro as their main port and cannery for generations. The canneries were long gone now because the fish were gone. Did these idiots commit mass murder of the sea life and these businesses?

Was there another reason? Who wanted these waters cleared of large vessels? The Navy? The port itself, which became the busiest in the United States?

There was fishing. There was the military. Although the Navy base was decommissioned in the 90's during the downsizing. There were the commercial lines. Maybe there was more than a simple bout of laziness. Maybe someone didn't want him, or anyone, to know.

He seemed to spend a week's worth of wondering on that day without an answer. First on the cliffs with the seagulls. Then, after meeting up with Skip, Mac might as well have been solo while they puttered out the harbor past the weekender boat slips. Out of the harbor the hull attacked the open waves, cutting then healing in the same moment.

Skip's cabin cruiser was decked out as a first-class dive boat. As beautiful as his boat was, the captain was the opposite. The boat's shiny deck and slick hull contrasted with the captain's unshaven, scruffy stubble and mussed deep gray hair that was currently pinned back from the wind. Skip gained the slightest touch of notoriety as the diver who discovered a single family of sea horses in the Long Beach pleasure boat harbor. Dabbling in becoming a content creator among all the social channels, Skip shot the local reefs with an underwater drone camera. He knew how to keep a secret because he didn't tell anyone where he found these sea horses, just shared the pictures he took every week as he dove to check on their status. He didn't use the drone on the sea horses because they were much too fragile to disrupt for a silly video.

Although Skip stumbled on that oasis of life in Long Beach harbor ten miles south, his boat moored in San Pedro. Skip was retired after spending his career as a research scientist following the tides and weather patterns for the NOAA. The National Oceanic and Atmospheric Administration. Interesting and rewarding, the pursuit earned him consistent income and a pension. Whenever Mac contemplated the pension, he wondered if he was too late to take advantage of those things. Truth was, Mac could never imagine not working, even if he was getting paid to not work.

Mac scanned the land behind them while Skip manned the top deck controls. The plan was to shoot out to the first batch of barrels dumped and get a digital eye on the DDT firsthand.

A loud whistle knocked Mac from his revelry. Skip knocked his head for Mac to come over.

"You're not wasting both our time on this adventure, are you?" Skip said.

Mac eyed him. "Really?"

Skip tucked one side of his mouth in. "This isn't a 'I

don't know what I hope to accomplish by floating above the cannisters, but I need to create forward momentum and maybe the trip will spark bright ideas' type of trip is it?"

"Now, why would I do something like that?"

"Tell you what, Mac. I'm happy to help but this DDT has been an open secret for a long time."

"Did you know about it?"

"Kid, the docks are the same as anywhere else. No secret is safe."

Mac considered the secret again. "But no one was talking about it."

"Nope."

"You know, Skip, I've been thinking about these barrels and am wondering if they were the culprit in the reduction of the whole fishery out here. That's why they don't talk about it."

"Do you have proof of that?"

"No."

"Any science behind it?"

"No. Just a hunch."

Skip's turn to eye Mac a moment. "Conspiracy theories don't help anyone. I thought you were a better detective than that."

He was a better detective than that. Mac wondered what it was about this particular job kept him wanting to cut corners, avoid the leg work. He was paid to investigate. Same as the scientists in the lab and reporters on the beat. Facts solved cases.

"Skip? Do you think anybody at the old job has anything more interesting about this stuff?"

"I can check but this would be more EPA than the weather people I worked with."

As they approached the first illegal dump site, Mac held the wheel while Skip prepped his little submarine drone. The same technology that made all those drones disrupting the airport possible applied to underwater tech, too.

Skip double checked the batteries and inserted an SDI card. He secured the seals on the mini-sub and did a test of the controls. Afterwards, he opened an app on his tab then engaged the sub's camera. Skip showed Mac the image displayed on his tab with a smile.

For quite a while they watched the deep blue on the tab, monitoring the drone's movements searching for the cannisters. According to the map they were close. But the haphazard dumping spots weren't revealing themselves to the searchers.

The ocean was vast and as they scanned the floor there was no sign of the dumps. Just sand. As they ventured further making larger and larger circles, Skip saw it first.

The continental shelf.

"I knew we were close," he said.

Mac looked between the tab and Skip.

"The shelf is why nobody found them before."

"Meaning?" Mac said. "I'm a land lubber."

"Look at it." Skip brought the drone past the end of an underwater cliff. "Those things are way down there."

Mac and Skip got all the way out here and it was deep. Just the same as the cliffs above the shoreline, this underwater cliff dropped off precipitously. They were reasonably close to the shore but right at the continental shelf. These dumping grounds reached to three thousand feet below sea level. Expensive as it was, Skip's drone couldn't reach those depths.

Hoping to salvage the day, Mac suggested they venture around Palos Verdes Peninsula and Skip agreed because a place like that could be interesting to his audience. The least, Skip was sure to get a few shots of a garibaldi, the bright orange state fish that are never shy of interaction.

Twice now Mac chased around looking for results without doing all the homework first. It was a waste Mac's time. Paid and billable time, sure. But Mac preferred that billable time be useful. He suffered from the rare malady of ethics. Honestly, it wasn't only ethics. His time was his own and he could do plenty of things that had nothing to do with pleasing Frankie and whoever it was that gave her orders. This whole thing was a wild goose chase. Everything was available in the newspaper stories that got all the facts from the NOAA. Nobody was hiding anything. No, there had to be other information or Frankie wouldn't have Mac on the job.

So be it.

As they motored closer, Mac studied the bluffs of Palos Verdes. Hundreds of picturesque homes gazing at the ocean's beauty with little concern with the reality of geology. All the cement and steel beams in the world weren't going to stop those cliffs from falling into the water below. But just like that Continental Shelf out in the water, it wasn't sharing any secrets.

Mac's phone rang. He looked at it long enough to think, not just to read the number, then answered. As soon as Mac hit the graphic they were in the middle of a conversation.

"They are protesting him, again." It was Delilah.

"People are pretty angry with him down there."

"That is why I hired you, Macondo."

"What do you want me to do about protests?"

"His reputation is in real danger. You need to do something."

"Sounds like he already did something."

"I need you to go down there and straighten this out."

His phone blinged.

"I just Venmoed you another ten thousand dollars. I expect your lack of immediacy will be corrected."

She hung up.

Mac looked at those cliffs again. They'd never even registered his existence. How could he win with these people? Mac looked at the financial app and saw the ten grand there. It was true. She knew how to get your attention.

"Hey, Skip!" Mac headed to the wheelhouse from the bow. "I just got an important call. Can we head back?"

"Can it wait? I wanted to get that footage while we were out. I'd hate to waste the trip and the gas."

Mac did a little Venmo himself. "I just sent you five

hundred bucks to fill your tank. Sorry for the wasted trip."

"I don't want your stinkin' money, Macondo."

"I know but that's all I can do right now. The Filmores just paid me off to solve a problem that I can't fix."

Skip looked straight into Mac's eyes and laughed one of those full body laughs. Full throated with his eyes watering. He turned toward the harbor as he laughed then wiped his eyes. "You are so fucked."

Chapter Eleven

The Protest Scene

When Mac jumped off Skip's boat, listened to two podcasts with all the answers to writing and selling books, he was no closer to figuring out how they expected him to end a protest, let alone clear Filmore. He was already sick of driving to Cuyamaca.

As he slowed to town speed at the stop sign, he rolled down his window to feel the chill air and he heard a ruckus. He turned the corner and a chanting crowd gathered for the protest. It was an active town.

Parked and walking toward the noise, Mac spied about a dozen people on the far end of Main Street, half with signs, one cowbell and a small bullhorn raising a clatter around the empty pedestal of the missing statue. As he got closer, he could make out the signs and the yelling. This was his group. They protested Filmore, seeking his removal as mayor and expulsion from city council.

The signs had messages of "Filmore must go!", "Filmore's a Cheat", "The Land Knows" and the like. The one with the cowbell banged in unison with the "Hey, hey, ho, ho - Dirty Filmore, he must go!"

Even while he doubted getting anything useful from a crowd like that, he couldn't help himself, and took a crack anyway.

Then, as he was less than a few stores away a woman off to the side had sound equipment and a mic held out recording. Yes, there was Zoey. She broke into a big grin at his approach.

Zoey removed her headphones and met Mac next to a bush just far enough away from the crowd to hear each other over the kerfuffle. "Howdy stranger! Fancy meeting you here," she said.

"I thought maybe you'd moved on."

"Oh, no. Not me. When I see a good one, I keep at it. And this looks to be a good one."

"Really?" Mac tilted his head and said, "What have you learned?"

"I'm not that easy, cowboy," then she laughed. "However, my offer still stands. You know many hands make light work."

"And you know I can't do that."

Here she put her headphones on, thought of something and opened one ear, said, "We could make a great team, caballero. Think about it." She winked and went back to gathering noise.

A phone call was in order. He needed to keep his anxious benefactor off his tail. He called Delilah.

"Are you here?"

There was a moment before she spoke. He couldn't tell if it was annoyance or if she was distracted. "No, I stayed in LA."

"Don't come down. This could get ugly."

"That is why I called you, is it not?"

"Well, I'm outnumbered. Someone's done a hell of a job of riling these people up."

"Olivera."

Was that the dad of the knocked-up girl? Mac wouldn't question Delilah on her daddy's sexual escapades, but Olivera must be pretty pissed about his own daughter's reputation. It was worth it to see what Delilah would share. "Who is Olivera?"

"He is another patriarch of the town. He and Daddy have history."

"And?"

"And it does not matter. Make them stop." The call ended.

He looked over at the protest. The leader gathered them all together in front of his phone. The whole mess of them were, there was no other way to say it, they were performing for the camera. If Mac didn't know any better, he would have thought this was a TikTok video for the silver set. They kept on at high gear for about a minute. The cowbell, yelling and shaking the signs.

Then the local sheriff slowly rolled up the drag and *whooped* his siren every little bit.

The intermittent siren scared them into submission. The siren meant, at least represented, that they could face consequences. Nobody wanted to upset the authorities. These were good people in this town. That's what Mac told.

The click and squawk announced the cruiser's loudspeaker which gave forth a metallic man's voice, "Break it up!" The sheriff hit park, stepped out and hung his arm over the top of the car door, "I said break it up! That's enough now."

The sheriff's words broke the spell. The crowd's shoulders slumped in tandem, and they settled back to their heels.

"Jesse. Billy. I see you. How about your better senses prevail."

A few headed to their own cars. A pair of pre-car teens zipped out immediately on their e-bikes narrowly missing the sheriff. He came towards the group after tossing the C.B. microphone like he was Buford T. Justice but with real authority and without the mustache.

Mac thought he'd get a load of this from up close, so he moseyed over. By the time he got there Olivera was finishing up with the sheriff.

"He's going to have to face up this," Olivera said.

The sheriff wasn't having it. "Whatever you want to happen, I expect you to get your permits. His breaking the law doesn't excuse your own law breaking."

The sheriff turned around toward his car as Mac came up. The sheriff stopped at a single step like Mac'd tried to sneak up on him and gave Mac the once over, with a single eyebrow raised for good measure then kept on. As he strolled to his cruiser, he shot spit between his tightened lips. Then took in the scene one more time eying the mob with his mouth a straight line, looked at the rest of the town, started up the cruiser and left without so much as another peep.

What was Mac going to do now?

Zoey tapped the shoulder of the leader and they headed for a bench presumably for an interview. As he listened to them, it occurred to Mac that podcasts were another form of independent journalism. That lady worked Olivera just like a reporter. He had to give it to her, she sure kept at it.

As for Mac, deciding to be useful with his time down here, he headed close to Zoey to eavesdrop on the interview with the old rabble rouser.

Mac caught , "...because the land knows. Even if the people don't, our ancestors know and so does the world around. There will be a reckoning."

A wind blew through that didn't move a single wet leaf on the ground.

Olivera's phone rang, and he answered immediately. He listened then said, "Hold on." Then to Zoey, "Excuse me, but I have to go. I have business elsewhere." Olivera joined his wife, they hopped in their old two-tone F-150 and drove off.

Zoey wrapped the cord around her headphones.

Shaking the chill from the wind, Mac approached, cocked his a head a bit and asked, "That's it? You weren't with him for long."

Another smile. This one a little more despondent. She said, "He had to go... Besides, it was enough to spice up the yelling and protesting. I can circle back if I need more."

"Fishing expedition?"

"I never know beforehand." She rolled the cable and packed it in her bag. "This stuff is all fishing, at least in the figurative sense. You can't catch a fish if you don't drop a line and you don't win the lottery unless you play."

Mac laughed. "Just feeling it out."

"Of course!" The mic had its own box then she also

placed that in her bag. "I really like talking to people for these things. I'm not built for sitting in a dark room editing sound. I'm a people person."

"Clearly." Mac couldn't help but like her attitude.

"I am." She focused on him for a minute. "Are you thinking about taking me up on my offer?"

"Now, don't get carried away. I just thought I'd make nice."

"Okay, okay. I won't rush you. I see you're the type to take things slowly."

"What's wrong with that?"

"No one-night stands in you, is there Mac?"

"What's that have to do with anything?"

"That's answer enough." She swung her purse over her shoulder and took a few steps, then peeked back over that same shoulder, "I'll see you around, Macondo."

"Looks that way." He watched her go and then caught himself watching her go. Why would she tease him like that? What do one-night stands have to do with him working a case, anyway?

Mac decided he was getting pulled in the wrong direction on this case. He took out his phone and dialed Delilah, who picked up on the first ring. Speaker phone.

"I need a face to face with your father."

"He will not meet with you. In fact, he does not know I have engaged your services."

"He probably knows that after I stopped by his hotel."

"Nevertheless, he will not take your meeting and I prefer you do not continue to push for one." Disconnect.

Rich people.

And a text from Frankie: What did you learn?

He texted: That it's too deep for us to look. That I have to take another approach.

In response, simply: Sounds good.

What the hell was that supposed to mean? Mac couldn't figure out what it was she wanted from him on this thing. Clearly, she wasn't sharing it with him. That was part of the problem, Mac knew how to dig around and, eventually, because she never told him what she wanted, Mac would come up with a completely unexpected and new idea. He was too ingenious for his own good. Since Mac found answers to no question, she tended to string him out there and wait for the inevitably useful results.

Clients.

A piece of pie waited for him at the cafe. He could strategize.

The protesters were all gone. The goats were still in their pen, non-plussed, chewing hay.

Inside, he sat at the same booth as before. The waitress approached with a carafe in her hand, "What can I get you, hon?"

"The pie still dairy free?"

"No milk, all fruit," then she winked. "And a little shortening." She motioned to the overturned coffee mug on the table.

"Yes, I'll take a slice and coffee, please," he said as he turned over the mug and she poured.

"Sugar's by the window." The waitress nodded and, as she walked away, "Pie's the best in the state."

"So, I've heard." Mac added sugar to his coffee. As he prepared to enjoy that first sip, someone placed themselves firmly in the booth across from him. The someone was the sheriff.

Mac lifted his eyes in question.

The sheriff answered. "I want to show you something. C'mon." He got up and walked out.

If Mac didn't follow, not only would he be a bad detective, he'd be a poor one. Mac dropped a fiver on the table. On the way out the door, he said to the waitress, "I'll be back for the pie."

The waitress was ringing up a customer at the register. She looked up and simply smiled and waved.

The sheriff was already in his cruiser. He ducked his head to make eye contact with Mac across the car and yelled through the window, "Get in."

What else was he gonna do?

As they drove through town away from the empty pedestal Mac asked him, "Where are we going?"

"Nowhere."

That was it? "Then what's with the ride?"

"Well, Macondo, there're too many ears in that dive."

"How—"

"Kid, nothing goes on around here I don't know about."

"I don't doubt it." Mac wanted to know what all these dramatics were for. People were annoying around here but no need to be a hostile witness, yet.

"You are looking to solve the wrong problem." Sheriff turned left into a section of little bungalows Mac hadn't seen.

"How's that?"

"Filmore's got you on the payroll, don't he?"

"Clearly."

"And, that daughter is looking to prove his innocence, right?"

"Well, ya."

"All the while she's got you focused on the city council and the bridge and how that's got nothing to do with him?"

"Batting a thousand."

"Have I missed anything?"

"You know I can't talk about that."

"So, you do have more. You found out about the girl?"

"Low hanging fruit?"

"Easy pick'ns."

"Is this a shake down to find out what I got?"

"Well, I wouldn't be doing my job if I didn't check in on a big city detective, private or not, coming into town looking to stir things up, would I?"

They had done a short circle and were headed right back in front of the diner.

"You wouldn't. You gonna give me anything worth me taking this little tour with you?"

"Yes. Watch yourself. That Filmore is up to something and it's worse than city corruption or knocking up that young lady. People around here are taking sides."

"I'll take it under advisement."

"These are good people around here." The sheriff pulled to a stop right where they started, "Go on. Go eat your pie."

They both sat silently watching the goats. Then Mac had a thought, "What's with the goats?"

Sheriff laughed. "Boondoggle. Jerry Fischer usually gets paid to bring 'em on people's property to knock down the brush but he convinced the city that tourists would love a petty zoo. So, the son of bitch stores them here when he's not getting paid otherwise."

"Makes sense. Either way someone else pays to feed the flock."

"Something like that."

The door wouldn't open when Mac pulled the latch and pushed. He silently looked at the sheriff.

"Oh, sorry." He unlocked the door and Mac got out slowly. "I mean it. Don't get in too deep with this guy. He's no good."

More advice telling Mac not to get involved. He should have listened.

"I won't." He always does. "I appreciate the advice." Even if he won't heed it.

Sheriff nodded. "I had to try."

"Did you?"

"It's for my conscience. I feel better this way."

"And as long as you feel better…"

"I sleep better. What you do is up to you. You're a big boy. I can only offer friendly advice." He shot his eyebrows up in adieu and punched it to close the door on his way out.

Mac watched him go then kicked the gravel under his feet. That pie could wait. The city records should offer useful mine information. All this stuff up on the mountain couldn't happen without pulling permits or environmental impact reports. People like to complain about EIR and permits and such but Mac believed what you did affected your neighbors. And those neighbors have a right to know before you go and start doing it. If a mining operation is going to spoil the stream, well, the people down the line have a right to know and a right to stop it. There's no such thing as an isolated area. Everything, by definition, is next to something else.

Upon visiting the yellow and brown city building Mac pulled the difficult door open and went right.

Inside was a chest high service counter. Behind, were metal desks and head high filing cabinets of indiscriminate and drab colors. He tapped the bell. Printed below, in too large font: "Ring ONCE!"

Which he did. He had to fight the urge do ding it a second time.

Momentarily, a thin lady with hair more grey than black shuffled to his aid, "May I help you?"

"I'm wondering if you have any public notices or filings regarding the old mine? The one Filmore is prepping up on the mountain."

"You aren't from the newspapers?"

"No, I'm not. Why?"

"Because they know that information is on our website and don't bother me with inane questions."

Mac smiled. He knew the type. The warning note should have clued him in. "I'm aware of the City Council meeting notes. I was hoping to be availed of somebody's expertise."

She eyed Mac. "Namely mine."

He offered a steady gaze back. Gentle but firm. "Namely yours."

A fluorescent bulb in the ceiling troffer zapped dark, strobed a few times then re-illuminated.

She cocked her head and pinned her cheek, looked up at the light. To him, she said, "Flattery will get you nothing."

Mac smiled. "No need. I'm coming to the source. Information, truth, needs no flattery."

Despite herself, she blushed. Mac may have started a defrost cycle.

She held up her finger, walked away, returned with a

bound folder, and hefted it onto the counter. "Here's what you're looking for."

"Is there an executive summary?"

"No."

"Have any advice?"

"No. But I can tell you nobody knows what he's doing up there. There is not enough gold in those hills. They never got it out in the beginning. And they won't now. There's nothing there."

"Okay, where can I look at this?"

She indicated a worn wooden table with a wooden chair pushed underneath. "I'd look at last month's. There's not much there. But you might find details worth tracking down."

"Any more clues?"

"I don't even know what you're looking for," she said as she walked away then on second thought.

"But happy hunting. I'll be at my desk if you need me."

Mac took the folder to the worn table and flipped through the pages. As he scanned, he realized there wouldn't be anything more here. She was right, the newspapers had already scoured and reported on these notes. This lady told him something just as important though. She told him what wasn't there and saved him the fruitless search. Nobody officially knew what Filmore was up to on that mountain. However, there was one more thing Mac had figured, and it didn't take a genius. Olivera might know what he was up to and didn't like it. Maybe the guy would talk to him. Placing the file stack on the counter, Mac yelled a simple thank you to the room with silence as the answer, then the plunk of the heavy door behind him.

Chapter Twelve

The Latte Scene

Mac exited his office building. Around him was a bright blue, cold day. A few steps away was Mac's favorite coffee cart. With a let up in the rain, Elise could count on customers again, hence, business commenced.

She greeted him as he approached. "Mac, can I get one started? Anything else?"

"Yep. And nope." He swiped his phone over her card reader after she hit a button.

"Two shots with oat milk," as she placed it on the corner of her stand.

"You know I appreciate it."

"I know you do."

He double knocked the metal counter surface, tucked one hand in his wool coat and went on his way. He had research to accomplish. But this was personal. He would pay himself, too, and walking the couple blocks down and over to the library was practically meditation for him even if there was the intermittent bus groan, newly developed high-rise condos and plywood boarded up storefronts. Still, sipping his coffee provided the separation for his compartmentalization. He needed to keep these things separate. His day job was too sensitive to share in his own fiction, so he relaxed by searching old stories and making up new ones, filling the blanks in the middle. And old stories lived at the library, if they existed at all.

You see, Mac wrote novels. Although he enjoyed his job, believed in it, and loved the connection it made to his grandfather, writing books gave him a sense of accomplishment. He was a paperback writer; dime store detective novels were his gig. Fiction. Well, Mac hadn't sold any of them. Didn't have an agent. He had email submissions out but nobody ever showed any interest.

One of the writers he loved was Raymond Chandler, of course. Agatha Christie. Arthur Conan Doyle. Mac liked to look at them separately: mysteries and detective stories. His habit, coming from Los Angeles, was to lean towards noir. The dirty grimy city. The corruption. The conflict between hopes and dreams that would be dashed on the rocks of the Pacific Palisades like a cheap sailboat. We even got rain once in a while, like these last couple days, to make our dusty city sparkle like the movies.

Mac hadn't stopped to think about it, but now that he did, this deal with Delilah Filmore reminded him a little of *The Big Sleep*. Spoiled kid, rich dad. No, it ended there. The dad was the one in trouble. And if we were to bite right in, most of the people he dealt with were rich. Poor people don't pay someone else to figure out their problems. That's something only the rich do. Like mowing lawns, cleaning pools, scrubbing bathrooms. Some of them call people to change a light bulb.

Los Angeles Central Library held court at the end of Hope Street. Officially it was on 5th, and the Maguire Gardens were off Flower Street, but Mac preferred to think of libraries as representing hope. In the most dire of circumstances knowledge supplied solace. Knowing other humans have suffered the same situation and lived to tell the tale. Don't believe it? Go find Viktor Frankl and know there have been better people in the world than you or I. To say nothing of people like Mother Teresa or Gandhi and millions of others named and unnamed.

Past Hope St. to Flower let you approach the library via the Maguire Gardens. Those gardens, lead to the library entrance with a courtyard and a long reflecting pool with varied stairs on both sides.

He liked to soak in the people milling around outside, sitting on the benches, tapping their shoes, searching and finding a slice of sun or shade depending on the day. Today, it was sun. The shadows were too cool but in a few months the search for light will turn to the search for relief in the shade.

A kindly, stern guard stood sentry to the entrance. He answered questions, was helpful in a pinch, but ask a question that was available by simply using your powers of observation? He had no patience for this. As Mac approached, a mother, toddler on her hip, asked when the library closed, and he just pointed to the hours posted on the door. She turned and Mac entered in the door and was hit by that library smell. Almond, vanilla, mold, conditioned air, wood, dust and a whole host of things he really didn't have to define.

This was a place of refuge and safety for Mac. Not because he came here to write but as he grew up, too. Even though G-pa had the office around the corner, Mac came here to study and research. To hide from the world and learn a little something. These stacks had everything to him. Facts and fiction, emotions and data. The best of what humans had to offer. The library represented the best our societies could offer and all for free. Because it was free.

Mac wrote most days, but he often couldn't make it here to the library. On the days he did, Mac liked to follow a maxim he learned from Ray Bradbury: To read a poem, a short story and a non-fiction article each day. The theory covered many areas of exploration and improvement and if you ever partake, you'll quickly learn the benefits, as did Mac. We'll never be able to read everything, but the habit helped to expand his tastes while inspiring.

Galway Kinnell had a bit of a hold on Mac lately, so he hit the poetry stacks and did a heartbreaking read of pulling nails and our connections over time and existence. A poem of such simplicity and magnitude can't help but change you just a little. Each step forward we are changed from what we were and closer to what we are.

Then with the feeling that time was short, Mac read the opening of Klara and the Sun then figured he'd read an article later in the day. That wasn't how the rules worked or what they were for, but rules were made to be broken.

Mac set his laptop down and his butt in a chair at a reading desk hidden at the far end of the fiction stacks between Au and Fe. Someone was going to interrupt him; he had that inkling which only made the rattle of resistance to doing the work more irritating. That nervousness and drive to procrastinate bubbled strongest when he attempted to do one of his favorite things. How could we have been made with a natural avoidance to doing things we love or were good for us? Writing, exercising, eating well, resting enough. The human psyche pushes against all these things. That resistance must be more than fear, more than laziness. It is central to our being but all the more confusing for its closeness, too buried within our own hearts.

But Mac needed to get his character through the next plot point. They just found another body and they thought the person was the source of an important clue. The laptop booted and Mac settled himself with his fingers on the keyboard, took a deep breath and he got a text, on silent, of course. He felt his phone rattle in his pocket. Then he felt three more. It was important. He pulled the phone to look, and Frankie dropped a string of half a dozen texts and Mac knew he wasn't working on his book today. The DDT thing took a turn.

All the cargo ships are still lined up outside the harbor like it's Saturday night at the club. Not too long ago, there would be times the ships got clogged up but since the pandemic, the lines never dissipated. They stretched for fifteen and twenty miles down the coast. In fact, not long ago one of the ship's anchors dragged along the sea floor and ruptured an oil line from one of the offshore oil docks a little south in Huntington Beach. That spill sullied beaches for miles both north and south killing wildlife and threatening the Bolsa Chica wetlands which sat right next to the rig.

Well, one of those anchors may have created its havoc in a different way. It looked like this cargo ship, *The Constitution*, drifted in the same tide as one of those dumping boats from half a century ago and had burst at least a handful of those drums full of the chemical. This idea that there was so much ocean, the water would dissipate the deadly pesticide was clearly a bad one because an entire school of fish was found floating by a pleasure boat. However, the fish weren't the only casualties. Two thresher sharks and a handful of sea lions also suffered fatal poisoning.

All of this was tragic, and the information was useful, but Mac didn't understand how he fit in the equation. He wasn't a reporter nor was he a government investigator. Most of that information had already been found and written up in the paper and to Frankie's department. She clearly had the preliminary report because she sent it over.

He texted her once he read that executive summary: 'What do you want me to do with this information?'

Her text: 'Why didn't you warn me this would happen?'

'Not my job.'

'It's a failure of imagination, Mac.'

'Right.' Maybe he was a sounding board today. He might get to work on his book after all. 'Good thing you have all that staff to pick up the slack. LMK if I can do anything.' Shit, he hit send before he could catch himself from being helpful. She'd always find more work for him. His phone rang.

Frankie started with, "Glad you offered."

Mac stuffed his laptop in his bag, "Hold on." He marched outside.

She filled his ears as he worked his way through the stacks, down a flight of stairs and onto 5th Ave. "There seems to be good information on all this DDT stuff in a storage unit in Torrance."

"Good, you know where it is. You don't need me. Subpoena it."

"No time. I need it now."

"I'm not breaking in. You don't pay me to break the law, Frankie."

"I'm not asking you to do that. You are resourceful.

There are many ways to get into a storage unit. Find a way."

"I sold my bolt cutters on OfferUp."

"I'm sure you'll think of something. I'll send the pertinent info."

"These projects are such a joy, Frankie."

"That's why you keep coming back!" Off.

Chapter Thirteen

The Storage Unit Scene

The parking lot of the WeStoreIt facility had a flattened box in the closest space, just past the blue placards spot, next to the manager's door. The box covered much of the area between the two lines and was marred with oil spots eating away the paper. That's where Mac parked. The drive-in gate to the facility was closed and he didn't want to waste time waiting for someone so he could jump their coattails into the place. Besides some of these places close after every car like a parking lot.

As a reasonably permanent structure, this place had an unshakable sense of transience. The whole vibe shook with untethered things forgotten but not discarded.

Mac pulled the aluminum framed glass door. Locked. He hit the grimy, no longer white buzzer marked "Ring Bell for Service" which buzzed. He found and waved to the camera tucked in the corner between wall, roof and spiderwebs. The lock now buzzed to a different tone and Mac pulled the door open. He was surprised.

This office, itself, was spotless. It smelled of cleaning fluid and cardboard, of which there were ceiling high stacks of boxes in three sizes awaiting purchase and assembly. But for the wear spots, the linoleum floor sparkled. A refrigerator cart and a pile of nicely folded moving blankets were all stacked in the opposite corner.

Officious and organized. Mac was going to need to be good to get the information out of this guy, but he was up to the task.

The man had a tuft of light brown hair on top of his head, a little too long. His bushy sideburns, mustache and goatee beard all moved with his question, "What can I do for you?"

"I just got hired by a company that has a unit I'd like to get into. Is there any way you can help me with that?"

"Those things are private property. We don't have access. If you have a key, you can get in. Otherwise, you're out of luck."

Of course, Mac knew all of that but some of these places rent the lock and, in that case, they have a master. Mac told him as much.

"Not here. The owner's old school. Bring your own lock. The only time we use ours is when they don't pay." He laughed a touch. Not a hard laugh, one of those knowing ones.

Mac agreed, "I bet. So, you don't have any restrictions on those locks."

"Nope."

"So, I could use any one I want?

"Sure."

"And the place is locked all the time?"

"You see that. Some places leave the gate open all the time but, here, they like to control access. We take security serious."

"Yep, I see that. You have to have a unit to get in."

"Just gotta have a unit to get in."

A single nod, "Ok. Thanks. Good thing I got one. Can you buzz me in?"

"Sure thing."

The guy buzzed Mac through as Mac pulled his car to the gate. First level defeated.

Mac followed the ascending numbers on the one car garage sized and half sized roll top doors, all bright green. He was looking for 465. Two turns and a short stretch dropped him to his destination. Mac spotted the security camera orb three spaces down and across the way. He pulled close in front of his spot.

As he bent to the lock, Mac checked his line of sight and it looked like between the car and keeping his back to those cameras, they wouldn't be able to discern his actions. Then Mac pulled out his pick set and went to work. The TV shows like to make picking a lock look easy. The truth is: it is. For those who practice. Just like playing piano is easy when you play an hour or eight a day. It's a matter of learning feel with the tools.

In short, this was an old lock with a door that had a tiny ledge that covered the mechanism. Luckily, it wasn't overly rusted. Mac inserted his picks, raked the pins a little until they set and voila! Unlocked lock. He pulled the lock, discreetly put his tools in his pocket and prepared himself for the inevitable reams of paper he was about to rifle through.

Grabbing the centered handle, Mac took a deep breath, who knew how long it'd been since it was opened, Mac hated dust, and pulled. Thwaaaa-vap!

It was empty. Swept and empty.

Craps.

Mac took a picture with his phone, door to rear wall nothing but shining concrete. He sent the pic to Frankie with nothing but a question mark.

Here's what she wrote: Oh. Thanks for trying.

A fat waste of time.

But Mac was circumspect. Frankie paid her bills on time.

He locked the thing up and, after sitting in his car, checked his emails. Mostly marketing messages and social media notifications. Then he swiped down to one from Zoey with the subject: Look what I found!

His phone rang. Dammit. Frankie. He clicked to answer.

"What's up?"

"I have another string I need you to chase."

"No more wild goose chases today."

"You're a detective. They are all wild goose chases."

"Until they're not."

"Isn't that what you're chasing, Mac, the solution to the puzzle?"

"Yes. What do you want?"

"Check your email, I sent it while we were talking."

"Great. Will do."

"You're the best."

"That's why you use me."

"Let me know what you find." Off.

He went to his email and not for the last time today, he was surprised.

These never work out the way you expect them to. Even when he didn't know what the heck it was he was chasing, Mac didn't think any of it would end up the way it did.

Upon checking, there was the email from Frankie. But what also came in his box at the same time was an email from one of the agents Mac had queried about his book. These were the emails he anticipated constantly and filled him with fear when they finally arrived. He didn't want to open it, but he was excited to find out. That moment between exhilaration, fear and not knowing, Mac was beginning to think being on that precipice was the thing that kept him going. The possibility. Like checking your lottery numbers.

Mostly, you're sure you don't have the right ones, but you could. What if you did? The lottery was buying a dream, paying a dollar not to really win the big prize. It was simply a dollar to dream about what you would do if you did. A dream that could break all chains and restrictions. Mac dreaded the rejection but loved the dream. He was a working man. His family were working people. He had been taught that the work is its own reward and he believed that down to his bones. Mac would continue to work on his books, build upon his dreams with words like bricks in a wall because he clicked the email. And the email began "Thank you..."

Do you need to read any further? You do not. It was a no. A well-crafted answer to his question of their interest but a negative response none the less. All about subjectivity and consideration and whatever. He would read it closer later when the sting receded. For now, it was just another rejection. And so it goes.

Before he dug into Frankie's information and with another taste of curiosity, Mac clicked on Zoey's discovery email. He wondered what enlightening bit Zoey had discovered about the Filmores.

But, of course, what came was not what Mac anticipated. She sent him a picture from The Herald when he was kid. She found the picture of Mac and his mom. They won a local chess club mother & son event and got their picture in the paper as a human-interest story. The picture was a wonderful one. Mac just nine years old, not even up to his mother's shoulders with his mother grinning the proud grin of victory. He closed it. That picture broke his heart, every time. Still.

Closing that door for now, Mac didn't want to delve into Frankie's documents just now. He knew he had to dig into all of whatever it was that she sent but maybe he could focus a little better after lunch. Procrastination wasn't going to get the case solved but it wasn't going to get done with a grumbling stomach, either.

As it happened, Mac remembered seeing one of those little huts on a corner a few blocks away. He loved those places. A parking lot and a four-walled kitchen. Because of his allergies Mac had worked out a system. He grabbed a carne asada burrito. This joint put in beans, rice, salsa and, to Mac's relief, they were offended when he double checked no cheese and if the guac had crema in it. Their burritos never have cheese. The offense not only meant the food would be good but that they didn't cheapen the guacamole by thinning it out, by which, threatening Mac's life.

Before the guy pushed his burrito and tamarindo drink out the tiny window onto the small counter outside, he announced it on the speaker. Mac was the only one standing outside the white and blue trimmed place. A place that made the announcements when nobody else waited? No other customers? Nothing was going to change how they did things.

Mac dug in and the beans were probably as much

manteca as beans, the carne was tender and tasty, the guacamole, perfect. Salsa hot but with flavor, good tortilla. He'd have to remember this one. Nothing like a proper burrito.

He chewed the latest developments while he did the same with his food. This DDT thing was headed nowhere. He knew it was mostly a discovery job meant to dig up what no one else could. Frankie expected him to find a nugget nobody had found, yet. This type of thing took a particular kind of patience. Invariably, Mac couldn't muster that peace of mind necessary to wait out the unearthing although the restlessness is what shakes the nuggets out. The yin and yang of it was ridiculous, as in all things.

Mac had the information everybody else had. He knew those barrels were off the coast and was still surprised at how little had been done about them, although, we all knew through experience, they weren't easy to get to. Now, he had been thwarted by a cleared out storage unit. After all this time could there really be that much information hidden? Of course, there could. Mac had seen how if a secret was kept for a certain amount of time, say a couple years, eventually everyone forgets about the issue and then that secret stays hidden. Chasing decades old clues takes serious, and precise, blasting.

Now the Filmores were another story. Getting hired by the daughter, Delilah, was a little out of left field but not in the realm of impossibility. Having Zoey and her podcast trying to jump into his efforts was an annoyance but nothing he couldn't handle. But those crazies around the town? Mac had already witnessed a protest. People had their dander up about Chester Filmore. And mark it. Mac did not think this would end well for that man. The sheriff seemed a law-abiding sort. Like he would be as non-partisan as the job would allow but when big groups of people are upset, well, let's just say even the rule of the majority is not always a clean fight.

Chapter Fourteen

The Restaurant Scene

At a table, a big round one, in the center of the restaurant, Mac talked with two friends from school. These were the old friends, the ones who knew him not from work or family, they are the ones who knew him from being a kid. You know, an idiot. But they also knew him as a big hearted, over committed asshole who would do anything for them. Whatever they needed. Anytime, anywhere. Nicki went all the way back to junior high school and Alan to elementary school

There were three of them tonight in the well-lit and open restaurant. This was a new, stylish place. These places didn't do dark and smoky. Now they did light and airy. But don't be fooled, even in a well-lit room there are shadows. Dark shadows where no one can see.

But this night wasn't about the shadows. This night was about food and friends, laughter and good times.

Zoey walked in the restaurant with a cute friend. Before she could address the hostess, she locked eyes with Mac across the open restaurant, he preferred to face the door, and Zoey walked right past the hostess and approached their round table in the middle of the place.

"Well, hello, Macondo!"

The table dropped silent, and the entire group faced her expectantly. Who was this?

That's exactly what Nicki said. "Who is this?" Nicki said with a smile she shared between them both that asked *who's this cutie and why haven't I heard about her?*

Mac rolled his eyes and braced himself while Zoey, well, did what Zoey does. Zoey loved this.

"Hi! I'm Zoey Forsythe. Mac and I are working a case together."

Here's where Alan popped in, "Zoey Forsythe? From *Tried and True?*"

"You're a listener?" Zoey couldn't have been more enthusiastic.

"I LOVE your show!" Except Nicki was somehow more enthusiastic. "Sit, sit, sit!"

Alan chimed in, "Of course, join us!"

"We don't want to intrude," Zoey said while she searched for a chair.

Now Nicki stood and the waiter brought chairs for their new friends.

As Zoey took her seat, she said, "By the way this is my friend Lori."

Greetings spun around the table and two of Mac's worlds swirled like flotsam at low tide.

"What job are you working together?"

"Well. We're sharing information about Filmore."

"Are you?" Nicki nodded encouragingly to Zoey and smiled at Mac.

"Not exactly," Mac said. Bouncing his own eyes between the two ladies.

Zoey leaned in conspiratorially to Nicki but said it to the whole table, "We're working together, he just doesn't know it, yet."

The table laughed. They knew it. Classic Mac. Everybody knew what was happening but Mac, who simply said, "What?"

Nicki didn't want to push too far so changed the subject to lighter fare. "Mac, did you get that pic I sent over?" She addressed the table, "I sent over a pic of him and his mom from the paper where they won a chess tournament."

A silence quickly hummed from the old friends. The visitors were lost, confused by the change in mood.

Alan said, "It is a great one."

"Love it." Nicki was testing the temperature.

Then Mac thought he could alleviate the tension. "They

are acting weird because that's the picture that gets paraded around when my mom's talked about. She died not too long after that."

"Oh." Zoey felt stupid. "I'm sorry. I thought it was cute."

Mac was thirty and people still felt sorry for him from something more than half a lifetime ago. Lots of bad things happen in people's lives. Much worse. Wars, famine, disasters.

"It changes like the weather. Sometimes he mopes and sometimes it's nothing," Alan said.

Except his friends. They carried him through that storm, they earned the right to a little ribbing.

"Hey now," Mac said, not sure if he should defend himself or just sit back for the ride.

Nicki jumped in. "She was great. Everybody loved her."

If his mother was here, he would be a different man. We can only be who we are. What we're born with and what we experience both shape us and will continue to shape us throughout our lives. Mac was a firm believer that what defined a person was not what happened to them but how they responded to the situation. As they say, it takes pressure to make a diamond.

Good thing because this situation was not for the faint of heart. It's not what you think. Mac can face death defying bad guys. What he can't face is the blending of his worlds. He had done a fine job of keeping everything compartmentalized. Work here, friends here, family there. Each confined to its own little space where he wasn't forced to confront any of them at the same time.

Around Nicki and Alan was the only time Mac didn't fight for control. Don't get it wrong, Mac never had control. In fact, his whole life felt like he was winging it but out on the job, he kept things tight and professional. He could let his guard down a bit with these few people. And now Zoey and her little friend were here. Mucking up his night and putting pressure on the job. No way.

This is when the waiter dropped off the check.

As Mac stood out of his chair he said, "Zoey, we're just about done. I'm going to have Brian get you a table. You don't want to sit around our empty plates and sappy goodbyes." He left the table before anyone could protest and returned with the owner who bowed with a towel over his arm and two menus in his hand.

The owner said, "A wonderful two-top just opened at the window."

Zoey squinted at Mac, but her friend popped up, embarrassed, and took him up on the offer. Lori said, "That sounds great! Nice to meet you all." She skedaddled like a puppy off the leash.

Zoey addressed the table and stood, "Sorry if I intruded."

"Nobody thinks you intruded," Nicki said. "It's just Mac's an asshole."

Mac smiled with nothing behind his eyes, "Good to see you, Zoey."

Zoey followed her friend to the other table, leaving two pairs of evil eyes directed at Mac.

"What?"

Silence.

"I like to keep my worlds separate."

"No, shit. All this compartmentalization is going to sink you," Alan said. "And you might have just found your iceberg."

Nicki said, "You really are a piece of work, aren't you? Get out of your own way, Edward Macondo."

"I don't want to talk about it. My business is my business. I have a legacy to carry on. It's about more than just me," Mac said.

Nicki wasn't buying it. "I don't pretend to know everything, but I know your grandpa wouldn't want you to be alone in your office all day then alone in your apartment at night."

"Do better, Mac," Alan said.

This was a losing fight and Mac had his own things to worry about, so he did what he does, "Okay, okay. I'll do better." He got up to leave and while he hugged them both said, "I'm going to roll. I have an early meeting and have to go back down to Cuyamaca." He then grabbed the check which had sat untouched across the table. "I've got this. Love you guys," he gave a wave and tucked some bills in the bill fold as he handed it to the hostess.

The friends watched him go and then Nicki said, "He carries that much cash?"

Chapter Fifteen

The Govt Meeting Scene

Frankie set this meeting for Mac with an executive level manager at the regional EPA office to see if he could work his magic on their deep documents. Mac didn't know what "working magic" meant and couldn't see why the EPA official would give him what she wouldn't share with Frankie's outfit, but as you know, billable hours pay the bills.

After checking in with security and getting his driver's license photo printed on a badge, an assistant escorted Mac. There was a buzz in the office, and more than a few faces peeked over their cubicle as he followed the assistant to wherever he was taking him. After a few turns, Mac waited in a conference room listening to the air conditioning blow. In these situations, he didn't like to look at his phone and be thought un-serious, so sat patiently under that fluorescent, government building hum.

Soon, through the floor to ceiling windows of the conference room, Mac watched a large woman dressed in a gray pantsuit and black shirt approach with brisk efficiency. She opened the door and spoke before she was all the way in the room. "Mr. Macondo, I'm sorry to keep you waiting."

Mac stood, "Please. I know you are busy woman. I appreciate you taking time out for me." She was nearly a foot taller than him, a decade older and a step faster.

"Since you're tight with Frankie, I can tell you. This morning we've had a surprising application made down south and I'm already inundated with complaints from all sides. And I mean ALL sides; politicians, the press, environmental organizations, the general public, even members of the staff are indignant."

In Mac's mind only one person in recent memory could upset so many people so ferociously and instantaneously. This just might be one of those times when everything in the universe touches everything else and the answer you were seeking wasn't where you looked but appeared where you were. He was going to try a little twenty questions. "Is this about that mine down by Cuyamaca?"

"How'd you know?"

"I'd hate to even tell you. What are they doing?"

"Nothing they'll be able to get approved. They haven't even done an Environmental Impact Report."

"Let me guess. They've filed to waive the necessity."

"Based on an emergency situation. You're good at this. Tell me more."

"Oh, I don't know anything more. I just have a gut feeling who's doing this and since it's Filmore, I have a pretty good line on how he does business. And his main S.O.P. is obfuscation and litigation."

"Well, you seem to know his playbook. But he's not the first of his type I've dealt with. I simply want to protect the people and the land. That's our mandate."

"And the politicians?"

"Are not my concern. I'm too smart to be scared and too old to care."

"We're lucky to have you."

"I'm glad somebody sees it! Now, to the real reason you're here. This DDT mess we've been left to figure out and clean up. What do you want? What are you looking for?"

"I don't know. Frankie has me investigating this situation but I'm not privy what her end game is."

"They do tend to be secretive over there. Comes with the territory, I guess."

"Do you have any particular insights you could share?" It never hurts to come right out with what you want to know. Or, more specifically, to allow them to share their expertise. People, all of us, like to show what we know.

"I know these guys fouled up our waters by dumping poison all over the place. It was bad enough they were allowed to dump in designated areas. To have had them create such a large dead space outside one of the largest harbors in the world which, before the time, was still one of the largest fisheries in the world, is an environmental disaster."

"Have you found all of the containers?"

"Not yet. But they seem to be along a similar pattern." She brought up a map on her laptop. "Here's what we have so far. I think it may be flat out laziness. Like they would leave the harbor make one big circle, dumping the barrels as they went and got back to port."

"You think they were saving gas?"

"Basically. This circular trip they made couldn't have amounted to more than a hundred nautical miles total. Those guys were on a company boat. And they were gassing up on petty cash. Maybe they simply skimmed the amount of half the tank."

"And bought beer?"

"No, they were doing this six days a week for three years. They would've pocketed a lot of extra cash like that. Probably doubled their take home."

"Besides the overtime shift every Saturday."

"Now you're seeing it. But this is all conjecture. Not an ounce of evidence to back it up."

An announcement came on the speaker phone, "Annette, we have Senator Shibata in the lobby looking for you."

Her eyes bugged out at Mac, then the voice that came out of her mouth was smooth as silk, "Please let her know I will be there presently." She looked at Mac, "I don't need to tell you, I gotta go."

"Clearly. Thanks for your time. Do you think we can swing back and talk more about this case?"

"Of course. You have my number," she said as she left the room.

But he didn't have her number. But he'd get it. He considered hanging around to see what he could overhear but the assistant appeared and escorted him down to the lobby. On the way Mac spoke up, "By the way, can you give me Annette's info so I'm sure I have it right?"

This brought a bit of a surprised, uncomfortable look from the assistant. "It's a policy around here that we don't hand out other people's contact information."

"I just had a sit down with her."

"I understand but I just can't give her information out. It is not mine to give."

"Can you give me your contact information?"

"Of course." He handed Mac a card as they reached the lobby where security confiscated his badge. Well, maybe he learned enough to appease Frankie for the moment and had a few things to investigate. He also had to get down to Cuyamaca and that mine. Something was afoot. Annette and the Senator confirmed that.

Chapter Sixteen

The Garden Scene

After that friends dinner the night before, an uncomfortable aura floated around Mac. He couldn't shake the feeling. Uncomfortable wasn't the right word. Sometimes you feel off, other times you feel the ghosts. It's like the ancestors were walking with you, expecting you to do something. Make it different. It's only the living that can change things while the ghosts must watch and hope to push activities in the preferred direction. Mac didn't know. He simply knew the ancestors were around on this day. Things felt weird.

One of the things he liked to do when he felt too much pressure from that great beyond was visit the Solano Community Gardens. Really, he liked to do it regardless. It was his dad's day off and there was a better than even chance he would be there. The ghosts there are simple. The pleasures are simple. Real. Don't confuse simple with stupid. Just like one shouldn't confuse kind with soft. This was a place of growing and nurturing. They had created the space for the neighborhood to grow fruits and vegetables when they didn't have room in their own apartments. It was a place of community and healing.

Mac drove up Solano Drive past the curb lined late model Buicks, Toyotas and Hondas. The two-lane street had a slight incline and was wide enough for the driving cars or the parked ones, but barely both. When he came to the stop sign just before the gardens, the DWP had a dozen guys with cones and sirens, digging and fixing a water pipe issue. With no passage Mac turned left and revved his car to climb the steeper Radio Hill. The massive red and white tower filled with antennas and satellite dishes looked from on-high, indifferent to what occurred below. He looped over the tunnel that used to be Figueroa and became the Arroyo Seco Parkway. The 110. The first freeway. He went down a hill into a cluster of bungalows and Victorians that were a mix of dis-repaired and beautifully restored with bright and contrasting combinations of greens, yellows, browns or blues. They were in the transition between the more experienced residents who had lived there for fifty years plus and the newer folks with visions of grandeur about what the past held.

You see, this neighborhood could rightly be called the last of a time wiped out by modernity. And not the type you may have imagined. This slice of neighborhood is all that's left of the place razed for an asphalt desert surrounding a verdant and azul empire: Dodger Stadium. The history of Chavez Ravine is long. Suffice to say, people still lament the loss of that neighborhood.

Mac dropped into a parking lot for those remaining neighbors. In the end, it is only those who are left that can be helped. The Solano Elementary school was barely a homerun away from the Dodgers and the LAPD Police Academy. And for the purposes of our story, you know it isn't far from Mac's pops. This elementary school had received much needed and imaginative funding where they blended the classic with the new. The brown, ornate old schoolhouse built around the beginning of the 20th century was kept and had blended with a multi-colored modernist addition right off the side. It was a rare example of the beauty available to Los Angeles when they took the time.

In any case, Mac parked, and walked past the school's Kindergarten play yard, down a long flight of short stairs into a pedestrian tunnel under the parkway, up the other side to arrive at the street side retaining wall of the garden. The wall was covered with a multi-colored tile mural of children, rainbows, flowers and butterflies.

As he climbed the flight of stairs into the garden proper, he could smell the earth and plants. The smell of Los

Angeles. Not just the smog and car exhaust. He was next to a three-lane part of a freeway, he also could smell the deep earth, the sage and citrus, mold, water and manure of a garden.

It was comforting to know, even in the middle of the big city, that the living, breathing planet could share its bounty. Humans need dirt. To Mac, that was an undeniable truth. Earth to earth, dust to dust.

When Mac reached the top step with a pause to take in all the terraced community plots, his dad walked up and touched his shoulder as he passed back out of the garden and said, "C'mon. I need you to come with me."

No need to ask what. He'd tell Mac on the way. And Mac knew when his dad acted like this, something was up. Mac also knew he'd have to drive.

After they took the tunnel, over the roof of his car, Mac asked anyway about what still hadn't been offered, "So, where're we going?"

"Frog town. Albie hasn't been by for a couple days."

"Oh. Got it." Albie was the white haired, long bearded founder of the community garden and Albie spent his days wandering around the garden acting like he was working. They were not eternally fruitful, those days, but Albie loved the place. He loved the idea of people working together. The way these small plots of land represented a chance for each person. Each family had it in their capacity to improve their lives. Even just a little bit. Not everything provided a reward for your effort. Plants did.

If Albie hadn't been by the garden, it didn't need to be said that something might be wrong.

They headed up Broadway, over the old bridge and a quite full Los Angeles River. "Look at that," Mac said indicating the heavy, muddy flow.

His dad was looking at the same thing. "It's why they cemented that river up. When the rains come, there's a lot of water. Ever hear the story of how that river changed from ending in Santa Monica to ending in Long Beach?"

"Yes, Dad."

"It was the one of the floods that convinced them to bring in the Army Corps of Engineers."

"I know, Dad."

"It's amazing."

Mac continued up Pasadena Avenue and back across the river after the roundabout onto Riverside Drive. Really no more than a dozen blocks from Solano Gardens but more than you want to walk, especially with a little worry in your heart. At Albie's age, when they don't show up, you naturally get a little concerned something might have happened. Since Covid, that trepidation seemed more valid and more likely to be proven correct.

As we pulled up to his little pale yellow and white bungalow, the curtains were all drawn, and three days of the newspaper piled on his driveway. Now, don't be surprised. Albie was a man of his time, and he required *The Times* daily. *The Los Angeles Times*, of course. Albie had a phone, and he used that little computer but, as he said, you weren't going to rob him of his morning cup of coffee with the diminishing newspaper spread out before him.

As they exited the car, an old guy walked by. "Haven't seen him for days." He paused and directed his bright eyes at them.

"Hey, Reyes," they both said at the same time. Originally a rock journalist in New York, Reyes spent the next two thirds of his life lamenting living in Los Angeles after he sold a script and moved out to be a star.

"He's not at the garden?" Reyes said.

Mac shook his head. "That's why we're here. We haven't seen him either."

Nodding his head in thought, Reyes moved again. "He's around." Then waved behind his head.

Dad moved along to the door to give a knock as Mac gathered the three papers wrapped in their plastic bags. No answer. They looked at each other confirming what they both thought might be the case. Dad was at the gate before Mac had even moved and led the way to the backyard then walked around the house to peek in the bedroom window.

Albie's old car tic, ticked with engine heat right when his dad *eeped.*

Albie stood looking out his window in a white undershirt all stretched at the neck and nothing on the bottom. He had a joint in his mouth and a question in his eyes.

"Híjole," Dad said.

The windows were the old wooden paned ones. Albie swung one open against the stick of the paint and creak of the hinge. "What?"

"Albie. We thought something was wrong," Mac said.

Here, his girlfriend showed up over his shoulder with a sheet wrapped around her and a muss of hair at the back of her head. Once she saw who it was, looking between their faces then into Albie's eyes, she shook her head, waved her hand dismissing them without a word and disappeared.

"A guy can't take a day off without you thinking he's dead?" Albie said. He still stood there looking at them naked as a t-shirted jaybird. At this point, Mac was glad it looked like whatever transpired, transpired a little bit ago and his soldier was at ease. "Jesus, Mac, ain't ya seen another man's pecker? Take a picture it lasts longer." He closed the window and the curtain.

They could hear rustling and a short murmur of Albie and his girlfriend's voices. Then, his hard footfalls echoed over the raised foundation's floor and followed him to the laundry room door.

Albie took to the stoop in his bare feet. "I appreciate you boys checking on me," he said apparently taking the time from bedroom to laundry to reconsider his frustration. He also found pants along the way.

"It just wasn't like you not to visit the garden for so long," Dad said.

"I know. I know." Albie stood on the landing of the stairs contemplating. "You boys want a cup of coffee? I'll get you a cup," and he was gone.

They looked at each other. Sat at the patio table centered in the square patch of grass between walkway and driveway. That's not exactly correct, it was a patch of dirt where once grass grew, and remnants held at the corners where dew gathered. The chairs were white plastic. The table white metal and glass.

Already talking as the door swung open was Albie and three mugs of coffee. "...messing with these people coming into Frogtown. It's not the hipsters I mind so much. They have personality. It's the money grubbers." He placed a mug in front of each and took a chair himself. "It's black — milk's sour — They don't care about anything but the money."

If you'd spent any time with Albie, you'd know he mostly had two topics. The garden and what's growing were the first. The second was Frogtown and its impending doom.

"None of these people go to St. Anne's. None of them come to the potlucks. They buy the houses and triple the rent."

Dad agreed, "It's happening all over."

"The Gutiérrez family over there, they tried to fight it but got evicted instead."

Mac knew them. The family knew a little more about tenants' rights, but the owners claimed they were moving in themselves which allowed them to kick the family out. The old timers had raised ten kids in that little place. Fixed it themselves for thirty years. Just kicked them out.

"The old man who owned it died and the rotten kids only saw dollar signs in that house," said Albie.

"What are you gonna do?" Mac said. He meant it as a lament.

"I'll tell you. I'm fighting for height limits. And historical designations. I know what they did over in South Pasadena to stop that freeway."

It's part of the lore of Southern California what South Pasadena did. Freeways have destroyed and split neighborhoods for generations around here. It happened in South Central with the 10, it happened here in Frogtown with that interchange. They lost half the town to a cloverleaf. The difference was those places were what people nowadays like to call lower income and what the rest of us call poor. South Pasadena was not that. Those people were rich and a lot of them were rich because they were smart.

The town was small enough that they couldn't stop this freeway with their connections.

What happened next showed what can be done when people of different backgrounds work together. It also showed that grass roots activism works.

The people in South Pasadena began getting houses along the proposed corridor designated as Historically significant. They then expanded those designations to the Latino neighborhoods to the south. Eventually, through a combination of environmental arguments against the traffic pollution and the historical significance of these homes and corridors, they stopped the freeway.

There are two stubs that go nowhere because the cities stopped the state and, eventually, the federal government from destroying their homes. It took twenty-five years to stop, and they have been working to repair the damage for another twenty years. The little guy can win but it takes gumption.

"Well, if anyone can do it, it's you," Dad said.

Albie cocked his head and drank his coffee. He would go down fighting if he had to. "There's more than one way to skin a cat. You know, the only people I've ever known to skin a cat was a med student. Why do we say that?"

They finished the coffee. Albie was fine. Always fine. They bid their farewells. Albie dumped his coffee on his newly trimmed rose bush. And Mac and his dad made the jaunt to the garden. Mac had spent enough time screwing around and had work to do. Bills don't pay themselves. He dropped his dad off a block away, just where the DWP guys dug a hole in the middle of the road.

"Alright, see you," Dad said over the rat-a-tat-tat of the street work. "And I'll water your plants."

"Whoa. Don't worry," Mac said. "I'll come by later

today."

His dad smiled with both 'sure' and 'I'm doing it anyway' behind his eyes.

Mac smiled, "Love you. Have fun."

He closed the door with a wave. Dad looked back, "You too," through the window.

Mac watched his dad go on his merry way. He didn't hear the jack hammers, just saw the sunshine on his father as he crested the rise.

Hang a right and straight down Broadway through old China Town, into new China Town, past what used to be Little Joe's because it used to be little Italy, over the Golden State Freeway, Mac came to his office. He found a spot, no need to pull his sign trick, headed upstairs through the rich smell of the old building.

Mac's office was like a fort when you were a kid. A place he could head to and think his own thoughts away from the intrusion of any other responsibility. Even the jobs he worked on. There was very little movement outside his door so he could dream things up without worrying about anything but that dream. Not client needs. Not bills. Not due dates. Right now, Mac sat down at his computer, the old laptop placed to the side, the one without internet, and turned it on.

While the dinosaur booted, Mac took off his shoes and socks. Stretched his toes. Felt the cool floor beneath his feet.

With a deep breath and the drive to create, he opened his book document at the end of the last sentence he had written. He didn't even read what he wrote, he started typing.

It was the only way he could do it. There were times when he needed to think and plan and manipulate but that was mostly away from his writing practice. He had been so busy this last week, he'd only made that interrupted trip to the library. No words. He'd never finish the thing without words. You gotta walk the first ten steps to cover ten miles.

He had no faith in his ability to finish at the moment, so he put himself in the world and started typing. Trust his instincts. Intuition knew the way.

He, his main character, just found a second body and it was the main suspect up to that point. Why would the killer get rid of the main suspect? Mac didn't know but he'd figure out a reason. That was some of what he liked about these things. The books. You create rational reasons for people's actions, and Mac knew, there was no reason in the real world. Just facts and animal instincts.

The words flowed from here. This space. It felt more like a journal entry than his story but, let's be honest, a lot of these words were a mix of the character thoughts, his thoughts and the needs of the story. The flow was more stream than river, but it was there. He felt that momentum, the swirling of the shape of an idea out in front of him although inside his head. Mac was lost to time. A couple hours must've passed because his well was close to empty, but he wanted to push just a little farther.

The phone in his pocket quadruple blinged with texts and rang. No, he was committed to the words today. No distractions. But the call went to voice mail then rang immediately. Out of his pocket, Stephanie's face filled the screen. His stepmother. What's so urgent?

"What's up, Stephanie?"

"It's your dad."

Never a great way to start a conversation. "What's wrong? What happened?"

"His heart stopped."

His what. His heart? Did she just tell him what he thought she just told him? "Wait. Is he okay? Are you at the hospital? I'll come right down." He pulled on socks, was tying the laces on his shoes. Didn't hear what she was saying. He needed to get to wherever Dad was. "I lost you, Stephanie. What did you say?"

"Mac. Stop. Slow down. Wait a minute."

For what. He had to see his father.

"Honey, he's gone." She blurted a sob.

"Where? When? How?" Mac stopped. The horizontal aluminum blind rattled and beat at the window. He couldn't see through the tears. Blobs of water. The world blurred around him.

"There was nothing anyone could do. Albie found a stream of water roaring down the slope when he got to the garden. The open spigot bubbled out of the watering can up the hill. Mac was already resting when Albie found him." She caught a fluttering breath. "Stop and gather yourself. We can't change anything. Not now. His heart just gave out."

He must have answered in agreement because she answered. But he hung up. He wiped his face and the fear that filled him from his toes to his overflowing eyes.

All the texts were from Dad's work buddies. They already knew. News like that traveled fast. The hospital knew him and the rest of the cops. It was their community. Their circle. Not a single one acknowledged the truth. They all asked if he was alright. They all knew what Mac knew. That he was gone. None of them would be the one to deliver the news. Not by text. They just needed the kid to know they were there for him. That they were there buoyed him but not much changed the fact that the only person he trusted was gone. Nobody else left. He had only memories of the most important people in his life. Nothing more. Visions. Ghosts. Ancestors.

Mac would go to the hospital and tend to his father's remains. He had done this for other people. Clients. Not for his own kin. Dad had done his own parents and Mom. Now he'd take care of Dad. That was the way. Regardless of how he felt, that was the way. You take care of your family until the end, which, of course, included the end.

Chapter Seventeen

The General Hospital Scene

The LA County USC General Hospital knew Senior well. The staff had laid him out in a room so Mac would be able to visit his remains before the whole process with the mortuary commenced. When Mac walked in the room, Stephanie stood over Dad, on the other side of the bed, a tissue to her nose. She lifted her eyes to Mac with the look of inevitable acceptance that only these situations muster.

The end. The end of the road. The end of Father's Day. The end of birthdays, celebrated. The end of lunches. Of dinners. Of off handed advise and well considered direction. The end of hugs and handshakes, shoulder slaps and knee grabs. No more sneaked cigarettes and clanked beers. No more. No more. No more.

Stephanie left Dad and hugged Mac. The longest physical contact the two had ever shared. Closer to her than he had ever been and would ever be again.

"Oh, I'm so sorry, Mac," she said as she released him and focused eye to eye.

"Me, too." Mac backed off and sat in the chair on the wall.

"By the time Albie found him, he was gone." Stephanie wiped a tear.

"I guess he didn't want any of those ambulances and hospitals."

"He'd had enough of the sirens."

"But he wasn't done."

Stephanie's tears flowed and she took a seat next to Mac. When she sat, he got up and went to his father's body. Even from across the room, Mac knew it was the shell.

Only a silhouette of the man who had done so many, many things for him. The soul, his soul, no longer trapped in his body. No slight rise and fall of his chest. Not a slight snore like that look on his face meant at every other point in Mac's life. He took his father's hand in his own, felt the meat but not the man. Set the hand on the gurney and touched the back of his own hand to his father's face.

Mac's chest was broken wide open. He had lost his mother, his grandparents and now his father. Still a young man. No wife. No family. Dad would never meet them. Only in dreams and stories. As an ancestor. The only ties Mac had to anything, or anyone was the business.

How long he stood there, Mac didn't know. A long time. A few moments. Time had simultaneously become meaningless in the present, filled with longing in the past and a bleak, featureless road in the future.

When finally, he couldn't be there anymore, he turned to leave. Blinkman was at the door. He stood motionless with his hands crossed in front of him. At ease in the military sense.

Mac threw him a chin. Blinkman threw one back and held out his hand. They grabbed hands and Blinkman wrapped Mac in his arms, "I'm sorry, kid."

"Ya. Me, too."

"He was a good guy, your pop. A good friend. A good partner." Blinkman and Senior were partners when Mac was a tyke, when Mom was still alive, although, Blink tired of the cop game and became a lawyer.

Mac just nodded. He didn't have anything else. "Spend some time with him. I can't stay here anymore." He walked past Blinkman.

"Take care, kid. Let me know about arrangements."

"Ya, he's had that paid off for a long time. After my mom, he said he'd never leave me with the problems of handling with those death dealers."

Blinkman smiled, no teeth at the thought. He knew. Then he thought of something else, "And, let me know if you need anything, too."

He acknowledged, “Will do. Thanks, Blink.” Mac waived over his shoulder as he entered the cavernous hallway. They were in the part of the hospital where nothing moved. Other sections filled with frenetic energy. With life. Here, nothing moved.

Stephanie caught him a few strides outside the room. “Mac, before you go,” she said. “Will you still come over for dinner on Sunday?”

“I don’t know. With this Filmore thing…”

“Senior said you weren’t taking that job.” She caught herself, stuck between a moment of normality and remembering he was gone. “He didn’t think so.”

All Mac could do was shrug. *Waddya gonna do?*

“Don’t go doing anything rash, Mac.”

“If anybody needed help, it’s them. It’s getting pretty intense.”

“Aren’t you going to take time to deal with this?”

“The arrangements are practically done.”

“I don’t mean the arrangements. I mean the fallout from losing your father. You probably need a break.”

“From what? I can’t. I’ve gotta pay rent. The bills don’t stop.”

“Mac, you’ll need to give yourself some time.”

“Ya, when I’m dead.” He caught himself. Looked to the room. “It’s just that I don’t have leeway here.”

“Well, still think about coming for dinner.”

“Ya, I’ll do that. Thanks.”

He heard his footfalls echo through the hall, detached, a spectator. The noise bounced off the walls to land in his ears alone.

His phone spelunked. Social media notification. Again. Then again. Then a text. Mac did his best to ignore the phone’s needs.

Until the phone rang. It was Zoey.

He silenced the device and pocketed it.

Chapter Eighteen

The Podcast Scene

By the time Mac got to his car, Zoey had sent four more texts and a link to her latest podcast. There was no quit in her.

As he sat in the car, another text. This one from Delilah: Come down. My father agreed to meet with you. Now.

Why now? And why would the old guy meet with Mac at all after refusing to for so long.

Then his Venmo account blinged with two grand.

What was he going to do, go home and cry?

Mac loaded up Zoey's podcast and started the trek to Cuyamaca that was getting older by the trip.

He started the podcast then quickly skipped over all her set up and sponsor rigmarole.

In short, here's what Zoey had to say:

Quick answers were not going to come quickly. I needed to get the scope of this whole situation in perspective. The city council fighting, the bridge, were simply a result of the disease. This tumor had been here for a long time.

This went back generations. Well, I would get to the bottom of it. And as with all things, and like many things in California, that history was a story about a very limited few. Rarely had the proper connections at the most fortuitous time meant more to both the present and the future than when California left Mexico and joined the United States.

One of our great public resources are public libraries.

When I visited the local branch, the Cuyamaca history section was so vast I stopped perusing the books and visited the research desk. Don't forget, libraries have librarians.

I introduced myself and, as luck would have it, I found just the person. Annette the librarian was the archivist of the Cuyamaca history section.

Some librarians, like some people, are not inclined to talk about themselves but love to share their knowledge. Good thing I was there for information. At first, the mic can spook people, or make them braggadocious, but soon enough they become themselves again.

Annette, our librarian, was a wealth. She started:

"The nesting dolls of consequences echoed through generations. When John Black moved here after the Civil War, he married a local Kumeyaay girl known as Silent Rain. She was the one who knew the gold grew in the river. John Black found out and it started the whole town as it is today. Despite confusion over land grants, that included a judge who didn't bother to check the actual borders over the years because of rains, there was a run on gold. But John Black lost it all including his claim when he couldn't pay for the equipment he purchased to dig the mine. You guessed it. That claim went to the person who made the most from the gold rush in these and all the other parts. The man who sold the shovel and picks and flour and salt. In this town that man was Brennan Filmore. He took that claim and John Black's land. Filmore dug that mine far and deep. He found gold but the operation barely paid for itself. Filmore abandoned the idea of striking it rich, but he kept the land, of course."

As I mentioned, the library had a deep local history section. And Annette was a history buff and liked to track and scour for information. Books, maps, essays, newspaper and magazine articles, the original land grant and subsequent court records. She had gone as far as to find a few recordings from a 1920's oral history project that discussed life in San Diego County fifty years before and two of the interviewees mention Cuyamaca in passing. Annette had transcribed and recorded those interviews in her archive.

"Well," Anette said. "The project had started with the

intent of writing a book, but I decided I liked gathering information more than formulating the dissemination of it."

Zoey nodded in podcast, "I can relate." Although I got everything I wanted about the history, and since Annette had opened up, I let the flood gates flow. "You said you grew up here in Cuyamaca. You haven't been a librarian your whole life."

Annette gave a knowing smile, her chin tucked to the side and a twinkle in her eyes, like a little girl. "No, my daddy owned a chicken farm down the hill a little."

"It must've been a different time. A lot of work."

"Oh, it was different, and it was work. Animals don't take holidays, you know. We came, my sister and I, my parents, we came from a time before power and phones. We had a well for water."

"It must've made you tough!"

"No, it simply made us capable of dealing with inconvenience."

She described the little farmhouse and the dusty chicken coup out in the yard. How they hauled water up the hill from the well to the house for cooking and cleaning.

"Did you dream of being a librarian when you were young?"

"Oh, no. I wanted to be a dancer. Even more so I wanted to fly. Picturing the old house, when our poppa let us play instead of work, which the sweet old guy did a lot. Some of my friends didn't have it so good. I would watch the birds fly off the coup. I even watched the chickens take more than a few flaps through the air. Feeling the wind in their wings." Annette reveled in the past then refocused. "It was their instinct, you know."

"To fly."

"To fly. Well, dreamer I was, I'd jump on top of that coup and as a skinny little bugger, I thought maybe I could fly, too." Annette laughed. "Don't you know, I landed on my bottom more than once trying to flap my arms hard enough to go a few yards. I was sure I could do it."

Annette paused a moment then said, "I haven't thought about that in years. Kids are so funny."

I finished by telling Annette we would make a darn good podcast out of all this. She wasn't the only one who liked to hear people's stories. I also feel a lot like Annette, if you don't take the time to hear about people's pasts, we lose them. It's not just President's lives that are important.

Come back next week when I will have more on this small town, big trouble.

Mac rolled down the gravel road to Filmore Ranch by the time it was all done.

Chapter Nineteen

The Locked House Scene

Mac wended his way along the well-tended gravel road. Driving the full way in risked getting trapped with no easy way out of whatever it was that was waiting for him.

His windows down, dry menthol perfumed the wind as it shook through the surrounding eucalyptus trees and a few mature oaks and sycamores. Leaves and gravel crackled under his wheels. The two-story home was set deep in the woods, surrounded by acres and acres of dry grass and those trees. The house was the type rich people build in the woods with big, exposed beams, overhangs and lots of gables.

The road he was on continued past the house to cut into the hills. Probably a fire road. Mac turned right into the driveway.

Before we get into Mac's part in all that happened next, we need to provide context. This was the first time the mob showed up to the Filmore Ranch Estate. However, this group was larger than those that had been protesting and were hell bent on getting what it wanted. They decided that Filmore owed them answers to their questions about the bridge funds and the bridge itself. Not as pressing, but, arguably to some, more important, they wanted answers about what his plans were for the mine. They were not prepared to accept politician's platitudes. They also were not going to wait for the next City Council meeting.

Filmore came back to town and that meant, to them, that he would answer to the town. The problem here became the townspeople had their own answer to the problem.

As it happened, another storm hit. Just a single night and day. It was one of those atmospheric rivers that drop rain like — a river. Two inches may not sound like much in other parts of the world but in Southern California, especially after a few successive storms? In most rains, the sandy, crushed granite nature of the dirt means the water runs right over the top. That's why you hear so often about flash floods around here. But if a couple storms stack around each other with just enough space between them, the ground becomes saturated, and that top layer can come screaming down the hill taking everything in its path. That's what happened to the bridge. And that's what happened to a fistful of homes outside Cuyamaca.

Losing the revenue, lacking a bridge and now, neighbors in a tightening bind caused consternation. Worse, when there's an instigator? As the chemistry professors say, all fires require a catalyst.

Olivera would swear he didn't mean anything by it. That he couldn't have known it would go this far. Mac believed him, to a point. Olivera wanted something to happen, it's just when a boulder starts rolling downhill, one shouldn't expect to control the path.

The protesters started downtown and Olivera had the family, his company, everyone he could reach from his Facebook was called, and surrounded the empty pedestal. When nearly a hundred people gathered and more continued to trickle in, his wife held her phone for a Facebook live broadcast then he began.

"Caballeros! Compadres! My friends! Filmore is at it again." Olivera paused, shook his chin as he looked at each member of the crowd. He knew these people. These people knew him. "You know and I know, this man's family took my family's land back in the Californio days. They take from us. And now, he has plans to take his land and do something even worse. He doesn't plan on bringing jobs and making our community healthy."

One of the crowd yelled, "What's he doing, padrón?"

"I'll tell you what he's doing. Chester Filmore has filed paperwork to turn that old mine into a toxic waste dump."

Here there was silence. There were many rumors, but nobody had heard about this stated so clearly before. There weren't boos and stage hisses like a political rally. The people were stunned and worried. Olivera knew it.

"Filmore wants to bring radiated waste from nuclear power plants to our home and place it over our water table. This stuff that is deadly for ten thousand years, he wants to store in that mountain so he can make a few extra bucks by doing nothing but building a vault and hiring a couple security guards."

One of Olivera's cousins, Mickey, who was standing right in front of him asked, quietly, at the pause, "You mean he's trying to poison us?"

Olivera looked down at him to acknowledge Mickey then addressed the crowd again, "Yes, Mickey. That's exactly what he's trying to do. Poison us."

Now, one of the women spoke up. It sounded like Yolanda, but Olivera wasn't sure. "What can we do?"

Pursing his lips, chin jutted up and down, Olivera looked over the crowd for a dramatic pause and said, "I say we go tell him how much we don't like his idea. I say we go to his house and let him know."

Everybody agreed. The crowd went wild. These people were locals. They all knew where Filmore lived and after they screamed their agreement, they streamed to their cars and trucks. The football and basketball team split between two pickups, all piled in the truck beds. There were workers and housewives, real estate agents and the kid who worked at the visitor center. A handful of ten-year-old boys and girls tried to follow along on their bikes until one of the trucks stopped and they hopped on the tailgate.

It was a short drive. His house wasn't far from the edge of town.

The arrival was remarkable in that it was so organized

and without discussion. The rows of cars parked along the drive up to the house. Right in the middle. No one would be coming or going.

The townspeople marched to the house with an eerily quiet shuffle. This was not a peaceful silence. More like the stray bubble in a pot of water before it exploded into a rolling boil. Once the trickle of people pooled in the front yard, Olivera yelled up to Filmore, "Come out and talk to us, pendejo! We know what you're doing."

Inside, Mac already sat at a large dining table with Filmore, who sent the security guard to the window.

The guard, Truman, went upstairs and addressed them from an open window. He said to the circle of people with Olivera at the heart, "He isn't here. You're wasting your time."

The entire crowd laughed. Olivera was unmoved, "He doesn't go anywhere without you. Let's talk. I'll come in. We can have a coffee and straighten this out."

The guard didn't answer, he simply closed the window. Some there had thought he took Olivera's statement as the offer it was and that the guard would bring it to Filmore. However, others took that silence as disrespect and dismissal.

Still oblivious to the mounting danger outside, Filmore sat at his table, slurped his coffee and addressed Mac, "So, what's so important you needed to meet face to face."

Mac arrived five minutes before the crowd, and, it seemed, he wasn't going anywhere. They surely blocked in his car. But he would have skedaddled had he the means.

"With all my legwork and all the news hounds, I needed it straight from the horse's mouth." Maybe these were the wrong words to use with this guy. "So, to speak."

Filmore considered it and said, "You don't trust me." Not a question.

"Should I?"

"Look, people say I'm one of the greatest businessmen this state has seen in many, many years. Isn't that reason enough to believe in me and my abilities?"

"Clearly, Mr. Filmore, you have are a good dealmaker. But that wasn't what I was getting at."

"What are you are getting at Mr. Macondo?"

This guy was unaccustomed to questions, even allusions, he didn't like. "I'm no magician. And if I'm to produce a sort of solution out of thin air, you'll have to let me behind the curtain."

"If that's the case..." Here Filmore smiled. He had one of those magnanimous smiles that the wearer imagines is utterly convincing and everyone else wants to smack right off his face. Filmore said, "I'll need to be sure that you are loyal."

Loyal? Mac was loyal to the cash. Mac was loyal to himself. But this blow hard? "I am loyal to my client's needs. It would be unethical to be otherwise."

A sour laugh gurgled from Filmore's stomach up his throat. "Ethics? Jesus, Delilah sure knows how to pick 'em."

Truman entered at this point. Big eyes and a flushed face. You might say this was not his typical look.

"Mr. Filmore," Truman nodded to both men. "Olivera wants to talk with you."

"And why would I talk with that asshole? Send him away."

Truman squeezed his lips together like he swallowed the first answer, looked at Mac once, realized there was no help there, and said, "He's not alone."

"Who's with him that would interest me in the least? The governor?"

"If I had to guess, I'd say most of the town."

That's when Filmore rose from his chair and went to the monitor in the kitchen area desk space. One of those built in desks in late model McMansions. The video screen was split in four sections with security camera footage from around the house. In all the places one expected to see a squirrel or blue jay, people mulled. Those people had the energy, even through the screen, the body language, of a mob.

And, as a high-level narcissist, Filmore could read a crowd. It didn't take genius EQ to know this was a dangerous situation. He didn't want them to even think he was here.

"What do you think?" Filmore said. He was buying time.

"It might be a good idea to talk," Truman said. "It might lower the tension."

Filmore feigned listening while equal parts fear and anger pinballed behind his eyes, deep in his mind. Not so much weighing chess moves as controlling a fight or flight response. Filmore was smart enough to know either extreme would stoke the fire. At least Mac hoped he was smart enough.

"Does he know I'm here? For sure?"

Truman was a pro. He probably wanted to strangle Filmore himself but, instead, calmly said, "I'm here so he assumes you're here. That's what he said."

Nodding, Filmore transitioned to what seemed a more natural state. Like he was negotiating already with himself.

Used to people hating him, this position was a well-worn trail for Filmore. He smacked his hand on the desk then made a declaration: "Ignore them."

Truman was a bodyguard, but he started his adulthood in the military, and it showed. He took his orders, spun on his heel and left the room.

Filmore adjusted his attention. Focused his gaze on Mac. Wordless. Assessing. What to do with him. Silence with a tremor in the air. Filmore's eyes darted to the screens behind Mac. Involuntarily. Like a cat tracking movement.

The security cameras reported, a handful of people, led by brothers Steve and Dan Steele, broke the latch on Filmore's tool shed. People streamed by while two set of hands gathered garden tools and handed them out to other sets of open hands.

"What the fuck are they doing?!" Filmore shot to his feet.

Truman dashed in the room. "Sir, if you don't want

them to know you're here, I'd advise against the outbursts."

Mac studied the screen over the other two's shoulders. "Mr. Filmore, I'm advising you to trust your security. You never know of what a crowd is capable."

"Don't you tell me what I don't know!" Filmore yelled.

That outburst was the final straw. The crowd heard him loud and clear.

That was when one of the crowd started screaming that Filmore better come out of his house. The hundred people, en masse, pounded on the doors. If they couldn't reach a door, they pounded on the walls with their palms. All in unison. The rhythmic pounding created the underlying heartbeat of destruction and menace. Boom, boom, boom. The crowd moved as one against the house. This was only the beginning. Soon the pulse dissipated and became cacophony. The even, organized upheaval disintegrated into mayhem and chaos.

Mac's buddy Truman stuck his head out of the upstairs bedroom window again, "He's not here."

One of the boldest of the mob spoke, "We know he's here."

"He isn't. Filmore wouldn't come back. Everybody told him you would react this way even if he didn't want to believe it."

"If we weren't sure before we know he's here because you are here. The coward doesn't go anywhere without his bodyguard, and he screams like a girl."

"Go on and get out of here. Nothing good will come of this."

The crowd surged and beat the walls with the shovels and hit the doors with their hands.

Mac didn't know what to do. He surely didn't want to get in the middle of a hostile crowd. Getting himself beat up wasn't going to do anyone any good.

A rock was the spark that set the fire which heated the water. That rock was hurled into the number two bedroom upstairs window with a smash-thump. That first damage was the last bit of heat needed. This crowd hit full boil.

This is also the last of the useful footage from Filmore's security cameras.

Bill and Tanya Roofus, front and center, pounded on the large, oaken door. Tanya yanked so hard; she broke off the ornate knocker.

The crowd teemed around each other like those bubbles in a pot. With over a hundred people, two hundred flat hands pounded on the walls, stomped the Cyclamen's gentle petals under the windows and screamed for an appearance.

From the house, only silence.

Then what could only be a bad omen, a pack of coyotes at the top of the valley yelped and howled in a tizzy, the excitement below too much.

Inside the house, Truman moved Filmore into his office upstairs and headed down to try to talk sense into the senseless.

Two young men, nobody would name them, were hoisted by others onto the roof and marauded to those high windows. One snapped the cameras at the first story roof line and a higher camera off the upper story. The more prepared of the two had a large flathead screwdriver and he pried open the swinging, wooden paned window. He whooped and hollered, the others screamed, "Filmore!" "Where are you?"

As the one ran to open that solid oak door, the other marauded through the house like Jack's giant fee-fi-fo-fumming Filmore's name.

Truman cold-cocked the guy, fist to chin to floor, as they met in the hall.

The crowd joined in with the same singsong taunting chants, "Filmore", with exclamations peppered in staccato, "Where are you?"

Filmore's security detail may have been trained but not in mob control.

The mob found Filmore in a closet of the fourth bedroom behind his ex-wife's dresses, formal types, smelling of cedar.

Filmore made himself out to be tough, but the guys who

pulled him out of that closet actually were. They took a particular joy in dragging the rich bragger by his Achilles heel, bumping his head as they pulled him down the stairs with their hourly workday hands, echoing the beat of their dusty, steel-toed boots.

They sat Filmore and his buzzing head in a dining room chair and asked questions for which he had no answers.

It was his actions he would answer for.

They tied him to the chair with an extension cord on his hands and an ankle on a chair leg, the other ankle with a curtain line torn straight from the wall. He was going downtown.

Since he wouldn't talk, they stuffed one of his socks in his mouth and duct taped it, tilted the chair back and put him in the bed of a truck conveniently backed to the front door, on the lawn, over the hedges. He lay on his back, his feet in the air, the blood draining to his head.

Still, nobody had mouthed the plan, but the wisdom of the crowd knew. They knew collectively what would be done, at least they thought they did.

Chapter Twenty

The Pedestal Scene

The line of cars stretched for half a mile, led by the truck and their quarry. At town square, the truck pulled right up to the empty pedestal, the one that held the old statue, and half a dozen of them placed Filmore right up there from the bed of the truck under the empty leafless sycamore.

That pen of goats just behind the pedestal didn't like all the commotion one bit. Clearly uncomfortable with the tenor, they gathered in the furthest corner away, bleating, rustling beneath.

Someone in crowd yelled, "And you thought it'd be a statue of you up there." Almost to the tee, they remembered that one. Nobody and everyone said it according to reports. Filmore looked out on a mob that must have reminded him of Frankenstein - the townspeople turned against his monster. His creation. His dreams.

Filmore screamed into that sock in his mouth as they left him up there and drove the truck away.

Cuyamaca taunted and jeered Filmore.

Even hog-tied, Filmore wouldn't have it. He was combative. Screamed his face red. Bulging, tears of anger streamed from the corners of his eyes. Some thought he would have a heart attack right there. He couldn't have seen his mistake. Not built that way, he looked as if he'd been betrayed. In a just world, Filmore would have understood his missteps. Begged forgiveness for his trespasses. Seen the error of his ways and experienced a moment of clarity.

Instead, Filmore rattled and shook the chair to gain

freedom. His hands fiddled behind him looking to untie his bonds. Behind the anger, he was righteous. Filmore was wronged and these people would pay. His eyes, raging beyond rage, calculated how he would destroy each of these people, marked each in his mental notebook for retribution.

Filmore rocked the chair, slowly. The chair couldn't hold his weight for long. Back and forth the pendulum swung. The chair bent each way like a rocker.

The crowd laughed, pointed. This was their revenge. To embarrass him. Nothing more.

A crackle filled the air. The leaves of the sycamores rattled and shook.

Filmore tilted with force, gaining momentum. Back. Forth. Back.

Forth. He rocked once too many, much too hard.

A wind streaked up the valley, a rumble and wave pulsed through the ground beneath their feet.

Filmore toppled backwards and tumbled from that two-men-high pedestal to a terrible crunch.

When the bystanders ran to help, they understood before they moved. If the broken neck didn't do it, his busted head did.

Humpty Dumpty would not be put together again.

Filmore was dead.

It was Cuyamaca that did it.

Chapter Twenty-One

The Immediate Aftermath Scene

For a long, strong intake of breath, time stopped. Silence but for the bay of the goats in the petting zoo pen.

The Highway Patrol rolled through town. Billy Brightwood knew everybody here. He grew up in Cuyamaca. Lived in Cuyamaca. Was raising kids in Cuyamaca, toddler twins. As he came upon the group, a bubble had formed abreast of the empty platform. Nobody broke the invisible force hiding behind that pedestal.

Billy couldn't see what it was but by instinct he knew it wasn't good. When he parked, the group heard his car door close, and the spell was broken. A handful ran to whatever had created the bubble of fear, many skedaddled and some stayed exactly as they were.

Filmore was in a heap. Blood pooled around his head and spread. Not a peep from him. Living, he would have been wailing or writhing. He was already meat outlined in scarlet.

Billy's police radio chirped as he hit the call button on the handset attached to his shoulder, "You better get the sheriff to downtown." He looked around at the thinning group. "And the coroner."

Instead of laying a look of disapproval on everyone, Billy checked Filmore's neck for a pulse. Though his neck was still warm, the blood was not moving through his body. Most of that was on the pavement. Just to be sure Billy placed his hand on Filmore's chest. Nothing. Filmore's eyes were open. Vacant. Glossed and gone, he was.

Thankfully, according to Billy, that was when the sheriff showed up. Whatever happened in this town. The town of

Cuyamaca. It was his show.

A second police car rolled up and a third. An ambulance, the fire truck.

You may remember the bard quote about all the sound and fury signifying nothing. The sirens and first responders would no more bring Filmore back than to return Horatio and his skull from dust.

"Who did this?" they asked.

"It was Cuyamaca that did it," they answered.

This was no play. Not a story from books. The sheriff was not pleased. His town was not Fuenteovejuna. And crimes were committed by individuals not communities. Perpetration is as basic as Criminology 101. Any kindergartner can tell you who did the deed. Unamused and concerned by what his town had done, even if inadvertent, the sheriff would get answers.

A current ran through these people. A knowledge that seemed unspoken to the sheriff but soon enough traveled through a whisper network, as well. They had decided that they all did it. Cuyamaca did it.

What a bunch of horse shit. These were good people. Not the type of people to do these things. The sheriff was sure of that. His town would not be one of those places. A hick town that did crazy things.

By the time Mac arrived at the scene, the coroner had Filmore in a body bag, the ring around the pedestal was cordoned off with yellow police tape and the goats still bayed.

Townsfolk chanted a monks refrain of, "oh, my god."

Others mulled and murmured. Hands over mouths, cap brims pulled low. Unsure of what had, in fact, been visited upon them. It didn't take long until Zoey spotted Olivera, the man she interviewed the other day, and made a bee line for him. Mac knew when the getting was good and followed.

"How are you?" Zoey said as she reached his personal space. "What happened?"

His eyes were downcast, and he shook his head while he

said, "I just don't know. It was Cuyamaca that did it."

"What do you mean?"

"It was the town that did it."

Mac didn't have the patience. "Something like this. It's one person's action. Someone did this."

"It was everyone and no one. The town."

They all accepted the blame and the credit for what happened. The entire town said, simply, "Blame Cuyamaca." When asked who did it, they said, "It was Cuyamaca who did it."

Whether it was an old maid, the goat farmer, or a young boy, they answered the same, never wavered. Cuyamaca. The city behind the clouds had extinguished this light.

Soon, around the pedestal, they were all gone. The townspeople. The police. The firemen. The coroner. In fact, it wasn't that the crowds were gone. The crowd changed in contour and content. Both around the pedestal and down, across the street, a few football fields away, a gaggle of media gathered and surrounded the police station.

Removed from the melee, Mac took it all in. He pieced together parts of what happened with Filmore. Guessed. *Deduction* as Holmes liked to call it to Dr. Watson. The main fact - and Mac wasn't sure there was any other pertinent fact - was the blood stain. Filmore bought the farm right on the spot.

It always disconcerted Mac, the amount of blood a body holds. Simultaneously it was so much, about a gallon and a half, and so finite. That so little of that liquid could sustain our fragile shells delivering oxygen and nutrients, carrying away waste from each hard-working cell.

Mac pursed his lips and considered his options until he defaulted straight to action. He went to see the sheriff. Zoey joined him and they walked past the car down the block. Zoey had nothing to say.

The small department building was the size of twelve men with their hands stretched out touching, all facing four different directions. There was a chain link fence surrounding the gravel yard with the two of the city cruisers and a police branded suburban. Spaced and empty like the town most times.

The street held a team of reporters with a handful of news vans to support those who did video, TV or streaming. That handful mostly recited on-camera gibberish about all they didn't know regarding the event. The print types. The written word ones. They mimicked their own process. Slow and methodical. They mostly sat on a squat cinder block wall talking about nothing. Chewing the fat. The three youngest had their phones open, presumably tweeting or facebooking or social media-ing in some capacity. Even their typing had the manic fortitude that social media required.

Reasonably sure they would never give him entrance, especially with Zoey in tow, Mac nonetheless strolled up and knocked on the door. There was always a chance.

It was a public building, but they had locked that door. Mac didn't blame them. But Zoey?

"What makes them think they can lock the door?" She was chewing gum now. It seemed to perk her up. Maybe she just had something that made sense to her that she could be upset about. An everyday thing she handled hundreds of times. "That man died. We need answers."

"Which is exactly what they are working on," Mac said as he cupped his hands around his eyes to cut down the glare and peer through the glass door. "They're not going to answer us. The one behind the counter looked up and looked away." He focused on Zoey, "Can't see the sheriff, either."

Mac chewed on what to do next. Indiscriminate action would be wasted energy.

No word from Delilah. He didn't expect any word from her. Her father just died. But the starting funds in his bank account meant his investigation probably just morphed into a supplemental murder investigation. There was no way Mac could get the sheriff to talk to him at this moment, but Mac needed to decide if he would work in tandem with the authorities or separate.

There would be advantages to both. With the authorities, they would lend him the weight of the badge and the government. Credibility. Gravitas, even. On the other hand, as an individual he'd be nimble. Untethered by pesky laws of evidence trails, First and Fourth Amendment rights, let alone the Fifth. On his own he could find answers to questions without the worry of ever having to prove his findings to a judge or in court. Because there are three different states: there is truth, there is justice and there is proving it in court. It is a rare court case that contains all three in balance and on the proper side of the scale. What is true in the real world to normal people is often colored by other factors of law and precedent. The justice system is not the real world. It is more, it is important, and it is ridiculous.

A voice spoke behind them, "What can we do for you two?" It was the sheriff who startled them. There's the reason they didn't see him.

Of course, it was Zoey who spoke up. "Why are you locking the doors? What if someone needed in?"

Sheriff offered a no teeth grin that he must save for only those he'd most like to stuff in the trunk but knows he has a voted position. Then he shifted his attention to Mac.

"You, sir, fit the description of the assailant."

Mac smirked like that statement might be an inside joke. The sheriff simply locked into Mac more.

"I didn't even get to town until after the incident."

"I have witnesses that place you at the pedestal when the deceased met his demise."

Zoey jumped in, "Who are these witnesses? I was with him, and he wasn't here."

"Well, young lady, I have professionals, members of my force, who can place him at the scene of the crime immediately following the incident."

The sheriff reached to the back of his utility belt and removed his cuffs. "You, Edward Macondo, are under arrest for the murder of Chester Filmore."

This is ridiculous is what Mac wanted to say. *I didn't do it. You've got the wrong guy.* He knew it didn't matter. This bonehead had decided Mac was going to take the fall. Mac needed to figure a way out of all of this. And he wasn't going to say anything to anyone.

"You have the right to remain silent. Anything you say can and will be used against you. Do you understand your rights?"

Mac remained silent just like he told him he could. If this fucker was going to frame him, Mac wasn't going to offer a syllable of acquiescence to this prick's game.

"Do you understand your rights?"

Silence.

"Okay. Somebody has read the ACLU handbook." The sheriff walked around behind Mac taking Mac's left hand with him then the other, cuffing them together.

Mac looked at Zoey.

Now, the media types took notice, and the clamor began. The first question at him, "Have you found a suspect?"

The sheriff turned square to the group. "The good city of Cuyamaca deserves better than to see one of its town leaders struck down in the town square. We will hold those guilty of the crime responsible. No more questions at this time. I will have more later."

He didn't go right out and say Mac was under arrest for the murder. However, the presence of handcuffs and Mac's dour expression let the reporters and the pundits and the public that this clown, Sheriff Beauford T. Justice, had found his man.

Sheriff shuffled Mac inside.

"Oh, so now you open the door?!" Zoey stood still but she wasn't the type to be silent. Mac could hear her over the gaggle. "I will get help, Mac. Don't worry, it'll be alright."

Mac was sure this was not going to work out fine. It was minutes after the attack, and they were building a case against him in public. That meant clues would be overlooked or ignored. That meant all other avenues would be seen through the lens of how Mac could have committed the crime. Things were most definitely not alright. And Mac had determined that if there was a time to worry, this was that time.

Inside, the three officers who actively ignored Mac and Zoey outside calmly awaited their approach inside the station. It was quiet in the building. The only sounds were the four feet stepping across the floor and Sheriff's belt and keys jangling at his waist.

Before a belly high counter, they stopped, and the sergeant awaited something.

Sheriff dug into Mac's pockets. "Pocket contents: Wallet. California Driver's License. Macondo, Edward. Key ring. Five keys, one fob. Amex credit card, Visa debit card. Thirteen dollars cash. iPhone. Anything else?"

Mac shook his head.

After a cursory pat down, "Shoelaces."

After pulling the white laces from his black Cons, Mac silently handed them to him.

Sheriff nodded once. "Take him to the tank."

The other two officers took an arm a piece and walked him to the rear of the station, through a door and let him into an open cell. Bars surrounding a bunk, toilet and ten by ten space.

Not a word. Mac expected some type of cheap shot or banter that he could ignore. Nothing.

They removed his cuffs and locked the cell. Exited the door with a window at eye level. One of those windows with wires all through it to keep from being broken. Like in a jail house.

Mac took a seat on the bunk and surveyed the room. Besides the door to the station house there was a metal fire door that looked to go outside, presumably, to more easily move prisoners out of the joint. There was a second cell same as his, empty. A short wall held a bench for six seated, each seat separated by a bar for cuff attachment.

The assessment took twenty-eight seconds flat. With a hip rotation, he threw his feet on the door side of the bunk and his head on the other. A run through the facts didn't offer much of a solution for why Mac was in the clink. He'd been to the town twice, three times counting today, doing nothing but interview people about Filmore, the mines and their past. The thought just wouldn't leave his mind: he was the scapegoat. A crime must have a perpetrator. The ground itself does not rise and kill a man with intent. Nor does a town. Crimes are the realm of man. Humans establish laws and humans break those laws. This sheriff lived by the immutable fact that someone committed that act against his town, not by his town, and someone would be held responsible for it. Mac would be that someone.

Relaxed concentration. Mac would fall into relaxed concentration and put the pieces together as he knew them. He was hired to clear Filmore of actions Filmore himself most probably nefariously committed against the township. On top of that, the guy was also doing his very best to further screw the area by forcing a toxic waste dump into the local mountains to get gold into his pockets that he was unable to get out of those same mountains. As far as Mac had found, not a single person in Cuyamaca supported the idea let alone the implementation of this plan to bring radioactive material to a place that could spoil the land and wastewater all while bringing very little benefit to those who lived here.

They were glad to see Filmore go. Cuyamaca, in fact, was happy someone did it.

However, we live in the United States of America and here in the U.S. of A., people are held accountable. This is no storybook land where food is plenty, land is free, and the woods rose up and struck down evil doers. Whatever lived in those woods did not act of its own accord. No faerie tale, was this.

Mac needed a plan. More than a dream of the cunning on a mystic trail. He needed evidence. Enough to prove his innocence and combat a sheriff who, at this moment, was surely building a bullet proof case against him. Not because

Mac was guilty, or the sheriff believed in justice. But because blame needed to be placed directly on a culprit so everyone could feel better and move on their merry way, forgetting any of this happened. Put a bow on it. Done. Mac would not be that guy. More was going on here and he would solve the puzzle. He would know who did this and he would not be the guy left holding the bag.

Doing this from a jail cell was a problem. On his own, he couldn't save himself. He didn't even have his Pops to count on and Stephanie sure wouldn't have anything useful. It was going to have to be Zoey. She would be his point. There was no other way to go. It was Zoey.

The decision for help created as many worries as it alleviated them. Now, he contemplated whether she had the capacity to get the bottom of this whole mess. What he really needed was a lawyer. On reflection, he may have introduced a larger problem with his complete silence. Then again, it was Mac's right, and he was going to exercise that right.

They would throw him in a room for interrogation soon. The clock was ticking the minute they arrested him. Forty-eight hours can burn off pretty quick and Mac had his constitutional right to know the charges against him. They would have to charge him.

Sitting here in the cell, they just wanted him to cool his heels. And that was what Mac intended to do. Not a word until he got his lawyer and got the hell out.

Chapter Twenty-Two

The Jail Cell Scene

Mac couldn't tell what time of day it was. He fell asleep waiting, but he couldn't have dozed for more than twenty minutes. Less activity outside that wired window had to mean day became night and Mac might not experience all that small town hospitality. Stuck in here long enough, he should at least get a package of saltines.

Sure, he was in for the long haul, Mac's eyes traveled the cracks in the poured cement ceiling like they were highways in the country, circling over and again the same roads. He had to hope Zoey was as capable as she seemed to be. Soon, the lights in the main area turned out, then in the cell. There was no reason for Mac to think something was wrong but a tickle in the back of his head told him something was very wrong. It was dark enough that his hearing sharpened. Too quiet. Just a wobble in the air around him.

He grabbed the thin wool blanket off his bed, imagined what might happen. He made it thick and wrapped it around both his hands, leaving an arm's length of slack between. It was no weapon, but he could defend himself somehow. Mac sat in the wobbly silence and listened.

The blanket was too thick. Too big in his hands. He worked through the same operation with the sheet and waited.

Time passed, measured only in Mac's breaths. He focused on his breathing. Worry would get him killed. He'd be amped and that adrenaline, if it passed, would get him tired and killed.

The door opened and a silhouette slipped through like a wraith. Dressed in all black, there was something white draped over the shoulder. A sheet with a noose tied at the end.

The lights came on. It was an officer, a towel over his shoulder and a tray with food. "I got this from Lucy's down the road. I had her make up a burger and fries. She remembered you had an allergy with milk, so she made sure no cheese and used the vegan bun."

Maybe there was something to small town hospitality. Places around the corner from Mac's office didn't remember he had allergies. The dichotomy of care for his allergies and being framed for murder was not lost on him.

Warm food in front of him activated his hunger. The worry pushed his pangs away, but the smell brought it front and center. Mac tore through the burger and fries, not a thing left after he was through except for the worry.

Fifteen minutes later when the guard returned for the tray Mac broke his silence.

"Am I gonna get my phone call?"

"So, the monster speaks," the guard said as he smiled and retrieved the tray. "I'll let the sheriff know you're back."

"I'm not talking to him. I'm talking to a lawyer."

The guard nodded as he opened the door on his way out when Mac remembered, "I'm being framed but I appreciated you caring for my allergies." The guard just kept nodding and let the door close with the spring hinge.

Mac listened to the catch settle into the jamb and stared at the silence that followed. The door beyond which everything that mattered existed while he wondered if he could solve all of this for himself from inside these walls.

Soon, the sheriff walked through that very door and said, "You're talking now, eh?"

"To a lawyer, sheriff. Not you."

"You're just making it hard on yourself."

Mac laughed. "Do you think I fell off one of your

avocado trucks? I have nothing to say to you. Just give me my call."

"Tough L.A. guy just gotta lawyer up. Like that's going to save you."

Mac was silent. He wouldn't be bated. Everything would be used against him. Even wanting a lawyer made him more guilty in this guy's eyes. "Phone call."

"Alright, smart ass. You can have your phone call." The sheriff took his cell phone out of his pocket and held it out to Mac.

Mac, of course, didn't touch it. "I'll take the call on that land line pay phone over there. Thanks."

Sheriff chuckled and unlocked the cell with a swipe of his arm. *After you.*

Now Mac had to try to remember Zoey's number. Which he couldn't. Mac hadn't dialed her number ever. He hadn't memorized a phone number since he was in grade school. They were all safely tucked in the contacts on his phone, never to be remembered without a name attached again. Who remembered numbers anymore?

So, he did what he had to. He called the number he memorized in grade school.

Stephanie picked up after two rings.

"Hi, Stephanie. It's Mac."

"Oh good. I'm glad you called. Are coming tomorrow for dinner?"

"I don't know about that. I can't explain right now, but I'm in jail."

"What happened, Mac?"

"Can you get a hold of Blink? Let him know I'm in Cuyamaca awaiting a murder charge. Also, get in touch with Zoey Forsythe."

"Murder charge? Wait. From that podcast?"

"Ya, that's the one. Get those two together. She can fill him in and start working on what the hell they can do to get me out."

"I'll do it. Don't you worry."

"Worry is about all I can do. Thanks a million,

Stephanie."

"Well, don't fret. You've faced enough troubles; this will settle out. Now, go relax. I'm on the case." The line went dead.

Mac listened to the buzz for just a moment. Maybe she really could help him. He placed the handset in the cradle then covered the handful of steps to his cell.

"Welcome back to the gray bar motel. I imagine you'll be staying for a while."

Somehow, Mac didn't find the humor in it.

The sheriff had a smile but there was no joy in those eyes. Malice. That was all Mac could see. He glowed with it as Mac's gaze followed him. The sheriff said, "Lights out," and hit the switches. The darkness fell while a small piece of it walked out of the room.

Knowing he was now in for a bit of a haul, he settled. There wasn't much sound. The hum and click of air conditioning, the vibration of electric power that was never apparent until you were stuck in silence. Mac dropped into a liminal state. Not quite sleep but rest.

At some point there was a metallic clicking then squeak and clunk of a door opening. He looked at the interior door. Nothing. It was the exterior door where a shadow entered the room. Mac was between screaming at him and hoping for the element of surprise. He spared a moment to imagine which would give him the better outcome.

It was obvious nobody was doing this on their own. No help would come. Surprise was his only advantage.

When the figure unlocked the cell, Mac feigned sleep and loaded for the attack. If Mac waited until the attacker was over him, he was toast. It was now or never. The man stepped over the threshold and Mac sprung. He held his sheet wide in front of him and in a single motion wrapped it around the man's face, swung behind him and jump-fell backwards. The mix between Mac's weight and speed overwhelmed the attacker who fell on Mac as he worked to wrap the sheet tighter around his face and neck.

The bad guy pushed hard with his legs, but Mac was

already up against the bars. He attempted to head butt Mac but only got the stomach. Mac had the upper hand.

"Who are you?"

The man attempted a twist Mac anticipated and turned with him onto his stomach. Now Mac had power and weight on him as he attempted to elbow and twist away. Then Mac felt a rush of pain in his thigh. Fear hit like lightning, but Mac lived with fear most of his life. Mac was a fighter, and that fear didn't force him to release, he automatically pulled the guy's head back then drove his face into the cement in triplet - bam, bam, bam. He felt what was probably his nose give way with a whimper then pulled harder on the sheet like he was riding a steer at the county rodeo then wrapped the arm with the knife up to the back of his neck. Too bad because his shoulder might have given way right then.

"What the fuck are you doing here?"

Nothing.

Mac rabbit punched him in the ear. "Answer me."

A muffled, "Fuck you," came back to him. This guy wasn't going anywhere.

"Hey!" And just as Mac screamed. "A mother fucker is trying to kill me you mother fuckers!"

The interior door flew open with the duty cop, "Shit." With a flick of the lights, he ran to the two men on the ground.

The sheriff was two steps behind. "What in the holy hell is going on here?" he said as the cop cuffed the intruder and sheriff sat Mac on his bed to look at his wound. "Get up. I have to take you for stitches."

Mac took a gander at the guy who just attacked him, his face bloodied and stunned.

"You know who that is?"

Mac had never seen him before, broken face or not, and said so.

"I'm not happy about this," the sheriff said.

"Nor am I," Mac said, wondering what the hell he was getting at.

The sheriff raised his voice to the dispatcher at the front desk. She looked up from her book and actively listened. "Tell Newburg to meet me at the clinic. We'll need stitches." The dispatcher simply nodded, a middle-aged, competent nod, as she raised the phone handle.

They walked through the front of the station and out the entry. It was dark out and the gaggle of press had disbursed. They took a right.

"You're under my control. I may have held you as a murderer, but you have a right to safety in my jail."

There wasn't much Mac could or would say to that. So many things went wrong under that statement that Mac would only get himself in trouble with an answer.

"It's only two doors down," the sheriff said as he assessed Mac's gate. "You okay walking there, Edward?" He sat on a wood and iron bench in front of a small clinic, large leaves gathered around the feet. The lights were out. "He don't live far." Silence. "Not enough people in this town to have a hospital open all night."

Mac was in no mood for chit chat considering the stabbing and murder charge, and all.

"It's good people around here," Sheriff said. "The type that look after each other. The kind that come out in the middle of the night to help a friend." The doctor appeared from behind the building and Sheriff looked pointedly at Mac, "Or a stranger."

As Mac stood, he rolled his eyes at the pain or maybe the sheriff.

"Let's get inside and take a look," the doctor said without even looking at them, unlocking the door with a set of three keys, one of which was his car fob. He was slight, not tall, with the sinew of a runner.

Directly inside the door was a waiting room with one of those nurse's windows and a door to the heart of the office. The doctor entered efficiently, flipping lights, moving through the office in as few steps as necessary. The doctor directed Mac to an exam table. He had never looked at his two guests until they were seated in one of the exam rooms but once he looked, they had his full attention, "Let's see the leg." It was like a spotlight had been shined in his direction.

Mac splayed his hands around the wound without a word. Seemed self-explanatory.

"Looks like a knife fight," doctor said with raised eyebrows and a question in his eyes that he wouldn't ask. He cut Mac's pants away from the cut and placed a chemical concoction on a patch of gauze, "Hold this on there while I get the gear."

He brought a tray next to the patient and cleaned the wound. It bled but not too much. Once they could look without much blood, it was more nick than stab wound. The doctor made quick work after shooting local in the spot, which didn't totally cover the pain, but good enough. "I'll give you more juice," he offered. Mac shook his head, "It's fine. Just finish."

That received a nod of approval.

Not another word until the doctor was done and cleaned up when he said, "Be sure to change the dressing daily and be gentle with a shower in a couple of days. You can have the stitches out in a couple weeks."

The doctor then threw his hand out to the side in an offer to escort them out. Mac guessed they were leaving because the sheriff hopped up without waiting for the hobbled Mac to follow. The silence of the encounter reminded him entirely too much of his own silence regarding his charge. It also made Mac wonder how often things like this happened. Does this doctor come down here often in the middle of the night to care for wounded prisoners?

In Mac's mind, none of this seemed to bode well for him. He was escorted to his cell accompanied by silence and maybe the lump of his attacker in the cell next door. Once laid out on his bunk, he worried on this whole situation. A nefarious charge, an assault and a night in jail, all for a job he knew he shouldn't have taken in the first place. He didn't think he'd get a wink of sleep, but exhaustion won out to provide his subconscious more imaginative ways for him to fret.

His blood galloped. He panted. His head swam. He flailed through the blackness, his legs wrapped and bound in a cold lather.

He tried to clear a space, but he was trapped. A ghoulish apparition of torn rags and empty sockets floated above him. Just outside his short and shallow breaths, the space trilled with the unheard tone of dread and pressed on his chest. Yellow rays split through a sycamore as orange and purple mingled on the clouds.

Mac opened his eyes again to a darkness with only his racing heart and the hum of air conditioning for company. Something in him had changed.

Eventually, he drifted off only to be awoken by the sprung hinges of the interior door. With a little luck it would be Blinkman ready to do his lawyer magic.

It was Zoey.

"Good morning, Sunshine!"

Mac rubbed the sleep from his eyes and swung his feet to the floor which reminded him of his stitches.

"What happened to you?" Zoey swiped her hand at his whole him then pointed at the leg.

"I had a visitor." He indicated the cell next door whose inhabitant seemed to have been carted away while Mac slept. The cell was empty.

Her eyes and mouth went straight into hard, horizontal lines. She turned around and banged on the door. Nothing.

She banged again as the door opened. "He was attacked?"

The duty cop ignored Zoey and entered the space. He addressed Mac, "I have a lawyer here to see you. We've made a conference room available." He unlocked the cell.

"Where's my assailant?" Mac said.

The officer slapped cuffs on Mac's wrists and lead him to the front. "He's already at county. He had a warrant; they'll just tack it on."

Zoey shook herself from her spectating and followed.

Sitting at the conference room table was Blinkman. He rose and Zoey introduced herself, "Zoey Forsythe."

Blinkman nodded as he shook her offered hand but swiftly focused on Mac, "What the hell happened to you?"

"I was just telling Zoey, I had a visitor last night," Mac said, taking a one-legged seat, his other stretched straight to avoid the extra pain.

"A bullshit charge and now you've been attacked."

"Pretty much." Mac was glad to have people on his side for the moment. He was feeling bleak there this morning. "Have you talked to a judge?"

"So, they gotta charge him, right?" Zoey asked.

Blinkman reassessed Zoey and said, "Well, amiga, the forty-eight-hour thing everybody believes about criminal charges is wrong."

"Is it?" Murder wasn't much in Mac's area of expertise.

"When under investigation for murder, or other serious crimes, they have ninety-six hours. Four Days."

"Even after he was attacked?" Zoey's tone rose a pitch.

Unimpressed with the outburst, Blinkman continued, "To top it off, that can get a little wiggly depending on the judge and court hours, weekends. That sort of thing."

"What's next?" Mac wanted a plan.

Blinkman said, "I wanted you to know I was on the case. Offer a friendly face." He addressed them both, "Don't worry, I'll get you released and with your safety a concern, I'm gonna raise hell." His voice didn't rise a notch, this came out in a measured tone, but there was a rattling rage behind his eyes. "This should never happen."

Mac was pretty sure it did happen. All the time. The attacks. The guy breaking into a jail to do it, maybe not as much.

A knuckle knock came through the door. "Sorry to disturb you." It was the sheriff.

Blinkman looked to the other two for confirmation, to which both nodded, and said, "Come in."

The sheriff stepped in the room, "We're cutting you lose, Edward. You are free to go," and walked out of the room, leaving the door ajar. He said over his shoulder, "Don't forget to pick up your stuff from Eric."

Blinkman had loaded for bear the moment the sheriff arrived and was all bunched up without the release but, Mac, he sprung up - with a wince - and walked right out to the duty cop.

Zoey, twice in two days, was speechless.

"You got my stuff?" Mac said coming around in front of the duty desk. Zoey and Blinkman went to the door.

The bag was already laid out on the counter and the duty cop, Eric, handed over the form to sign. Mac signed.

"This all of it?"

"That's what your signature says. I'd double check." Eric said as he ripped out the carbon copy below and handed it to Mac. "Also, take that container. It's your breakfast."

Mac looked inside the styrofoam clamshell to discover hash browns and chili with three slices of bacon. Mac instinctively grabbed a slice and shoved it in his mouth then pocketed his wallet, phone and keys.

Eric said, "Since you were allergic to dairy, Alice didn't think you'd eat eggs. No farm stuff there."

He didn't tell him eggs weren't dairy, amazed to be given a safe breakfast. Besides, he didn't like eggs.

Mac gave him a quick salute and skedaddled. He knew when the gettin' was good.

"I'd like to have a word with that sheriff," Zoey said.

"I'll fight it out when I'm far away from those bars," Mac said as he walked out the doors.

"We'll have this out in court," Blinkman said.

"I just want out." He looked both ways and saw what he needed and walked straight towards it.

Zoey looked after him, "Where are you going? The car's over here. Your car is over here."

He didn't answer. No one was going to tell him what to do at this moment. Even twelve hours made him adamant about what anyone else could or could not tell him what to do.

Mac sat on the wood slatted and iron love seat in front of the clinic. While he opened his clam shell and shoveled a bit of chili and hashbrown into his mouth, he watched them catch up.

Blinkman stood silently but Zoey sat next to him, leaning forward, intent on speaking then stopped. She leaned back and let him be. Maybe he had earned a moment of silence. Maybe he needed a moment of breeze on his face and to catch up on what the hell had sprung him after that night of bullshit.

Mac said so, "Why would they spring me, Blink?"

"Could be as simple as no evidence."

"Or new evidence." Zoey said this and sat forward again, eyes lit. "Another suspect."

"Someone was trying to take me out." Mac couldn't say 'kill'; it was too true.

Blinkman agreed. "Dead men tell no tales."

"You would've been even more of a patsy. Really taking the fall. Jeez, we gotta get you outta here." Zoey looked at them both but neither moved. Only Mac's mouth worked the bacon or the scoops of chili. Wheels were turning and churning here. "So, what do we do?"

"First thing is I'm going to finish my delicious breakfast," Mac said. "Then we are going to get the fat fuck out of this town."

"And after that, we are going to nail the son of a bitch who set Mac up."

"Ah, Blink. I didn't know you cared," Mac almost choked on his food from the laugh that rumbled up as he said it.

Zoey could see it now, there was drama ahead. "This is going to be a hoot."

"They thought I was stirring shit up asking questions. Wait until they see me when I give a shit." Mac stood and headed towards the cars. He dropped the clam shell in the trash can and headed to his car with what could only called a strut. No trace of a limp from his stitches. Not an ounce of weariness from sleeping in the jail house. Mac moved like a bear stalking through the pines and sycamores. Top of the food chain. It was on.

Chapter Twenty-Three

The Angry Scene

What came next for Mac, he wasn't sure, but they put him in the middle. He was no sacrificial lamb bleating meekly on its way to the block.

All his anger was useless. The energy should be put to use.

As he walked to his car, he turned on his phone expecting a flood of information, which he received. An entire blurt of texts funneled in and the phone rang.

Delilah.

"I'm sorry about your father." Mac was pissed but he wasn't a monster.

"Thank you," she paused. "I am sorry you have been placed in the middle of all this. Come by my father's house, I would like to help."

It was as good an offer as any. "I'm on my way."

Mac stopped. Blinkman and Zoey were still twenty paces behind. Once they were close enough, he said, "I'm headed over to Filmore's."

"Are you sure that's wise?" Blinkman said.

Zoey had another idea, "Was that her?"

Mac ran his tongue over his teeth, nodded.

Blinkman took in Mac's whole attitude, "Don't go starting any other problems with that family. You aren't clear just because you're out."

"I'd never," Mac said with a shake of his head. "Really, I want to feel her out. Besides, she's paid me well, I have a responsibility to her as a client."

"I'll come with." Zoey was already getting in the passenger seat of his car.

"No." Mac didn't need her nose in his business any more than it already was. "I got this."

"Well, I do, too." She grinned as she sat in the car and buckled the seatbelt. "Besides, I want to fill you in on the dirt I found while you were in the hoosegow."

Closing his eyes for strength, Mac then looked at Blinkman who said, "Whatever. You're a grown man. So far, you don't need me. Don't do anything else to make it so you do."

"I appreciate you coming down."

"Just don't break anything, Macondo."

"Make no promises, tell no lies."

"Good luck. We all know there's dirt flying around this town, I recommend, as your lawyer, to stay out of it. But I know you won't." Blinkman leaned down and gave Zoey a wave, "Y'all got my number."

As they watched Blinkman drive away, Zoey said, "He's a good guy."

"He's an asshole."

They both laughed.

"But he's got my back and I appreciate it," Mac said. "Now, what'd you find?"

"We have entered a generations old fight, Mac. Did you know Filmore's ancestors basically stole their land from the Oliveras?" Besides what was in the podcast she filled Mac in on what she learned about the Californios and land grants. It was obviously the tip of the iceberg.

Mac, of course, knew all about the boondoggle for the friends of the governor back in the day. The scramble to get land must have been epic among that moneyed class. They played their cards for generations worth of property and, as it stood, the only people that were sure not to get the rights were the indigenous tribes. In this town, Cuyamaca, that was the Kumeyaay.

Driving through this land, Mac couldn't have imagined there was too much fight for this area until that gold showed up. Before metropolitan water districts this would have been rough country. Not a lot of running water. He was sure the pine would have been alright for the timber people but once again, not enough water for them to replenish easily. Southern California never could have grown like it did without pulling from the Colorado River and Los Angeles taking the lifeblood from the Sierras. They spent so much time in drought nowadays they were losing the Easterners who moved here for the rich grass lawns twelve months a year. Water restrictions kill the lie that California was tropical. Arid pushing towards desert, not the Hawaii-lite those postwar vets tried to reinvent after winning the survival lottery.

These trees had seen a lot, most of that time without so many humans to ruin the good times. This continent had developed a reasonably balanced approach between humans and nature until interlopers from the other hemispheres imposed their exotic ways on the land and each other.

When they arrived to Filmore's entrance there was a big white suburban parked across the road. The security guys explained no cars were allowed to approach the house.

"I work for them." Mac didn't like how this was going already.

"Good. Then you understand." The guy waved his hand. "Just park it over there and you can walk in. No cars."

"No cars."

"Nope."

After they parked and started the half-mile jaunt to the house, the only sound was silence. Not exactly silence. As they ambled along the voices of the forest surrounded them. Birds chirped and whirled, a few sticks and leaves crumpled from what was probably cotton tails but deeper behind there was the wind. The voices through the trees whispered secrets, offered answers. Inklings of what all of this would come to.

Zoey pointed out a single coyote loping across the ridge, staying a respectable distance away from the humans it knew to be dangerous.

"You haven't said much," Mac said looking at Zoey,

not adding that it was out of character. Don't poke the bear.

"I figured you probably needed a little space," she said, twirling an arm length stick she picked up as they walked. "You'll talk when you're ready." She seemed to enjoy the bounce of the far end of the branch and its single leaf. "Between jail, then what happened there, and your father, you've had a traumatic few days."

He thought about that for a few scuffles and steps. All he had was a nod for that. She was right. Mac hadn't been able to apply words to any of what he faced. He figured he'd have time enough to parse his feelings when it was all through.

There was a rev and tailspin behind them, the sound of gravel flying. A white Land Rover raced towards them then came to an abrupt stop, window even with them, it quickly opened.

It was Junior. "Hop in."

Zoey and Mac met eyes and shrugged in unison. She said, "You take shotgun." And they climbed in, and Junior shot out of the chute.

Mac regarded Junior then, "We haven't met—"

"I know who you are, and you clearly know me." Junior didn't have one in his mouth, but Mac could imagine a piece of grass sticking out. Like he'd just come out of the barn after a romp; happy, relaxed.

"Despite what happened to Mac, I want to give you my condolences on your father," Zoey said from the back seat.

"Tragic. Tragic that people would do such a thing." Now Junior had an idea. "You here to talk with Delilah about all that?"

"Yes, we are here to talk with Delilah about all that." *All that?* Mac had felt like the hand of grief was pushing him into the mud along the River Styx about his own father. Like Charon the Boatman wouldn't pick him up but laughed at Mac blundering in the muck. While Junior looked like his shoulders had shed the weight of the world. Intellectually Mac knew the difference, but his heart couldn't fathom that scale's tare.

Junior whipped into the driveway to a clean stop at the garage door of the house. Even with his freewheeling, Mac never worried that they would crash into the thing. This brat had a professional driver's confidence.

Junior cranked around to look at Zoey then Mac and said, "I know it don't track for you but I'm glad the bastard's dead. Delilah, she's taking it harder. I think she has more of that paternal love and belief than I do. Did." Here he paused to see if he'd get a reaction.

There was none so he continued.

"I may not have liked him. He may never have given me a fair shake, but I'll tell you, I'll protect his legacy and, more importantly, our fortune. You do what you must to help Delilah get through her stuff but if you have problems around here, come to me. I'll settle them." A dark look passed through him. Mac noted it and kept attentive, Junior continued, "I ain't risking this family."

Mac was confident that, to this kid, family only meant money, but he toed the company line, so to speak, "Its my job to look out for the best interests of my clients. Not to worry."

Since that was settled, Junior loped out of the truck to the front door while Zoey and Mac followed at a slower meter. The place was dark. Quiet. Last time he was here, they dragged Filmore right into the back of the truck. In fact, the tire marks further marred the trodden sod and flowerbeds. As Mac paused to inspect the mess, Delilah appeared from the dark interior into the daylight. Mac could play it cool up to this point, but he moved from simmer to boil as he walked toward that front door.

Delilah wore an A-line dress. All black, head to toe with a pair of thick sixties sunglasses, save classically red lipstick. She took a drag on a cigarette, watching them from an emotional distance. There was sadness in the slope of her cheeks but there was more.

He waited for Delilah to say something then when nothing came, Zoey broke the spell.

"You set him up."

This received but a turn of the chin and, from the shift in her cheeks, what must have been a squint behind those eye hiders.

Mac joined in, "Well. Is that what you did? Get me involved so the outsider could take the fall?"

"Edward." Simply in the way she said that one word. His name. Mac couldn't equate her with the girl he had been dealing with. This woman had gravitas. Power. "Why in the world would I do that?" She turned around, took a step to the threshold, then over her shoulder said, "Come inside. You can bring the girl." Then she was enveloped by the darkness.

A few big rain drops fell around them like an introduction to the downpour that commenced. Without a thought or consideration, they went inside.

As much as the yard was in disarray, the interior was worse. The furniture had been placed back where it belonged but the details of Filmore's house were marred. Scrapes and holes in the walls, a missing vase in the entry. The stairway banister missed teeth from its wooden grin. A smell of disinfectant spray and lemon furniture polish permeated the room.

Delilah headed toward a single wingback chair that faced a love seat in the living room. The type of room that received guests and seemed to have gone out of style at least a generation ago. When she turned around to sit, one arm wrapped across her torso, her elbow touching her left hand while the right held the cigarette aloft, smoking. Delilah sat, straight backed, while only moving her hand to feed the cig to her lips.

In what seemed to be the only option, Mac and Zoey sat tight, shoulder to shoulder, on the love seat.

"People have been asking why you were blamed so quickly in my father's demise. I wondered the same."

"It's nice that you wondered, Delilah, while you left me rotting in that cell."

"You were hardly in the cell long enough to rot."

"Long enough for an attempt to take me out."

"I have no knowledge of that."

Like they were in court. It was like these people were unfailingly building a case, obfuscating and adjusting the point of view.

"No knowledge."

Zoey had been sitting quietly, but she couldn't spectate. "Do you mean knowledge of it happening or knowledge of who did it?"

As Delilah leaned forward, pulled off her glasses and uncrossed her legs. The leather squeaked. She said, "Doesn't matter."

"It does to me," Mac said getting up and circling to behind the love seat. Then he asked for something that at the time seemed unlikely but learned later was impossible, "You're going to have to do better than that. These shell games almost got me killed."

"Oh, Mac. It isn't the first time," Delilah said.

Zoey was speechless. For a girl who was never at a loss for words, she sure lost them today.

If Mac had his head on straight. If he had a decent night's sleep. If someone hadn't just attempted to murder him. If his father hadn't just passed, he would have left then and there. If he didn't need the money.

It's a sad state of being when we'll do just about anything for money.

"Why did you call me out here, Delilah?"

"I thought you'd never ask." She relaxed in the chair again. "I asked you here because—"

"WHAT IS GOING ON WITH THIS MINE DEAL, DEL?" wailed from upstairs. It was Junior.

When Mac looked up the stairs, it occurred to him that Truman, the security guard, wasn't around anymore. The threat in Junior's drive down the stairs put Mac in the mind of those rioters that last time he was here.

Delilah simply sighed.

Junior had a laptop open in the crook of his arm, "Carmichael just sent a kill letter. Did you see this? Why didn't you tell me?"

"Because I wasn't sure it would happen and that today being Saturday, if it was to happen, they would do this all when courts were open rather than to give us a head start on the week."

"You're going to lose this whole deal."

"It doesn't matter."

"How does losing a massive deal not matter? I can't understand why you are left in charge of all of this."

"Which is exactly why I am in charge because you don't understand anything Junior. There is a twenty million dollar kill fee for pulling out."

"Why didn't anyone tell me?"

"Consider yourself told." She turned to Mac, then back to Junior and said, "Now go away, the adults are speaking."

"But with Daddy gone, how could they…"

"Junior, the deal is with the corporation not him. We are here and they have cold feet. They pull out, we get remunerated. End of story."

"Edward, it was important that father was cleared and had strong standing in the community so he could shepherd this deal. He is gone. The deal is dead." She looked between her two guests to create dramatic pause. "You are no longer needed." Delilah rose, picked up a gift bag from the kitchen table and handed it to him. "Thank you for your efforts on our behalf." She left the room and Truman appeared.

Mac, flabbergasted, didn't speak. The guard led them to the door. Mac was now free from this entire Filmore train wreck of a family. This could be because she didn't need him or because she wanted to create public distance from him. Was he going to be charged with murder? Set up as a patsy all along.

"Truman, am I the fall guy here?" They'd known each other a long time. They were never friends but it's possible he liked Mac better than this ridiculous family.

He answered that line of thought. "Look. I don't know anything about what they do. All I know is they pay me well and in a couple of years, I won't have to listen to any of you people moving your chess pieces. I got nothing for you, Mac."

Now, as he looked for the car, Mac realized it was at the road entrance. "Can you give us a ride out?"

The entry door was already closed.

"Adding insult to injury, amiright?"

"Zoey." Mac looked at her and had nothing productive to say so he looked in the bag. It was bundle of twenties, still wrapped like at the bank. Probably twenty grand.

"Looks like you can afford the legal fees now," Zoey said without a hint of a joke.

"Ya." Cash. A payoff, payout, an untraceable chunk of go away.

Positive this was the beginning a wave of bad tidings, Mac tried to clear his mind. These jokesters were one thing. Mac had more than a murder charge to deal with. His dad's funeral was tomorrow.

As if she could read his mind, Zoey said, "I'll be there tomorrow."

Mac focused on which tree a woodpecker tap tapped.

"You know, I knew your dad."

"You can't know a guy just because I talked about him once or twice."

"No, you twit. He helped me when I was in law school."

"You're a lawyer, too?"

"Passed the bar and decided I hated it. Too many compromises for my taste." She pointed to a Sycamore to the right. Up high, just next to a patch of mistletoe growing out of a branch, was the woodpecker. "I was in law school and already getting an inkling that it may not be for me, so I started poking around all the different types of lawyering. We only met in passing but he had some kind words when I was shadowing an Assistant D.A. He told me everybody needs a helping hand once in a while."

"Everybody needs a helping hand." Mac didn't exactly say this to Zoey but himself.

"To be honest, he also said whatever I do, it's less about dollars than sense."

"That was a favorite of his. He loved the wordplay, how it forced you to flip perspective."

"The D.A. said the same thing. In that wing, he was famous for solving cases just because he had that ability to attack the problem from a unique point of view."

"I admired that about him."

"You weren't the only one."

They walked surrounded by the shuffle of their feet and whirl of the woodpecker until Mac said, "I've been mired in my self-pity about the arrest and my dad, but you know, he'd already have been telling me to flip this thing on its head. We've been too straight forward in our approach. Let's flip the script."

"Did you just say 'we'?"

"That's what you took from that?"

"Yep. But I like the other thing, too. What do you suggest?"

"I've been learning about Filmore and all his antics but what I haven't done is find out why Johnson Long Chemical was so hot and heavy and had now backed out."

"If it was a good deal before he was gone, why is it a bad deal now that he is. You think they were pulling the strings?"

"As much as Filmore saw himself as a player, he was a big fish in a small pond. Let's find out what the real big fish wanted."

"Are you sure you want to get in deeper? They already put you in jail."

"Ya, but I wasn't charged with anything."

"Ya, not yet."

"Not yet. Let's see if we can push their hand."

"You're playing with fire, Macondo."

"Why else would I do this type of thing? If it wasn't for the fun stuff, I'd be chasing insurance fraud claims all day."

"Isn't that what you do?"

"Not when something like this comes up, I don't."

Chapter Twenty-Four

The Funeral Scene

From the gargoyle above, water dripped onto the metal outcropping below. Tap tapping, the sound beat on as Mac lay in his bed unable to start his day. This day. The time ticked, forcing him, inevitably, to act.

Shower, then he dressed piece by piece. Black socks. Black suit. Black tie. Black shoes. After a double check in the mirror, his hair was still black but so were the bags under his eyes.

Entering the gates of the old cemetery, just around the corner from Elysian Park and the Academy, Mac could almost see the spirits lined up at the property, all along the road. Apparitions were scrawled in charcoal relief eagerly awaiting visitors under the limbs of the reaching oaks, alders and sycamores.

When he got to the cemetery plot, Blinkman was already there. Mac should have known he would be. Dad had set all the arrangements, so every step simply fell after the first domino. And it was Blinkman who flicked that first domino.

"I'm lucky you took care of this for Dad. Thank you," Mac said as he gave Blink a hug.

"I wouldn't have it any other way. Good thing, too, what with that mess down in Cuyamaca."

It may have been his dad's funeral, but Blink would say what had to be said.

"I'm out. It'll blow over."

"Shouldn't-a taken a job with that—guy." Blink searched Mac's eyes. "A drowning man will take you down with him."

"He's already drowned, Blink."

"There's still gonna be blow back."

Stephanie walked up as Blink finished. Mac was worrying about Blinkman so much, he missed her coming.

She hugged Mac then Blink.

"I can't thank you enough for taking care of this," she said, tissue to nose.

"Everyone had their orders; I was just the first in line. There's the priest," Blink said and left them.

"Me, too." Mac wanted to speak with the priest and didn't want to leave Stephanie the moment she arrived. But he did. "I'll be back."

Stephanie stood still as she watched him leave.

Mac walked right past the priest and Blink to the burial site. The casket wasn't here yet. A tarp was set up with a half dozen chairs. He was here to see his mom. It wasn't a place he visited often. Being a Californian, the family never did the Día de los Muertos. They just loved all the art. And the idea of it. Honestly, he hated the cemetery and couldn't visit on purpose.

This place was for when you had to come. Just looking around the space made him sad. On top of his sadness for his father, Mac could picture coming here for his mom's funeral. The people, the tears, the overwhelm. The weight of all those anonymous apparitions leaned on his living soul, feeding hungrily on life's breathe.

Rather than bow our heads it is when we look up that we see the angels. When Mac did so now, the sunlight broke from a cloud and a sparkling spirit seemed to pass in the air above as if his mother was there. Mac couldn't find a feeling for his father, yet. It was too soon. Too raw. Too new to the next realm. Family spirits visit more when family passed or was about to. A rumble in the liminal space between here and there.

Right now, missing her only left more room to miss him. Emptiness, hollow, echoing. Mac's hands felt a thousand pounds.

He turned around to see the hearse park and the slow

stream of solemn faces approach. A sad day. Nobody liked to acknowledge the end of the journey.

Mac felt a light touch on the shoulder. He turned to see Nicki and Alan dressed in black funeral garb.

She squeezed him. "Oh, Mac, sweetheart. I'm sorry."

Alan, without a word, took Mac's hand seeking something in Mac's eyes then gave him a bear hug.

"I'm sorry, Macondo."

"Me, too. Thanks, Aguilar."

Alan grabbed Mac's shoulder in his hand, pushed back to arm's length and stared straight into his eyes again and nodded.

As they finished, Nicki said, "Anything, Mac. Just tell us." Nothing more needed to be said. Could be said. They all wiped a tear. Well, Nickie dabbed so as not to smear her whole face with mascara and said, "We'll see you after."

His friends walked toward the burial site and Mac stayed still. The air held a light mist that settled over the grounds in a blanket. The clouds ate and muffled the sounds of the mourners' speech with an occasional laugh. The traffic outside roared past like another world. Disconnected from the entire scene, Mac felt like a spectator.

"Hey, partner." It was Zoey.

In a spot where Mac would probably have witty banter or, at least, the anger to deny they were partners, he simply nodded.

She enveloped him in her arms and said, "My deepest condolences, Edward. I'm sorry for your loss." Zoey held him for a moment longer, released, gave him a pat on his shoulder as she looked into his eyes, then left him.

Once he talked with a batch of people as they streamed in, he realized what a relief it was; a simple kindness for his friends and Zoey to give her condolences then move on.

So many of the exchanges felt like they were giving him their grief rather than relieving Mac of his own. Offers of sorrow blended with stories of their own fathers and mothers, sisters and brothers, relative or child combined to overcome Mac's entire facade of control.

When he touched the casket, it was cold as the freezer cabinet at the grocery store, inanimate. Mac wanted there to be a spiritual connection but this thing, it was the opposite. By definition, he figured. Dead.

He took the front left corner and Blinkman and four other officers picked up with him. Once again, he imagined they might float the distance to the gravesite, spirits on the clouds. It was heavy. They struggled with small steps under the weight of his father and the casket.

Mac wondered if he had the feet or the head. It must have been the feet because the old westerns talk about leaving places feet first. His dad loved those old spaghetti westerns by Leone and the sort. Good guys that weren't so good. Bad guys that were all bad. Except many of them went long, like this funeral. He was ready to be done and they were just setting the thing on the stand.

Mac took his place in a chair next to Stephanie. He studied the arranged flower stands in red and white, blue, of course. Roses, orchids, lilies. They all began to swell and extend; became animated objects, growing and multiplying. Reaching like tentacles, they wrapped each person in an embrace. The sprouts extended to his mother's grave and his grandparents' over the knoll. He focused on the petals, the variation and difference in contrast to the stamen until he was lowered in the ground. Even while the guests spoke and grasped his hands or patted his shoulder, Mac could only see the flowers as they grew and the ancestors as they waited.

Mac had few tears to feed them. A stray drop formed during Blinkman's words during the ceremony as he recalled Eddie Sr difficulties in getting his son through high school without his wife. The only mention of Mac's mom during the burial, officially or unofficially. During Mac's own eulogy, he remained in control with a few laughs provided in his remembrance, but tearless. He held in his heart that his job was as emcee not the bereaved although the entire event revolved around him without his involvement. Blink handled things. Stephanie cried and was consoled by her sister. Mac remained a rock in the stream that flowed past him.

What stood out most to Mac was how alone he was in the world. The single mooring he had checked with and tied to in a storm would soon be left alone in this place. Silent and abandoned.

"Hearing all these stories about your father…" Zoey had snuck up next to Mac. "I can't help but think he was a better man than you."

Mac turned to look at her as she continued.

"Better sense of humor. And God knows a better detective." She laughed. Mac smiled in appreciation of the effort.

"I might be able to accept the detective part but sense of humor? C'mon."

"It's true. He'd break the ice with humor. Try to make you comfortable around him. Give you a view into his humanity."

"So, he could get the goods out of you."

"Well, that was the detective part. Your methods tend to lean toward the obstinate and defensive."

"Now I feel seen. This is skirting into my love language now. Insults and insecurity."

"I know, Mac. I know."

"Thanks for this little talk. I feel better."

"Good."

"You're still not my partner," he said and walked straight to his car and drove away while she watched him go, corner of her mouth pinned in her cheek.

Nickie walked up with Alan.

They watched while Zoey said, "He's gonna have to stop doing that."

Nickie said, "Mac's got a way of doing that."

"Cut him some slack," Alan said.

Nobody looked away but Nicki said, "Nobody can run from their problems. No matter how far you go, you are still right there."

Mac turned left out of the gate and wended his way over to the gardens.

Once he walked up the stairs between mural covered retaining walls, he found Albie sitting on the bench below the persimmon tree. He wasn't doing anything. He looked to be meditating on the plants around him. The fava beans that hung heavy already and the serrano chilis green and full. Albie gave a wave as Mac came over.

"Coming from the thing?" Albie said.

"Ya." Mac sat next to Albie on the wood slatted, wrought iron bench. The slats had a little more give than he would have liked. "I had to get out of there."

"Don't like 'em myself. Life's for the living."

"Funerals, too."

"I hope you're not upset I didn't come."

"I'm here, aren't I?"

"Too many tears."

"Too many."

"He was gone when I found him, Edward. Nothing I could do."

"I know, Albie. I know."

"Sometimes it's just your time and it was Eddie's."

"I don't think he would rather have been anywhere else. He loved these plants."

"There's a joy in caring and tending for something. The rewards are more than the fruits of our labor."

"Albie?"

"Ya?"

"What am I gonna do now?"

"Be sad for a bit. Then feel a little less sad as time goes on. But that space in your heart, it never fills up. We create new spaces but our loved ones, they never leave."

Mac reached down and pulled a dandelion next to his foot out of the ground. "I'm a suspect in this murder case. Dad died. I owe a bunch a money I'll never be able to pay back. I don't see a way forward."

"Who needs it. You start and then find your way. You need to start fighting, Mac. I've been watching you lately.

Listless and depressed. Not taking care of your plants. Not taking care of your business. Not taking care of yourself. Take a new look at those shoes."

Mac recognized the frays he'd been avoiding.

"Your Dad and I, we'd been talking lately about what we could do to get you going again. Well, he ain't here and all I got is this talk, but you need to square up these problems and kick the shit out of 'em."

Mac didn't even imagine that he'd be a conversation topic between those two.

"You be sad. That's fine and good. You also do your stuff. Life don't wait for you to lick your wounds. That clock keeps on tic, tic, ticking. Get busy living. That's the only way to respect what your ancestors did for you."

Albie slapped Mac's knee, "Now what's first?"

"I'll have to think about it," Mac said. He sat and looked, rooted to the spot.

"Don't think," Albie said. "You spent enough time thinking. Now it's your time to do."

Albie stood up and grabbed Mac to pull him up, too. Those sinewy arms were stronger than they looked. Gardening really was good exercise.

"You be sad while you figure this out. But you have to go figure this out. Trust your instincts. Believe me, those things are steered by spirits, telling us where to go. Walk out of here and do the first thing that occurs to you because jail will not be a good look on you, young man."

Mac walked down the steps and pulled out his phone, "We need to talk." He listened for a moment. "Okay, I'm headed to my office now."

Chapter Twenty-Five

The A Little Help Scene

Mac closed the blinds behind his desk as the video conference linked up. There was total silence from the program until Frankie's face flashed onto the screen.

"You've been busy, Macondo," Frankie said. "I don't have to tell you a murder charge will hurt our professional relationship."

"They're scapegoating me," Mac said. "I didn't kill the guy."

"Personally, I think the world's better for it."

Mac needed to expand the scope of his project a little. If he could get the heft of the fed behind him, it'd be easier to move mountains.

"What would you say if I told you there might be a connection between those drums of DDT and Filmore?"

"Continue."

"I'm still pulling the strings on the knot," Mac had to set the bait because he'd barely considered this as a possibility but, like Albie said, he trusted his gut. "It looks like one of the shell companies involved with those chemical drops is tied into this waste dump Filmore was trying to get down in Cuyamaca."

One to call it as it lays, Frankie said, "Are you getting me involved to save your ass?"

"No. It started as a hunch. As I met with your wonk about the barrels, the senator showed up when it all blew up about the EIR for Cuyamaca. There was a string there. More links these cases than the EPA."

"What do you want from me?"

"I needed you to know I'm chasing this lead. That I

might shake shit loose. And, for once in my career, I'm asking your permission before I do it."

"A night in jail has changed you, Macondo."

"It might well have."

"Respect for authority doesn't suit you. Go rattle the gates of hell if you must. Even your father would have approved of that." That was her way of giving condolences.

"I think he would. Thanks, Frankie." That would be one hell of a deed if Mac solved these cases together. He could feel a little more energy. Taking control of this situation was the only way he would escape jail or worse. He didn't know what the stakes were, but he did know they had to be much bigger than just his future. People were moving chess pieces Mac didn't even know existed and he was sure to be a pawn.

Since he was in the VPN for the secure chat with Frankie, he decided to dig again on the DDT issue from this new standpoint. He didn't need links to the toxic chemical waste, he wanted a connection between the plant in Wilmington and the mine in Cuyamaca.

Most of what he found in the cursory beginning were the images of DDT sprayed from large trucks on beaches while families tanned and frolicked. It brought to mind how they used to spray malathion on all of Los Angeles in an effort to eradicate fruit flies. According to the World Health Organization, it only caused brain damage in children and the DDT seems to carry through females for generations. They have found traces of the chemical in the wombs of grandchildren of women who were exposed in places like that beach. Fish and birds are damaged, and so are humans. He was looking in the wrong place or searching in the wrong way. This science was important but not the point.

It all started with business. Money. Also: obvious. Companies made money while risking the health of their workers but that, also, was as old as time. See slaves and wars, for instance. Taking advantage of others was sport for these people. If there was one thing that was old as the state of California, it's not oil or chemicals, even people, it's the land itself. Real estate.

Who owns the land that houses that chemical plant in Wilmington?

A search in San Diego County was possible online. However, one could only access the information for Los Angeles with a visit to the county registrar. He already knew who owned the land down in San Diego. It was up here that things were murkier. He was going to have to go to the county registrar.

A wind blew through his office, and he looked up to a silhouette in the doorway. Zoey. "Where are you going?"

"To city hall. I've got an idea about the land. It's the only place I can research it."

With a step into the light, and hands planted squarely on her hips she said, "That's crazy talk. You need to take a breath. You buried your father today."

"And I'll join him if I don't puzzle out what is causing all this commotion in Cuyamaca."

"Edward Macondo. You need to deal with your feelings, or they will never go away."

"I'm dealing with them while keeping myself out of jail or worse, Zoey."

"You do have to do the research and solve this. But you also have to give yourself a moment."

"I had a moment sitting in jail. I'd like to avoid a sequel."

Mac didn't want to step through her to get to the doorway so stopped directly before her. He said, "Now step out of my office so I can lock up."

She did as he asked, and Mac locked up and left without another word. He could feel her eyes on him as he walked down the chessboard hallway. It wasn't the first time he thought he was a pawn in someone else's game. He may not be rich. He wasn't connected and he didn't have a big job. But Mac had two things: He was smart, and he was dogged. Now, with his dad gone he had nothing to lose and no one to keep him on the blue side of the law. If he had to cross that line to get these bastards who tried to frame him, well, he was never one to do things in half-measures. Go big or go home. Things were about to get really interesting around here.

Time to go do the least ass kicking thing he could think of. He went to the county clerk to research real estate titles.

Chapter Twenty-Six

The Registrar Scene

A decision to travel after 2:30 in the afternoon in LA results in delayed gratification. Mac lived in downtown, but the registrar was in Norwalk, not quite twenty miles south. And unless you were a commuter, the idea of traveling south on I-5 at 3:00 on a Tuesday was a bad one. He didn't check their closing time, but it must've been 5:00. Nine to five sounded like government hours.

Of all the ways he could go, he hopped on Fourth for two reasons that represent the drama that is Los Angeles. First, skid row reminded people of how sideways things could go and they avoided the street as if the plague still traveled amongst the tenants, COVID notwithstanding. Traffic would be lighter. Second, he could look at the newly completed Sixth Street Viaduct. They tore down the old one, built in '32, and replaced it with a new arching grand structure reminiscent of the art deco L.A. was famous for while echoing the repeating arches above adding a modernist feel. The people of the city had become excited about the new bridge causing closures from the combination of drag racing and Instagram pics under the lit arches.

As he crossed the Fourth Street bridge, which had itself hosted more movies, tv and commercials than you could count, the storm-fed LA river charged through its cement container. Quickly turning right then on-ramping to the 101, he joined the slow roll of afternoon traffic.

Since he had tied Cuyamaca to the DDT with Frankie, this could go on Frankie's bill. Was that double dipping? Maybe just killing two birds with one stone. Getting fired by Delilah didn't change the fact that he also needed to know what was going on down there to protect himself.

At a creeping pace, feeling like the traffic worked against him, he merged with the 5. Regardless of the lane Mac chose, the other lanes moved faster. Dark clouds lowered the sky above, making the whole trip claustrophobic. The car behind was on his tail and in front the guy was on his phone, drifting and moving forward in fits and starts. The rain began light and steady as if they were in the cloud rather than the water drifting from above.

This twenty mile per hour pace wouldn't give him much time researching. Maybe an hour if they closed at five. Mac didn't need much. Detectives aren't much more than gawkers and paid researchers.

When he finally reached Imperial Highway, popped off the freeway and paid for parking, he walked up to a locked door. The sign said eight to four. Maybe he should rethink this spontaneity.

Stuck in Norwalk, he didn't relish another hour and a half heading home so he pulled out his phone for some food close by. Of course, his phone showed him two places each a block away and being his father's son, he skipped the chain and went to the small pho and banh mi sandwich shop.

The rain stopped but he drove to a strip mall, next to a mega-plex that might not show movies for much longer and parked.

The rich broth filled smell of pho made his mouth water, but Mac was feeling restless with his time. He grabbed a banh mi and a cola to go. The sandwich looked perfect when he got in his car. A baguette with pate, mayo, ham, cilantro, pickled veg and chili's he hammered two bites and merged on the freeway. This fruitless searching couldn't continue. This case needed to be solved. Mac needed to prove whatever it was that needed to be proved to absolve himself of the crime he wasn't yet charged with.

Danger surrounded Mac like the stench of freeway exhaust. Running around wasting time wouldn't solve it.

He needed decisive action. The problem was, he had no idea what that action could be. But he was sure he would take it.

After he got out of the freeway traffic.

It did cost time, this ill-advised excursion. Closer to home, he kept to the 101. Film crews lit both the Sixth and Fourth Street bridges. A blockbuster must've pulled permit magic to get approval to close both. No through way there.

As the denizens of the 101 curled over the Los Angeles River, Mac thought of a story his father told. He passed the spot where Sha'var once stood. El Aliso. The Sycamore. The tree, at one time, presided over the valley's most important human endeavors and succumbed to that very city's success. Over hundreds of years, the majestic giant survived floods, fire and disease as the spiritual center of the entire valley. The trunk was as wide as four men arm to arm and three times as tall. Adjacent the freeway, its branches would have shaded the interstate. Now, in the light industrial area, there was the Sha'var El Aliso copper commemorative sidewalk plaque.

Mac became more and more concerned that was lost. His business was in trouble. No social life to think of. No branches in the family tree living above him or below. In this very moment, the only worthwhile things he had to focus on were tangled together: working on this case and getting out of trouble. He was full of the need for action. His energy, a ball of lightning with nowhere to discharge. Who was he kidding, he was deflated and defeated. With nowhere to go, he exited and headed to Solano Gardens.

The night was already dark, but a bright moon peaked between the dissipating storm clouds. Sweat peas were climbing the arch over the entry to the gardens. Mac knew the space well enough. He used the blue lunar light to walk past the bench, through the low gardens where Mac talked with Albie earlier today and climbed the terraced hill. Cactus twice as old as him stood sentinel at the running patch that was his father's. He had prepared a handful of rows, seed packets propped up in the dirt denoting the future bounty Dad would never see. Tomatoes, carrots, spinach, cucumbers. An old serrano nearly hip high with blooms and drying chili's both weighing down the branches.

Mac sat down in the dirt cross legged and picked at the inevitable weeds sprouting in the fresh earth. He soon had a small pile by transitioning to his hands and knees, working down the line. Dandelions, crab grass, and the red and green spotted spurge that seemed to pop up and multiply overnight, as this had to have.

His father had been working this ground not a week ago. It would be weeks for any of these plants to sprout, maybe Dad dropped radish seeds to provide a quick spurt. Radishes popped up fast. Not fast enough for him to appreciate the work this time. But the plants lived on whether Senior was there to tend them or not. As long as somebody gave them water, they'd thrive regardless of the hand that did it.

The pile of weeds grew to the size of a single trip to the mulch heap. He would do no more this night. He put in the time and would be back to do more. The plants needed constant care but only so much of it a time. But they did need the care.

Chapter Twenty-Seven

The Morning Scene

Swirling chaos like a boat in a squall surrounded Mac as he awoke. Opening his eyes, he lay there to settle the vertigo. To place himself. To feel his own bed and realize he was home. He could smell the latent years in the lathe and plaster walls and the dusty old lampshade next to his bed under which his phone waited.

He needed to go down to the registrar. That was top of the list. Knowing who pulled the strings on this whole thing would go a long way towards understanding their end game thus exposing the motive.

A text from Zoey: You up?

As he contemplated answering, there was a knock at the door and this, "I know you're up. Let me in."

He stayed.

"Macondo. I'm going to wake all your neighbors."

And he opened the door. "I realize you won't go away."

"Why would I?"

"Because I don't want you here."

"I know, I know. The big strong detective can do it on his own."

Mac still stood in the doorway. Zoey squeezed past him and said, "It doesn't matter. I found out who owns that land."

"Which land?"

"In Cuyamaca."

"I know that. It's Filmore. Or his trust or a corporation. But Filmore."

"That's where you're wrong." She waited.

"Are you going to tell me?"

"Isn't the suspense killing you?"

"Zoey, please."

"The land is owned by Johnson Long Chemical."

"Like the Wilmington DDT guys?"

"Ya. Parent Company."

A whole run of dominoes fell. He never guessed he'd get to this point without a bunch of legwork. "How did you get this?"

"I looked it up at the registrar this morning. San Diego lets you look online so I gave it shot. You never know unless you look. I like to catch and question my assumptions then bat them around like a cat with yarn."

Too excited to be frustrated, Mac said, "This shortens the distance between Filmore and trouble. But, why did he sell? And why didn't anyone know?"

"It looks like that's what we're going to find out." Zoey went into the kitchen. "Where's the coffee?" Her eyes searched the counters for a maker until she lit on it. "Oh, no." A stove top espresso pot next to a tea kettle. "You use one of those?" she said to Mac through the wall. He was getting dressed in the bedroom.

He knew what she found. "Yes, I do." They both laughed. "It's delicious," Mac said.

He laughed because it was true. She laughed because she thought he was an idiot.

She told him. "You're an idiot."

"Where's your romance? I enjoy the process."

"You enjoy making things more complicated than they need to be." She found a metal coffee container. "How much?" she said while she dumped what seemed a good amount into the filter area while she spilled on the counter, ran the water, locked the contraption together. She lit the stove to high and placed the gadget as Mac entered.

"Wait. How much coffee did you put in? Hold on." He turned off the stove and grabbed the kettle. "I need to heat the water first." He put on the kettle.

"You need to boil the water for your coffee maker?" she said as he took the thing apart.

He checked the coffee level and dumped her water. "It tastes better. It can get bitter if you boil it in the pot."

"Isn't that thing just a glorified percolator?"

"Trust the process." He placed the contraption on the counter in three pieces. "Want toast?"

"Do you make it in the oven?"

He threw two pieces in the toaster. "Have any ideas where to go from here?"

She was in his fridge. "Sun butter?" Zoey held up the container.

"I'm allergic to nuts and sunflower seeds have good protein. More than peanuts."

"Hmph."

The water boiled. He poured it in and built the contraption, put it over medium heat. She sluiced the sun butter on the bread and Mac poured the coffee with his first bite of toast.

She took a sip. "Have any sugar?" she said as she found it on the counter.

"Have any ideas where to start?" Mac said.

"I'm wondering if we can hit up your government client for info."

"What government client?"

"The one who pays you to investigate these things. I know you weren't at that press conference unless you were getting paid, Macondo."

"What if it's a lawyer?"

"Then you would have called them when you got locked up. Can we get a meeting?"

"Slow down. Let's see what we can find online."

"There wasn't much on the internet."

"Oh, no. I have access to more research than the world wide web."

"Oooh, secrets."

He lifted his coffee in a toast and finished his breakfast. Then Mac realized, "You know we still have to go back to Norwalk."

"Back? I thought you went down yesterday."

"Don't ask. They have early hours. I still need to know if that's the company that owns Wilmington."

"You know they do."

"That's not what I assumed on Filmore's mine. You proved me wrong." He plopped onto his red sofa and booted the laptop and VPN. "You seem to have an idea on where to start?"

Zoey joined him on the couch, "I don't know how deep you can dig but, long since I started researching for my podcast, it's seemed that company was shady."

"Everything I had pulled up pointed to simple disdain for the environment and love for the cash their copyright earned them making poison."

"What can you see?"

"I'm not a spy, I don't get people's emails. A lot of what we have specifically on the situation are in the EIR's from the EPA. Same stuff that we can all pull down off the public site. I can send them to you."

"I'll stick to your executive summary."

Mac held his fingers over the keyboard. Hovering there he waited for inspiration. Don't think. Do. Inspiration appeared while he was working not when he *thought* about working. "Let's dig."

The system didn't anything new on Johnson Long Chemical. These are the times when you start from the beginning. He exited VPN and brought up the California Secretary of State and did a business search. Every corporation has an entry with requisite information if they're doing business in the state.

There wasn't much but there was a filing agent for the Delaware corporation. Surprisingly, the agent was here in Los Angeles and not too many turns around the block from here.

Which turned out to be an empty storefront. Dead end.

Luckily, they drove over instead of walking the baker's dozen of blocks so got in the car to nose over to Norwalk. They were past morning traffic. Freeway open, Mac put on an album he'd liked, Parquet Courts "Wide Awake".

"So, this is the kind of thing you listen to all the time?"

"I listen to everything. But this one is on my rotation. What do you listen to?"

Zoey looked at him for a moment. Was this a test? "I lean toward whatever's Top 40. Or one of those love song stations."

Mac just hmhmmed and listened to the song. "I'm a bit eclectic in my music. I like listening to whole albums to get a feel for what the bands are up to."

"Music is just kinda background noise."

"What?!"

"What?"

"You don't hear what these guys are doing?"

"Sounds kinda loud for me, to be honest."

"The guys are a great mix of a current post-punk with classics from the early eighties like The Jam and maybe Talking Heads. I almost picked them up just because they had called themselves Americana punk. That had to bring in Violent Femmes and X, didn't it?"

"You're just making up words, Macondo."

He pulled past the front to make sure the Registrar was open this time, which it was based on the hour and the people milling in and out.

All the running around and finally getting a computer station, they searched and found the bank owned the land. Johnson Long Chemical had defaulted on the loan, of course. This was a waste of time and effort. Nothing would come of this. He should just stick to the insurance jobs and stay out of the way. This job had only caused him trouble.

His phone rang. Delilah's face showed up on the screen. He showed it to Zoey.

He answered with a finger to his lips for Zoey, "Hi, Delilah."

"Are you coming to the funeral?"

He thought about that for a moment. He'd been taught to lick his lips three times before he said something he shouldn't. "Why would I do that?"

"You were our close adviser. I would like you to come.

My father's innocence is still important, and you will have the opportunity to meet our other advisers. He is to be buried at the old cemetery in Cuyamaca. I will see you there tomorrow."

"Have you forgotten you fired me?"

"I am re-hiring you."

"I'm not sure that's a good idea."

"It is not only a good idea, but it will also get you off the hook. The sheriff would not expect me to allow you to come to his internment if I suspected you were at fault."

"He would if he thought you wanted your father dead."

"That is ludicrous."

"In a case like this, the first suspects are the family."

"Nevertheless, I will see you here." She ended the call.

Zoey scrunched her face in and said, "You aren't going, are you?"

"You know I am."

"Well, I'm coming with you. If they arrest you, at least I'll be ready this time."

Chapter Twenty-Eight

The Funeral Scene II

What Mac hadn't considered, truly considered, was the how-many-and-whom of who would show up at the circus that was Chester Filmore's funeral.

Besides the family, his buddy the sheriff was there. In a bit of a relief, he paid Mac no mind. At least, outwardly.

The one who gave Mac too much attention was the Filmore son. Junior was a big bundle of pent-up rage. Which Mac couldn't quite fathom. The kid grew up with all the money he could need, three mothers, if we count the new models, and the run of their tiny little town. When he stepped back and looked at it, Mac's grandpa was right all along. Your family's love purchased a happy life for a child, for their entire lives. The money to buy a bike or a car only digs a deeper hole. More money creates a gap that they think more money will fill but the gap can only be filled by the parents. The elders. The family. Even the rest of the community. But it all starts at home in their hearts where they can feel wanted, needed and cared for. That really was the springboard.

Junior really was a first-class prick. When he abruptly left whoever he was talking with and approached Mac, he said, "So, she did have you come."

"Hi, Junior. This must be a difficult day." Spending time at a funeral did give Mac a bevy of platitudes for the future.

"Mac. Every day is a difficult day in this family," Junior said then indicated the assembled people. "All these people didn't care about my father."

Listening in a moment like this is an unappreciated skill.

A rant will often evolve into unprotected thoughts and that was where the gold was.

"Now, Delilah thinks she runs the family. All the businesses are as much mine as they are hers."

"I assumed everything would be wrapped up in a trust," Mac said. Nothing wrong with leading a little.

Junior caught himself at the mention of trusts, grimaced and walked away without another word. Maybe he's not as dumb as Mac thought. Well, at least more secretive.

Looking around the gallery, if a measure of one's life was tears at your funeral, Filmore was a poor soul. There was a full house with stone faces behind the plethora of sunglasses.

"Did Junior have anything good to say?" Zoey said when she sidled up to Mac.

"I thought he was warming up then he clammed up when I mentioned the trusts."

"Maybe there's more to the trusts than we initially thought."

"Could be. We should take a seat."

The congregation settled in the pews of the small pioneer chapel. The pastor said all the things pastors say at funerals about mortal coils and valleys of death. It was Delilah who took the lectern to deliver a eulogy. She regaled us with Filmore's supposed business accomplishments, his political aspirations, even the trail of wives then finished with the flourish of "he will be remembered not only as my father and mentor but as one of the great titans of business we have or will ever see. I promise to carry on your legacy, Dad. I promise to finish what you've started. Goodbye. I love you."

Knowing it's not encouraged to speak ill of the dead, Mac reserved his eye roll to his imagination. The hyperbole was one thing but the legacy stuff he didn't expect. Mac's read on Delilah was the loving daughter who enjoyed having her whims paid for.

Now, between the speech and Junior, she seemed to be more driven. Was the spoiled brat just a character - a role she played to appease her misogynistic father? Was that why Junior was so upset? Did the dolt assume he would take everything over from the old man and his ditsy sister outflanked him?

"I was just thinking she's smarter than she's been letting on," Zoey whispered while they rolled Filmore out feet first.

"Thinking the same thing," Mac said after the family passed. "I better seek Delilah out. She didn't get me here to show off the casket."

"Maybe she's got another bag of money for you," Zoey said out of the corner of her mouth.

"It wouldn't hurt."

Zoey got in his line of site and faced him, "Be careful with her. I'm not sure she didn't orchestrate Filmore's demise. I'm getting black widow vibes from her."

"Based on what?"

"Call it woman's intuition."

"Well, if she keeps up with the bags of money, I'll keep coming. I've got debts no honest man can pay, as they say, and I'll take the help."

"Except that it drags you into the mud with the Filmores and makes you less than honest. Even if you aren't involved in her dirty dealing, you're tainted by these idiots."

"It'll get me in the black."

"There's more to life than money."

"Which is only said by someone who has it."

"Or is pious."

"I am neither. I am broke and scrambling." That was too close to an admission of his real feelings for Mac's taste. There was an opening with Delilah, and he approached. "Am I back on the case?"

"No condolences?" Delilah practically purred this.

Mac'd never heard condolences sound like she was looking for a very different type of comfort. All he could muster was an, "Uh", Blurred by his own grief, and surprised that she could act that way at her father's funeral. He also didn't grasp the very real, and unexpected, interest he had in that particular purr.

"We can't discuss this now," she said with a smile and slightly dimmed eyelids. "But find me after the internment. I'd like to discuss this over a drink."

Mac felt the offer that was missing in the words as she walked over to a bald guy in a suit that probably cost twice Mac's rent. As much as he argued about his bills with Zoey, this current interest with Delilah was somewhere below the belt buckle.

Speaking of: "Was that a come on?"

Zoey.

Looking at her confused, Mac said, "What was what?"

"I thought she might have you right there."

"Are you crazy?"

"Are you? Don't even think about hitting that. That girl is trouble with a capital T."

"I wouldn't even think about it."

"I can see when pheromones are floating in the air. There was commingling going on there." She stopped. "I'm serious, she already has you in the sheriff's gun sights for the murder charge. Don't go hopping in bed because you're feeling weak."

That may have cut a little close to the bone. "I'm not hopping in bed with her."

"Not now that I've broken the spell. I'm telling you: Black widow."

"I'm not disagreeing with you."

"You know they call them black widows because after sex, they eat their mate. The females. They eat the men."

"Ya, I'm somewhat familiar with the practice."

"I bet. You seem like the type to get eaten up by his woman."

"That hurt! I was talking about the spiders."

"I'm not."

"Okay, okay. I get it."

"I'm not entirely sure you do but if I've stopped you for the moment, I've done my good deed for the day." Zoey shook her head. "Besides coming to this damn place. Was the only reason we're here was for a booty call?"

"No. We have to hang around to the end. She has something she wants to discuss."

"Besides the booty call?"

"In addition to the booty call. I'm not gonna do it but if I do, I'll do it with my eyes open."

"You sure think you have it figured out."

"I've made it this far."

"A blind squirrel gets a nut once in a while, too."

"The line of cars is forming for the trip to the cemetery. Let's go."

"Let's go. Let's go. Sure, change the subject, Macondo."

Mac ignored her. He didn't need to be nagged about right and wrong. He was a grown man. He knew what he was doing.

When they got to the car, his bluetooth wouldn't hook the phone to the car. Mac started messing all the different ways to get them to reconnect. All different versions of turning one or the other on and off.

"Can you, please, just drive?" Zoey wasn't having it.

With a knock of his head, he dropped his phone in the center console and pulled out of the spot.

The internment was uneventful. Delilah and Junior may have shed a tear behind their designer sunglasses, but they didn't wipe them away.

All attending were invited to the house.

A very similar line of cars proceeded to the homestead in the same manner. They parked on the side of the entrance road and when they reached the house the turnaround driveway was full.

The guests were directed to a terraced piece of land above the house and stables. Designed for entertaining, there was a picturesque view of the valley and two built in bars at separate ends and meandering paved paths surrounded by a manicured xeriscape landscape. Filmore truly was planning for more political functions in his future.

Guests congregated around the occupied bar with the better view.

As Mac and Zoey entered the personal space of the crowd, Delilah caught Mac's eye with a spark. She strode toward him like a mountain lion, then past, took his hand and kept going. He followed. Couldn't help himself. The only thing that would stop him was his good sense and he didn't want anything to do with that.

She silently dragged him to the barn. They entered the tack room where she kissed him hard. Their hands ran over each other's bodies then she dropped his pants. She dropped her panties and lifted her skirt as she turned around never leaving him far away. One hand on his thigh the other planted against the wall. Her red manicured nails shined against the rough wood. It was frantic and fast. When they were through with a mutual, guttural, moan, she kissed him. A dry kiss. A peck. She ran her fingers over his lips, pulled on his bottom one, smiled like the cat with the canary. She cleaned herself with her panties, dropped them in a receptacle and left, a skip in her step. Not a word.

Mac pulled up his pants. That wasn't what he came here for.

Or was it? What else did he think was going to happen? This had been building since he visited her at the hotel. Since she came to the office. Now that he was on the other side of the obsession, he didn't know if it had been mutual attraction or if it was a manipulation. He was no fool. It was a little of both.

A neigh and shuffle echoed from the horses out in the stable. The room, filled with bridles, harnesses, a few saddles and blankets, was quiet. A bunch of implements of both care and control. The horses must be well-trained to put up with all that stuff.

The crowd had already thinned when Mac summited the stairs. Did he leave the funeral too early? This was too much, too close to his own troubles. What could he do with these spoiled brats to save himself? He wasn't thinking straight. Was this clarity or worry?

Zoey's bemused expression didn't alleviate his confusion. "So, that was the smart thing to do, was it?"

Torn between fighting for his own right to do what he wanted and to prove that right didn't make him a fool, Mac decided to lie, "Nothing happened. Why would you think I did what you think I did?"

"Because I saw the way Delilah re-entered the crowd. The predator caught her prey."

"No." He couldn't picture himself controlled like that.

"A lamb to the slaughter, Macondo. You better get a grip on yourself." She surveyed the guests, searching. "I'm out here to get dirt. I need an interview to round out the podcast."

"So, while I'm out here risking my neck, you are career mining?"

"Why else would I be here with your sorry ass? I want to help you, but I also have to pay my cell phone bill. Unlimited texting isn't cheap."

"Are you pissed because you're jealous?"

"There are more things in heaven and earth, Macondo..."

"Meaning?"

"If you don't know, I can't help you." She shook her empty glass at him and headed to the bar.

Mac needed to find out why he was here. None of this made any sense. He couldn't have driven down here for nothing but a quickie.

Scanning the crowd, he found Delilah sitting at one of those gas firepits filled with glass beads. Junior was part of the group as well as a batch of ritzy looking geezers. Judging by the jewelry, their wives were huddled two arm lengths to the side, standing.

He sauntered toward the gathering. Delilah picked up his movements while she stayed engaged with the conversation. The appraising look reminded him of Zoey's warnings. Was he being daft?

Not wanting to appear like he didn't belong, Mac approached the circle of women. They all fell silent. He was not welcome to whatever it was they were discussing.

These ladies were rich like he figured but they weren't

soft. Mac assumed this group were rich city women who could barely lift the rock on their fingers. These women were probably horse riders judging by the tan skin, good balance and strong hands. Ranch women. He saw the jewels. They saw a low rent P.I. who was, worst of all, from the city. Weren't women supposed to be the more cordial of the sexes?

Of the four, three turned their backs on him. The fourth only felt obligated because he addressed her directly. "May I ask how you knew the deceased?"

She answered, "Well, I didn't know him well. I knew him by reputation."

"And what was that reputation?"

"My husband partnered with him on varied business ventures." She took control, "Is this a police interview?"

"Of course not. I'm sorry, I should introduce myself. I am Edward Macondo. I've been doing work for the family lately."

"You are in the middle of all this mine business."

"You could say that."

"Filmore pushed my husband to join in, but the details weren't right. Well, look at the result."

"Do you mean his death?"

"I don't mean the beautiful house. If you'll excuse me, you've given me the chance to break away and tinkle. Us old lady bladders don't last long."

Mac turned around to find Delilah and Junior alone in their chairs. The geezers had left them, and Mac took a seat.

"Hello, stranger," Delilah said and demurely recrossed her legs one to the other, shifting her hips with a grin.

Junior looked between the two. "Hi, Mac." This time he knew he was missing something but didn't seem to care. He must've spent his life watching his sister manipulate the men around her. "I must say, I didn't expect to see you here."

"Delilah asked me down." What's with the performance? Mac already had this conversation with

Junior. "Besides, it seemed proper to pay respects."

"Considering how much my sister has paid you."

Ah, it was their power struggle. No need to take that bait.

"On that topic, I've changed my mind," Delilah said. "I will continue to retain your services."

"I believe we moved beyond that. You axed me." Mac still stood, holding the back of a chair, the fire between them. He watched her eyes through the wavering flames.

"Mr. Macondo. I will allow you to keep your severance fee and double your day rate."

"If I'm to stick around, you'll need to explain what is going on with these deals."

"I am be happy to, non-disclosures notwithstanding."

Mac circled around the chair and sat. This was going to get good.

"However," she continued as she stood. "This is not the time nor place for that discussion. Please come by in the morning and I will answer all your questions."

Mac was caught. "Except those you can't."

"Clearly," she smiled a winning chess move smile and was greeted by a mourning guest.

Junior got up, "See ya tomorrow, Mac." He waved and headed toward the stairs to the house but was corralled by another set of mourners.

Zoey grabbed the seat next to him. "Still on the clock, huh?"

"How'd you know?"

"Some predators don't eat their kill right away; they bat it around for a while."

He examined Zoey's face, "You think she's having fun with me."

She was serious, "Lions play with mice to protect themselves. When the lion comes in for the kill that mouse could infect them with a bite."

"Unless they are too tired."

"And distracted."

"Ah, jeez."

Zoey smiled. "But don't worry, I'm your personal nature show host. I've got your back."

"Like when I just ran away with my pursuer?"

"A little harmless sex never hurt anyone, Macondo."

He laughed a nervous laugh. Mac wasn't used to a woman talking openly about sex.

"Are you embarrassed? You know the women enjoy it, too. And we talk about it."

He broke her gaze. "I don't want to know." Watching the flames flicker around the glowing glass beads, he changed the subject. "She wants to meet in the morning. I don't want to make that drive there and back. Can you stay the night down here?"

"Change the meeting from me to us and I'm game."

"That goes without saying."

"Let's find a hotel before she invites us to stay here."

"Maybe we could find more clues. Close quarters and all."

"All we'll find is you moaning and groaning all night."

"Who says I'd sleep with her again?"

"I meant when she shut you down, Romeo."

"You think you've got it all figured out."

"When it comes to women manipulating men, there are some go-tos and giving it up then keeping away is in the playbook."

"Another thing I'm better off never knowing. Please, stop." Mac rose. "Let's blow this popsicle stand."

"Let's. But you can leave the 30's lingo here. For real, that's like a hundred years go."

Mac laughed as he walked away. For real this time.

Chapter Twenty-Nine

The B and B Scene

While Mac drove to town, Zoey checked the availability at the local motels. Every one of them was booked up. The national media was still in town from the funeral, and it didn't take many TV news crews to take up the meager offerings. She did find what looked like a couple rooms at a bed and breakfast, but their website wouldn't allow a booking for the same night.

The place was beyond the end of the main drag on the other side of the goat pen and the greasy spoon, just where the neighborhood began. It was the picture of a B and B. An old Victorian in yellow and white. The electric tingle of coming rain and the smell of petrichor filled the air as Mac passed onto the property. They walked under a winter, bare-branched wisteria growing on the arbor connected to a white picket fence and gate to the click and chirp of a single cricket.

Back in the day, the place must have been the home of one of the big names in town. It still carried the grandeur and weight of the need to impress.

At the top step of the front wrap-around porch they were met by an opening large red door, behind which stood a woman nearly as wide as she was tall, sturdy with kind eyes. "Welcome to my home. Come in, come in." She waved them through the door. "No bags? Well, I do love spontaneity."

Once they were through the door, the two took a spot next to a hall tree in the foyer.

The hostess continued, "I have good news and bad news. I'll cover the good first. There's room for you tonight.

You asked for two rooms, but I only have one. That's the bad news."

Mac looked at Zoey just as the proprietor said, "It's one bed but we're all adults here, right?"

She wanted the room rented.

The rain fell hard and fast at the same moment. It went from silent to a deluge.

"Looks like we're staying," Zoey said.

The lady already had her phone out with a square attachment to swipe a credit card. "Or I accept Venmo?"

Zoey waited for Mac.

"Oh, of course. I've got this." Mac pulled out a credit card.

"I've already straightened the room and laid out towels on the bed." She said as she completed the transaction. "Bathroom's last door at the end of the hallway. I'll show you the way."

"That won't be necessary. Which room is it?" Zoey took back over.

"Top of the stairs."

"What time's breakfast?"

"Seven thirty."

"See you in the morning." Zoey was already working up the stairs.

"Good night!" the lady said after them.

When they got to the room, it was as they both expected. A small double bed in a room crammed with antiques and flowery accents.

Zoey said, "I couldn't stand the thought of seeing this room with her eyes on us."

"She seemed nice enough."

"Her cozy little mystery brain was picturing sparks between us."

"Not all women are romantics."

"The ones who own flowery b and b are. I could see her little gears turning. Ooh, look at the 'share the same bed' building up."

Mac moved the towels to the dresser and pulled the

comforter open on the nearest side of the bed. He sat on the exposed sheet and untied a shoe.

"What are you doing?"

"Getting ready for bed."

"You're on the floor. I'm not sleeping next to your stanky ass."

Was it really going to go like this? "Are you kidding?"

"Am I kidding? You weren't kidding when you hit that brat in the barn."

"You said a little nookie was healthy."

She sat on the other side of the bed and took off her own shoes. "That's not what I said but I have no problem with someone hitting it. What I have a problem with is sleeping next to your pheromone slathered self." She stood again, removed the flowery comforter and threw it and a pillow on the floor at the foot of the bed. "Sleep tight."

"I paid for the room."

"And I'm doing you a favor."

"What if we tic toc?"

"Tic toc?"

"Head to toe. You know reverse positions."

"No way. Your business would be too close to mine."

"I'm not going to try anything."

"I'm not worried about that. I don't want any of that evil woman near me. And you've got her all over you. Nope. That's a nice rug down there. It'll protect your hip. You probably aren't even the first person to sleep there."

"You're serious about this."

She took the bathrobe off the hook behind the door. "I'm going to change."

"Into that?"

"I'm not sleeping in my dress and pantyhose." She closed the door after her.

Mac considered the pile on the floor. Dropped all his clothes in a pile on a chair and climbed into the bed.

He must have been asleep by the time she came back because he woke in the middle of the night with the comforter stuffed up as a wall between them. Whatever she had to do to make herself feel better.

In the morning, Mac woke with the sun. The storm cleared and left a dappled sky of clouds and sunshine behind the sycamore protecting their window. Not much to do yet but he hadn't touched his book in almost a week, and it was nagging at him.

Dressed, he searched for a note pad. It wasn't a hotel. Downstairs the only rustle was in the kitchen, so he investigated.

A gray-haired man rolled dough and cut it into a dozen sections. Mac approached softly. It was as if he disturbed his meditation. The man noticed his movement and gave Mac an acknowledgment.

The spell broken; Mac sidled to the kitchen entry. "Making cinnamon rolls?"

"They're our signature."

"I don't get many of those."

"Diabetic?"

"Allergic."

"These are non-dairy, unless you're allergic to wheat."

"No, I'm dairy. I can't believe you make non-dairy."

"Our granddaughter is allergic, and we see so many things she can't have, so we decided to avoid as many allergens as we can as a practice. Most people never know the difference and, for the people who need it, it means all the difference. No nuts, no dairy, eggs only on the side and we can avoid gluten if we know ahead of time."

"That's very thoughtful."

"Well, if we can make a patron's day, it's worth it."

"You're a rare breed."

The man put the rolls in the oven ignoring the complement. "And you are up very early, and you aren't dressed for a run or a hike. Do you need paper?"

"Are you detective, too?"

He laughed, "A certain type stays at b and b's. Couples. The adventurous. And writers."

"Guilty."

"We have all you need at a desk in the common room."

They made their way and the man introduced Mac to the desk. A roll top with a cup of pens and paper tucked in one of the compartments.

"You're welcome to use the desk." He opened a drawer and pulled out what looked like a clipboard without the clip. "Or you can use this to settle out on the porch if you'd like to avoid the other guests. Many of them start hovering once they smell those cinnamon rolls."

"That'd be perfect."

"Hide around the side. No one will see you there. Legend has it the old man who built the place used that piece of porch for the exact same purpose."

"Was he a writer?"

"No. He used it to hide from his family." They both laughed. "Let me know if you'd like anything else. I'll have the coffee ready in a few minutes."

"Who was the original owner of this place?"

"That'd been my great-grandparents."

"No kidding. Your family's lived here for all these generations?"

"Don't look surprised. Black people lived back then, too."

Mac shook his head. "It's not that. I can't believe a place stayed in a family so long."

"It hasn't. My wife and I bought this place a few years ago when we retired." He used hand quotes on the retired part. "We needed to keep an income while we slow down, and this place came up. I heard stories about it from my grandpa and made a habit of keeping an eye on it. The timing was right and here we are."

Mac thought about how many of us looked forward to a working retirement.

"What did they do in those days to have such a big house?"

"The old guy was the first to find a big gold vein here. You could say we wouldn't have a town if not for him."

"I thought it was Filmore's family that found that gold."

"It was Filmore's family that gave my people the loans to chase the gold. They did pretty good at first. Look at this house. But when they, my ancestors, lost the gold vein, they couldn't pay the loans. Then it was Filmore's family that took everything from them, including this house."

"So, you don't like that family."

"Water under the bridge. But I didn't like that man. He was a crook. And, funny I said it, that man stole our funds to fix that bridge. He almost bankrupted this whole town."

All Mac could muster was a shake of his head.

"I better get the rest of those cinnamon rolls in the oven. I'll leave you to your business. Go find that nice spot out there."

As described, Mac found that solitary chair around the side of the house. Birds he couldn't name chirped and twirled in the small line of bare aspens at the plot line. They must be quite a site shimmering in the summer full of leaves.

He tried to quiet his mind like the branches of those trees. Lose all his commingled thoughts of possible trials, jail, his father, the business, the Filmores. All of it. Writing was a different place and he needed to quell all those interruptions. Give himself a chance to step away from all those competing needs.

His practice seemed simple, but it took practice. Don't think. That was it. Ray Bradbury had those words over his own typewriter. Don't think. So, Mac tried it every time. He attempted to just get going. The approach allowed a beautiful freedom and lent the deeper feeling of storytelling rather than the sense of completing homework that so many imagine working toward a piece of fiction to be.

Instinct pointed to a big plot point in his story and without the rest of the book to check against, Mac went for it. The words, this morning, felt like a well pump. He knew they were there, but he had to work his way towards them. If he started, they'd flow. No thinking. He began.

"What a beautiful morning!"

Zoey.

He would never finish this book.

"And look at you hiding over here with the best seat in the house."

"Ya, the owner told me it was a good spot to not be found."

With a laugh, she pointed to herself. "A detective."

She was a morning person. High energy straight out of the gate. By nature, Mac was not and only through sheer stubbornness had he learned to wake and be productive early. It was the way of the world. But he did not cotton to anyone too cheery in the morning. "Hmph."

As we all know, his attitude would not deter Zoey. "What are your working on?"

He flipped over his page with three words on it. "Nothing."

"I was gonna say notes but now that you're defensive..."

"Who's defensive?"

"Okay, protective. You went and hid your words right away."

With a quick look down. "I did not." He flipped the paper over, then back again.

"Do you write stories!?"

"Why would you say that?"

"I love that. You are one cryptic dude, Edward Macondo. Are they short stories? Books? Romance?"

That was too much for Mac. "Romance? I wouldn't know where to start. Dime store detectives."

Zoey had the presence of mind not to celebrate her small victory of learning something personal from Mac, but she wouldn't stop there. "Do they echo your cases? That'd be a fun way to work out the logic while you're in the middle." She thought about that for a moment. "Like journaling."

"No. I do not echo my cases. This is a break from these things. Actually, I set this one - this is my second book - in the forties. In the middle of the zoot suit riots."

"No kidding." She leaned in.

"My guy is investigating the Sleepy Lagoon murder." Mac stopped all of a sudden.

"Go on."

"I can't. I'll tell you later. I can't talk too much about a story while I write it, it steals the momentum. But, talking about this out loud made a connection."

"What connection? The Sleepy Lagoon?"

"No. The media."

"I don't know what The Sleepy Lagoon is."

"The way the papers handled a murder stoked the fire for those riots."

"Mac, I'm going to fess up. I don't even know what happened in those riots. Other than hearing the words and a song about it, I know nothing."

"Do you know pachucos?"

"Pachucos?"

"The zoot suiters. Young kids who were making money and buying big ol' baggy suits to show it off."

"And somebody didn't like that."

"It was the war and a whole bunch of military were gathered around L.A., looking for blood."

"And, as they did at the time, they were restless, and they decided to take it out on the folks different from them."

"With the help of the newspapers riling everybody up. A few choice editorials set the Mexican American kids up as disrespecting the war effort by using wool for their suits. So, they made it patriotic to stomp hardworking people for wearing a different cut suit."

"Okay, so the media created outrage. 'If it bleeds, it leads, right? It sells papers."

"Right and had consequences but another thing the owner said earlier stuck with me."

"What's that?"

"That bridge almost bankrupt the town and the coverage turned against Filmore."

"So?"

"So, his deal with whoever the deal was with. The

power broker may have wanted the city desperate so they could push through the storage facility."

"And the bad press put too many eyes on the city."

"Making the EIR actual news before the fact rather than after."

"Thus, stalling the project."

"Are these all diversions?"

"Maybe we'll find out. One thing I do know is there's a lot of yarn in this mess and pulling a strand just keeps tangling it more."

"You gotta start somewhere and one strand is as good as any other."

"Okay, I'm not getting any writing done now. Let's go get one of those cinnamon rolls before they're gone."

"I already did."

"You didn't bring me one?"

"Figured you already had one. I couldn't walk past 'em without grabbing one."

"One should never assume, Zoey."

"Ok, Sherlock." Zoey rose from her chair. "Did you know they're vegan?"

Just to clear the air, those cinnamon rolls were as good as advertised. Better. Icing on a wonderfully spongy pastry dough surrounded by cinnamon and sugar. A touch of orange. Mac had two.

While Mac munched on his second cinnamon roll, they walked over to the general store on the main drag. Both were still dressed in funeral attire and didn't want to continue to be. High heels and suits were not the way to blend with the locals in Cuyamaca.

Opening the door was a surprise.

Tuned to G7sus4/D chord, a guitar hung over the entry and when the door was opened, instead of a bell, they had a stick with a pick on the end. Played that way, Mac was astonished that it evoked one very popular song. Many a guitarist knows it. Vruuuuunnggg! It's been a hard day's night...

Zoey pointed at the guitar and smiled at the guy who

looked like the owner behind the counter. "Did you do that?"

"You like it?" He was pleased, gray and balding with a slight paunch.

"Clever. Very clever."

"That guitar was for sale out at a rummage sale for two bucks and I wasn't going to play the darn thing but no reason it couldn't make music."

"I love it!" Zoey threw her eyes around the store. "Do you have any clothes?" She placed her hand on a Cuyamaca is for lovers t-shirt.

"Just those tourist t-shirts and sweatshirts. Also, assorted work clothes along the back wall."

Zoey chose a pair of white painter's pants with a hammer loop on the right leg and that burgundy lover's t-shirt. It was the only one in a ladies cut, plus a sweatshirt. Mac couldn't find pants his size but went for a pair of overalls and a long sleeve t-shirt with a skull over a crossed pick and shovel on it. *Searching for the original pirate treasure. Cuyamaca mines.* Mac picked a cheap pair of boots, but Zoey had to settle for water moccasins. Better than high heels.

The old guy puttered silently behind his counter while they searched and shopped but he'd look intently at Mac occasionally. No judgment, only curiosity.

After Mac and Zoey changed into the clothes, they brought the tags to the counter.

It was the owner's chance. "Are you the one they's framing?"

Mac was glad to hear the bull shit called out but not glad to be reminded. "The one and only."

"I don't know who's worse for this town, Olivera or Filmore."

"No doubt." Mac agreed.

Though Zoey wasn't wallowing in her problems, the old guy had a bone to pick, and she saw an opening. "What do you mean? Olivera, too?"

"He's been playing both sides since I can remember."

From a little room behind a thin blue curtain came what looked to be the man's wife. "Oh, don't you start with all that, Maynard. These people don't care about small town politics. Leave them alone."

"He's the one getting framed. I think he would like to know about why he's gettin' railroaded."

His partnered shooshed him. "Sticking your nose where it doesn't belong," she said as she escaped through the curtain.

The old guy added up the figures on a scratch pad and announced their total.

Mac worried they might not take credit with the pencil and paper treatment but as soon as he offered his credit card, the old guy busted out a cell phone with a swiper doohickey.

Then the guy just couldn't help himself. "You probably already know the animosity between those two families goes back to this town's founding. Do you want these shoe boxes?"

They both shook their heads.

"What you wouldn't see—"

The old lady put her head through the curtain, "He's no good. Never was."

"She taught him in the fourth grade. Both of them, in fact. She's retired now."

"If you want to call running this store retirement."

"I run this store."

"Well, I'm working all day, just like you."

"Anyway," he looked at her until she disappeared again. "Those boys were peas in a pod then. The town was hoping there'd be an end to the feud."

She appeared, "Started to feel like the Hatfields and the McCoys."

"Are you going to let me talk to this poor guy?"

She retreated.

"Even though the dads were apoplectic about it, those kids didn't care."

"Until high school. Everything changed." Yes, the wife

appeared. "There was a girl."

He nodded. "There was a girl. Now, all the details are gossip but it tracks."

"I've heard it too many times the same way to be too far from the truth."

Zoey knew when the gettin's good. "We're not in court. Just talking."

The lady smiled, "That right."

The proprietor rolled his eyes at Mac. "It started like Romeo and Juliet and got darker."

"Stop it. They didn't kill themselves."

"It created a tragic circumstance, nonetheless."

"That it did."

"So they's this girl and the boys had a thing for her. She moved here from somewhere else in high school and she was pretty as a picture."

"And those boys chased her like dogs hunting a fox. Although, at first, I don't think she minded."

"Well, it turns out Olivera takes her to a dance, then Filmore starts dating her and knocks her up."

"And he forces her to have an abortion. Olivera and Filmore get into a fist fight and never speak again without a hint of spite."

"Well, soon enough Olivera falls inline to support her in her grief."

"And is still married to her."

Zoey's eyes were wide. "You're kidding."

"God's truth."

Mac looked between the storytellers, not quite buying it. "You mean to tell me they've carried this animosity for all this time?"

"That's just the beginning. Like I said, the families already hated each other. That pushed 'em over the edge."

"And the sheriff would frame me, why?"

"Oh, I don't know that." The old man.

"Maybe 'cuz you were helping them, and he didn't want someone to clear up Filmore's things."

Zoey jumped back in. "Or maybe because he wanted to

protect the town. Like we thought in the beginning. He couldn't stand that his town had done something like kill Filmore and he needed a scape goat."

"Could be."

"He does love this town."

The guitar hit its chord and a small family's chatter broke the spell. Mac and Zoey thanked them for the help, and the story, and left for the Filmore estate.

Chapter Thirty

The Coffee Scene

A goal makes these things easier. You have a better chance of hitting the target when you aim the arrow, right?

The beginnings of a plan were developing. With their realization about the players involved, Mac and Zoey could push further with that hook on what they needed to learn. Delilah and the brother had to be more forthcoming. She had promised she would be.

They would learn who the players were. Get answers on the trusts and corporations upon corporations. Where all the money was sifted and redistributed. Delilah had to answer for all the problems she created for Mac. Both spoiled brat kids needed to answer for all the problems her father had created for this community.

However, there seemed to be a problem with the day's plan already.

A gaggle of news vans gathered on the highway at the Filmore property entrance, and a police car blocked the way. Portending even worse news, the on-camera talent dotted the ridge above the ranch giving live reports of the "goings on" at the late Filmore's property.

Mac and Zoey couldn't drive in but the cop guarding the entrance had instructions to allow Mac to walk in. Another impromptu hike. It was a good thing they changed their clothes.

The knock then twirls of a woodpecker filled the trees above the shuffle and clump of Mac's boots and Zoey's silent moccasins. This section between the highway and the house held silence like a secret.

The tempo of their footfalls got Mac thinking, if he was

to have Zoey traipsing along everywhere, he might as well bounce his ideas off her.

Though it was Zoey who broke the quiet. "You are wrapped up in some generations long bullshit."

"But what does that mean? Animosity among families is as old as time. Why was I dragged into it?"

"Denial is mostly a sub-conscious response. Deep-seated hatred can seem as natural as that creek bed down there. Always there, barely noticed."

They ticked through what was known. The families hated each other. The sheriff wanted to protect the town. Filmore had a deal brewing and probably didn't have as much control as he thought.

The way to the house was long enough that there was a physical transition in the space. Closer to the highway were the sycamore, oaks and a cluster of pines. As they neared the house, it was the smell that really made Mac take notice. His mind had been too cluttered to notice before. They moved into a eucalyptus forest that continued to be dotted with oaks. The menthol smell and simple crunch of the thin leaves under their feet surrounded them as the home came into view.

Parked in front of the house was a nondescript government issue cruiser.

There couldn't be any danger for Mac but that didn't stop him from worrying. The last trip to the jail house was unwarranted, too.

They were met silently as they approached and led into the house by Truman, the security guard.

Mac took his spot opposite Delilah on the love seat.

She tilted her head in greeting. "Good morning, Mr. Macondo."

This game of cat and mouse with her was beginning to grate. But on reflection, he didn't know why he expected anything different.

Zoey chose a seat across the coffee table from both and readied for the tennis match. The interested observer.

Sitting on the coffee table was a full silver coffee set,

cups and a plate of danishes. Delilah prepared herself a cup, cream and sugar, selected an apricot danish then turned her attention to Mac. "A little Austrian man makes them. They are the best in the county."

"Delilah—"

She threw Mac off his game a little. "Don't you want a little something?" Delilah smiled then said, "I promise they aren't too sweet."

"Look. Delilah." Mac leaned forward. "This isn't social call."

"Do you like coffee?" Delilah waved her delicate cup at those assembled. "You should try this one. I only have it on special occasions. They call it Monkey coffee."

Zoey leaned in, poured a cup, gave it a smell. "The monkey poop kind?"

"No, that type, kopi luwak, is made with caged civets. It is a bit inhumane, and they are a bit like a cat. This coffee is made from Taiwanese macaques who live wild, chew up the fruit and spit out the seeds. Like we would with a cherry pit."

Mac looked between the two women and couldn't decide which was worse, the one who was drinking it or the one who was thinking about it. He wasn't going anywhere near that coffee.

"Does it really taste different?" Zoey smelled it deeply but just needed a push off the edge.

"See for yourself." This was surely the most genuine moment Mac had witnessed from Delilah. She took great joy in pushing someone past their boundaries.

Zoey sipped. "Ah! It's less bitter. Rounder. Mac, you have to try."

"I don't swap spit with monkeys."

"It is far removed from the macaques," Delilah said. "You may enjoy the complexity created by the macaques' enzymes on the seed."

"Hard pass." Mac picked up a blackberry danish. "I'll have one of these. Thank you."

"You should try it, Mac. When will you ever have the

chance to taste it?" Zoey enjoyed this.

"Hopefully never."

Delilah said, "We are considering adding a coffee crop to our avocado groves. Some have said the longer seasons for a California coffee give the crop a more complex flavor."

Zoey leaned in. "Tell me more."

"We would run the coffee trees between the avocados. They have similar water requirements." Delilah chewed her danish. "I believe coffee could be like wine in the 1970's while allowing people to support local agriculture."

"What about water?" Zoey, typically inquisitive.

Delilah looked between the two. "We are researching ways to use less water while ensuring a premium crop. Things like drip irrigation, wind breaks, fruit vines that diminish waste, encourage soil moisture and protection."

Now, Mac saw an engaged businesswoman. Were these kids better people without the blow-hard father around? If nothing else, opening up about these other projects might encourage looser lips in the real conversation. "Clearly we're paying more per gallon for coffee than gas but is the crop as lucrative as avocados?"

"An astute observation," Delilah said. "It is nearly as profitable. By choosing highly rated varietals, we can increase our yield. Research shows it can go as high as one hundred fifty to two hundred dollars per pound. However, you miss what is most interesting about this. For the same water and land costs, we increase our return significantly."

The gardener in Mac couldn't help but ask, "Would it strip the land?"

"That is another interesting part of this equation." Delilah was in her comfort zone. "I have followed research that suggests fava beans may be a viable crop that will also provide nitrogen similar to the old farms that planted clover when cycling their plots."

"We use fava beans that way in our community garden," Mac said. "But a couple people think, depending on the plant, the plants grow big but bears no fruit."

"That is exactly what we are attempting to ascertain. We are looking into funding our non-profit to study exactly that."

Here's what Mac's been searching for. "Do you use the non-profit for many projects like this?"

"I would like to, but our board does not support it."

A door and jam smacked their separation upstairs while Junior appeared on the landing. He was followed by a middle-aged woman. They looked to be finishing up an interview, at the least, the woman had a pen in her hand with interesting tidbits scribbled on a legal pad.

Nothing but smirks came Mac's way from Junior and the lady. An interview? Why all the roadblocks and news vans outside? Who dropped the dime and who should care about questions for the family?

While they proceeded downstairs Delilah stood and said, "Mr. Macondo, I'd like you to meet Yolanda DeSoto. She is the Assistant District Attorney." Delilah then indicated Zoey, "And his associate Zoey Clayton. You know my brother, of course."

"I'm glad to meet you in the flesh, Mr. Macondo," the ADA said. She held her pad at the bottom of the stairs and did not move for any glad handing. "I didn't know you would be here." She turned to Junior. "I have what I need for now. I will leave you to the rest of your day, Mr. and Ms. Filmore." That lady did not want to be in the same room as Mac and that made Mac nervous.

Why would the Assistant District Attorney be here anyway unless they were making progress on the investigation?

The first suspect is the one who has the most to gain from a death. As much as Delilah had to gain, Mac couldn't read some other motive. She was the pampered princess with him alive. She had more work with him dead. Delilah would have more recognition now but, he guessed, to be infamous was still a type of fame. Delilah's father's death, Chester Filmore's death, didn't meet the criteria for part of any real great historical record. To Mac, this was mostly an unfortunate circumstance for everyone involved.

"I was telling them about my plans for our land."

Junior took a seat on the sofa next to Mac. "Dad thought all this farming was a waste of time."

"He only saw land as a place to extract value or create development." Delilah, the dilettante, was an environmentalist?

Junior eyed his sister. "Nor does the board support it."

She stared back. "Things are changing around here."

Zoey couldn't help herself. "What does that mean?"

Delilah adjusted her weight, uncrossed and recrossed her legs. "I am executor. I lead this family and the enterprise now. They do what I say."

"That's not how it works, Del. They're not going to let it."

"I am going to make it work that way. I have ideas about how to right this ship." Here she turned her full-faced attention on Mac. "Don't be confused, you aren't here to be involved with our non-profit."

Junior said, "We are in the midst of a large transaction."

Mac waited for one of them to continue. Silence was often better than encouragement.

Delilah filled the silence. "You were here to make clear my father's innocence. That is no longer necessary, obviously."

Junior jumped in with unexpected fervor. "Now you need to clear the runway for our storage facility."

Mac grimaced. He didn't expect them to admit to the mine. "I don't understand how I'm supposed to do anything for you. You don't even own the property."

Junior sneered. "Macondo, we own Johnson Long Chemical. It was a paper push to distract simpletons like you.

In what seemed like an opposite version of herself from a moment before, Delilah said, "Your job is to keep people focused on the mine and it's benefits, not the legal aspects, nor on the search for my father's killer."

"That's a double whooptie-doo, then, because you need a pr firm for one and the cops will handle the other." Mac stood. This whole job was a dead end. "You wasted my time. Again. Thank you."

"Now, Mac." She practically purred this. "I thought there was something between us. More than business." She smiled one of those smiles. The kind some people have that open doors that are closed.

Good thing Mac didn't fall for that type of trap. He took in the room looking for — something. Junior was disinterested. Zoey was taking notes in her mind. Nobody was helping and Delilah simply wanted to swat him around like that lion. Money wasn't enough. And the sex? Well, the sex was good but not good enough to do whatever the hell she had him doing. "You need to hire someone else, Delilah."

She changed tactics but the sex was still there between them. "Look, Mac. I've got a soft spot for you, and someone needs to do this. I know you're in between a little bit on your jobs and I'd like to help. Let me help you. And you'll help me in the mix."

"I do research not public relations."

"And that is what you're going to do. I need to know more about how this Environmental Impact Report is going to turn out. I simply need more information on the firm that has been contracted and I'd like a sense of how the EPA will lean. You'll simply research the information and present me with your findings. I have professionals to keep the public discussion on point."

"So just research?"

"That is all. Just research. I'll be up to LA in a couple of days. I'll swing by your office, and you can present to me then." She stood and offered her hand. "Deal?"

He couldn't think of a reason to say no at this point. It was easy money for nothing but footwork. "Deal."

They shook on it and Delilah unconsciously pushed them toward the door.

Zoey spoke up. "We wanted to ask you a few things."

"I have another important meeting on Zoom. If you'll excuse me." She shuffled them out the door.

Mac and Zoey were on the stoop in silence.

Zoey said, "She's got you wrapped around her finger."

Mac offered nothing but reticence and an eye roll.

She continued, "Now, if one was of a suspicious nature, as I am, they'd ask what was going on here?"

"Nothing but crappy business by rich trust fund kids is what's going on here."

"No, it's fishy. I know it and you know it. I can't quite put my finger on what the play is here, but someone is definitely getting played."

They began the trek to the car and the highway.

Mac offered nothing.

"I don't mean to say it's you who's getting played, Mac. That girl in there is playing chess. I have a feeling a whole lot more people than you are in this game. You and I, we can't be more than pawns. Well, you. You're a pawn. I'm not even on the board." She laughed. "Thank God."

"I came out here for this?"

"Maybe she assumed you'd be alone. She'd have the chance to manipulate you and get a little on the side."

Mac kicked a rock. "She had three coffee cups out."

"I noticed that," Zoey said as she twirled her hair.

"Maybe the DA had a cup."

"No. It would have been on the tray, used. Besides her lipstick was still perfect."

Mac looked at her. "Delilah planned on you being with me."

Zoey stopped. "I don't think so. Maybe she planned on Junior joining the conversation. She had the three cups for you, Delilah and Junior."

"Well, whatever it was, nothing was accomplished. I didn't get any new answers and she didn't either."

"Maybe the DA visit wasn't planned."

"Then why leave when we arrived?"

"Why, indeed."

"They're up to something."

"Which they?"

"Delilah and Junior.

"Obviously."

"And it has to do with this company. All that coffee talk is bullshit. They're up to something with that and I want to know what it is."

"Maybe she's just trying to raise money. You know, prime the pump for those rich bastards we met at the funeral."

"You're probably right. I'm just seeing ghosts. Filmore's death was an accident and I just lucked into a high paying gig with a couple trust fund kids too lazy to work for themselves."

"If that's the case, you won the lottery and don't look a gift horse in the mouth."

"I don't trust anything that comes too easy, Zoey. What's the motivation? My dad taught me that everyone has a motive for what they do. And one of the only things of which I am sure of is that Delilah has never done anything out of kindness in her life."

They rounded a bend and the property entrance at the highway became visible. It was empty. No cops. No news vans. Just the car and the whistle in the trees.

"At least they could have given us a ride out."

Mac disagreed. "The less time with them the better."

Chapter Thirty-One

The Research Scene

DDT: *dichlorodiphenyltrichloroethane*. Banned in the US since 1972, the chemical was thought to be a boon at first. It was an effective insecticide and was used to battle mosquitoes especially. Eventually, it was found to harm animals up and down the food chain including birds, fish and eventually humans.

There is a particular legacy in Southern California because that was one of the main spots where it was manufactured. Southern California was also the location of a large repository of the chemical at the time it was banned.

Now, it's been discovered by environmental groups and intrepid reporters that millions of barrels of this stuff were dumped off the California coast. This group of people were looking to understand what type of effect this dumping had on the ecology of the area.

Mac was interested in the who's and what's of the situation. He was confident it was there and the definition of "a bunch" was the same if it was one million or three million. It all sounded bad.

Who did all this dumping and who knew they were doing it?

There was a certain way Mac liked to accomplish his fact finding. Many people checked the papers and scientific records and, as you know, that was one part of his process. Another part of the process was to find the real people around all that dumping. He was no cop, so if he could get them to talk, it was gossip and myth. But we all knew, every myth was based on a little bit of truth.

While headed to San Pedro, Frankie gave him an

exploratory text. Mac was sure one of two places would get him the info he and Skip, the boat guy, couldn't get in their sea voyage. First, the docks were a possibility, but those guys were all trying to work. And Mac didn't want to interrupt them. To be honest, they also aren't very conversational when they're working.

However, there was another place people talk and, hopefully, too much. The bar. There weren't too many people involved but the reporting had mentioned a large amount of industrial oil waste was dumped along with the DDT. Old leathernecks and pipe fitters were a good bet to know what happened or at least know a good story about what happened.

There were a couple bars that would fit the bill but the boat guy, Skip, had taken Mac to one a few years ago after a day of fishing and Skip seemed close with the bartender. Well, the bartender knew his name. The friend of a familiar is marginally better than a stranger off the street. He headed to The Rusty Can. A true union man beer hall with sawdust on the floor and enough darkness between the lights to remember to not worry about what was hiding in those shadows.

The place carried the specific smell of simple green cleaner and booze. A floating hangover.

The bartender was watching a TV hanging in the corner of the room. A pair of fogies sat at the bar, another by himself at a table and two other geezers played pool on a short bar-size table, the brightest spot in the place.

Mac took a seat a few removed from the pair at the bar and two seats from a three-gallon jar of purple pickled eggs. He ordered a draft pint and said while the bartender pulled the beer, "On second thought, I'll take one of those eggs, too."

The beer landed in front of Mac in a chilled glass. "You like to get started early." The bartender scooped an egg out of the jar. "You like the chilies?"

Mac nodded. "I only eat the egg for the chilies."

The bartender fished a chili out, too, and placed both

on a cake-sized paper plate in front of Mac, a napkin tucked underneath.

"Most people are scared of those," one of the old guys at the bar said.

"I'm scared of those," said the buddy.

They all laughed.

The buddy continued, "I've never seen them change that brine. Hell, it's probably been there since my pappy came to this very spot."

"Hey, hey. We follow county law here." The bartender could have been offended because he cared for his reputation or because Mac might be a health inspector.

The two guys just shared a look.

"I don't carry a badge," Mac said. "Besides, if those chilies don't kill me, they'll kill whatever shouldn't be in there."

The bartender reset. "What does bring you in? We don't get many fresh faces in here." It could be a threat, or it could be conversation, depending on the demeanor. This was conversation.

"I was stuck on this side of town," Mac said, ate the chili and knocked the egg back in a bite with an approving nod. "I came in here with Skip not that long ago." Here Mac grinned. "I liked the friendly vibe."

They all liked that one.

"Skip the boat guy?"

"That's the one."

"Son of bitch hasn't been by in a while. He okay?"

"Oh, ya. He's caught up in his YouTube channel. Can you believe he's making money at it?"

"I watch it. He's pretty good."

"Probably making more than his retirement. He's got a lot of subscribers."

Just 'cuz they're old doesn't mean they can't use a phone, Mac reminded himself. But that did give him a transition. "Ya, we went out last week looking for those cannisters."

"Jesus. Those things," said old man number one.

His friend agreed. “What a mess.”

“Somebody’s gotta know what happened,” Mac said, dropping a line, hoping for a nibble. Always the fisherman.

“Not me. But ol’ Jack over there says he was on a crew that used to get overpaid to get sauced and throw barrels overboard back during Reagan.”

One shot the other one a look. “But he don’t like to talk about it.”

“Which guy?”

The first guy turned around with effort. Bad back. Maybe, a hip. “The one getting paid out.”

That was good. He’d be in a good mood.

“Thanks, guys,” Mac said as he got up, tilted his beer and headed to the pool table. Mac engaged him right away. “Looks like you caught your limit.”

The pool player watched Mac’s approach. The man appeared mid-seventies but lean and still moved athletically. Forearm ink. Faded. “No limit here.” He lit up a cigarette.

“Hey, Jack.” The bartender from across the bar. “You know you can’t smoke in here.”

Jack waved once with the cig hand. “Sorry. Forgot.” He winked at Mac. Everyone’s part played to a tee; the bartender shined glasses.

“Are you up for another?” Mac said.

“I’m not sculpting a masterpiece,” he said while he racked the balls.

“The name’s Mac.”

“Jack. Lag for break?” He set the cue ball to the side and met Mac’s gaze.

“Your table. You won last,” Mac said. “Take it.”

Without comment Jack moved the white cue ball and struck with one of those smooth shots packed with power. He broke with a crisp clack. Sunk two stripes and a solid. “Stripes,” then sunk two more until he missed a bank shot on the eleven ball.

As Mac eyed then stood over his shot, he said, “Those guys over there tell me you used to work boat salvage back in the day.” And sunk one in the corner.

"That's a funny way to put what I did. But I don't talk about it. I signed some sort of NDA, you know."

Mac sunk another. "Who the hell had a Non-Disclosure Agreement in those days?"

"People who don't want you talking."

"Sounds more like corporations that don't want you talking."

"Good point."

"If you were doing what I'm guessing that company is long gone."

"Ya. Nobody likes talking about what they did wrong, friend."

Mac stopped and looked at him, "Want a drink?"

"Nope."

Nodding Mac lined up another shot. "My pops had a friend, used to tell stories about hanging out with his dad." Mac promptly missed as he said, "An old-time leatherneck, that guy. He used to watch them take God-knows-what in fifty-gallon drums and just dump them into those marshes over in Long Beach."

"By the power plants?" Jack took over and sunk one.

"Yep, those." It looked like Mac might wait a while. He leaned against a barstool by the wall. "I don't know if any of it's true or urban legend. But it sure sounds likely from a time when they acted like nature was where we threw stuff away."

"They did used to do that." Jack sunk another.

"Not that anyone talked about it."

Jack finally missed. Mac had a lot of balls to catch up.

"And aren't going to."

Mac chalked up his cue. "I'm no cop. I'm trying to find out what happened and get the people who are responsible on the hook."

The old guy laughed. "Like they did with those January sixers? Not that I support the bull shit — it's a disgrace, really —, but those dummies at the bottom get jailed up while the people who planned it are sailing free. A story as old as time."

"Well, I'm not saying you did any of this but if someone were to do it, what do you imagine they did?"

"Hypothetically speaking, the guys in the boat were paid triple time to dump drums at first. Take 'em out a few miles, throw 'em overboard."

"Like the law said."

"Ya, but soon enough there were so many, there was no way to keep up. And they changed the work from hourly to per barrel."

"So, the trips got shorter."

"Of course. We'd get past the shelf and dump 'em. If they didn't sink, we'd take an ax to them so they would."

"On the sealed drums?"

"What else? We didn't worry. Man, we was covered with that stuff when we was sunning. You've seen the pictures. They used to have tank trucks rolling down the beach, spraying us all while we played in the sand. Hell, I'm still here now. How bad could it be?"

"You know that answer."

"Not then, we didn't. Hypothetically."

"What'd you think later?"

"It bothered me. What happened to Star-Kist. We used to have schools of tuna, didn't we? And those crazy assholes surfing off PV? I hear a lot of guys there and down at San-O get cancer."

"It's not all these cannisters." Mac wondered if he should go talk to those guys off Palos Verdes. If there was a group that gossiped like a bunch of hens, it was a gaggle of surfers.

"It didn't help the situation."

"What was the company?"

"Nobody. They paid cash." He looked at Mac. "That's not exactly true. We all knew who it was. We got those chemicals from Wilmington Chemical - they made the stuff. They had to get rid of the stuff. And they didn't care as long as it was gone. Corner." Jack sank the eight ball to win the game.

"Who'd you work for then? Hypothetically."

"The Nike. He named the boat long before the shoe. Just an old fisherman. None of the small guys could make enough anymore and the cash was good. He's long gone now."

"Lots of them are long gone."

"Excepts for those drums. The drums are still there." He leaned his cue in the corner. "I gotta take a piss. You have a good day, now."

Interview was over.

Mac got a name. The Nike out of San Pedro. Follow every thread. Eventually, one answer leads to more. He could go down to the beach and chat up the beach rats.

On second thought, the surf spot could wait. Despite what people say, blond hair or brown, straight or curly, regardless of accent, a gang's a gang. They are territorial and they trade in intimidation. He was in no mood. He was tired.

There are studies that attest to the health benefits of a siesta. A quick nap will do wonders to attitude and energy. Mac worked for himself. If he needed a break, he took it. He pointed his trusty vehicle towards the office.

Also, with many masters to please, he still wanted to work on his book. The daily words had been interrupted and if Mac wasn't progressing, he was never going to finish the story. Jail, bills, and mourning be damned.

Oh no, he remembered, he also had to visit the garden. A few days since Mac stopped by, his dad would be disappointed already. To the garden it was. The rains brought sprouting grass in his rich brown earth. The plot was a place where only what his dad wanted to grow, grew. Mac plucked a shopping bag from the bouquet of plastic hanging from a nail on a post. A bunch of the fava beans were ready and he filled the bag with his dinner then went to work pulling the grass that was already a tender finger long. By the time Mac had pulled them, shaken the dirt from the roots and created a pile large enough to fill a five-gallon paint bucket, he hadn't thought about anything but the task at hand. It all smelled of moisture and green chlorophyll, bright and alive.

It was a welcome respite to be free from his worries, only focused on a task that served humans for millennia. Prepping and caring for the home of sustenance tended to settle him in a way few other activities did.

As Mac gathered the waste into a bucket, Albie ambled into the garden and tooled around at the base of the hill picking and plucking at his own plot. He offered Mac a wave but left him space enough to do what he was there to do. Albie was there to do the same. There was an unwritten rule at the garden that if the person already at the garden didn't approach you when you arrived, you leave them be. It was a way to let others know you had work to get done.

Albie also knew Mac would have to come by. Albie was by the compost bin and Mac had a pile of weeds. His Dad's plot was clean, and Mac did a cursory sweep of his own plot, but his heart wasn't in it. He fished out a couple dead sycamore leaves trapped on the ground, clipped a handful of brown leaves off the plants and headed for the compost bin. Not even a glance up, Albie worked away. But he did say, "How you holding up?"

"You know."

"Don't worry I won't fawn all over you. If you need to say something, say it."

"Thanks, Albie."

"Losing someone is hard enough than to have to deal with people getting all uncomfortable when they see you. *Do I say something? Do I not?* The bigger the loss, the deeper the grief. It's easier to wrestle the bear. Wrap your arms around it — feel it — then let it go."

Mac nodded. He had nothing.

"We all have our own ways. Eddie did a good job with you. You'll be okay, Mac." Albie patted him on the shoulder and went back to his plants.

After dumping the waste in the bin, Mac left with a wave and the sense that the bear would win this match. Working the plot gave him that respite, sure. Even made him closer to the old man for a minute but it also brought that unexpected open space right to the front. How Mac wanted to tell him about watering and clipping, how good Suzie's plants at the next plot looked. Frank's cactus was blooming early, or was it late? Missing the advice of the old detective as he still seemed to be under the blade in this case, guillotine poised. How did he get caught in the middle of these bastards? He should have listened and stayed out of the whole thing.

Walking down the stairs he almost walked right over Kiko, a diminutive chef who worked at a local restaurant that grew many of their herbs and what vegetables they could in their plots at the garden. She was intense in the way of a young, driven striver but still had a smile in her eyes and a moment for people. She'd go far.

"Mac!" she said through her laugh as he caught her by the shoulders to avoid knocking her over.

"I'm sorry! I didn't mean to take you out," Mac said. Smiled.

She lowered her eyes. "I'm sorry about Eddie, Sr." Then met his eyes. "I just heard. And wondered when I'd see you here."

Mac blushed a little. "Thank you."

"He was a good man who died happy. I say, feel proud for the life he led."

"Ya."

"You're lucky. Look at it this way, when my grandfather died, we spent two weeks at my grandmother's house."

"Buddhist?"

"Yep. It was good for the family and for her. And for me. But not so easy with work."

"The star on the rise!"

"No-o."

"He's letting you come here alone? Trust me, he doesn't let everyone do that."

"Whatevers. I'm just trying not to get fired. When are you coming in?"

"I don't know."

"Come in soon, I'll buy you dinner. Come in early so we can eat together."

"No, you don't have to do that."

"Gimme a break. David loves you. He'd be mad if I didn't invite you. Now that I think about it, you come after service. We'll have a great time."

"Ok. I'll get back to you."

She smiled again. "Text me. I'm serious. Besides, not many people get to have dinner with a world class chef."

"That's true. David is getting pretty popular."

Kiko winked. "I was talking about me." She turned, waved behind her head and crested the stairs.

Looking to the space she left, the sky was gray. Low clouds settled over the garden and a light mist dusted his shoulders like powdered sugar. Mac felt a swoop of air like crow overhead but saw nothing.

Time was ticking so he pointed his car down Broadway, wended through Chinatown and the street markets. For a moment he considered stopping to shop for food but felt the pull of his book. The story wouldn't write itself.

He lucked into a spot just a block from his office, parked and climbed the stairs.

These were the types of days his dad would be waiting, leaning against the door frame. Lunch on his mind.

Mac's door frame was empty. He keyed his way in, and a few days of inaction hung in the air, nothing but stale dust crept into his nose. Keys and wallet went in his desk drawer and Mac went straight to his computer and his imagination. He had an old, clunky one without internet, only a word processor. Like he was a new age Sherlock Holmes beating the world with his quirky, original thoughts. There was no extravagance to his effort. Mac used the workstation and his will power. He also used the Bradbury mantra: Don't think.

As soon as the program was open, he looked at the last words, added a few to the previous sentence then he started typing in earnest. The story came like it always did. Turn on the faucet. But it only worked with no expectation.

Embrace the process and know the strands eventually intertwine to create a story full of truths, lies and a small amount of amusement. Trusting what some like to call the muse, his unconscious, his daemon or sprytes, developed a tale with all the twists and turns. The blend of oral storytelling and written story weren't as far as many think or so Mac thought. He was yet to sell one of his grand tales. The work was its own reward and, right now, his detective was in a bind, unsure where to turn. Like Butch and Sundance, he jumped.

Chapter Thirty-Two

The Debts Scene

Well, "Don't think" is fine for writing but not life. Mac was thinking, on the bright side, with those cash payouts from Delilah, for a little bit, rent was no longer a problem. Wait, he should pay that.

Digging to the bottom of his lowest desk drawer, Mac found the cash and counted out enough for the next three months office rent. He thought better of it and put back two months' worth. Cash in his pocket was preferable to cash in theirs. Remember, if you are going to work for yourself, it was best to pay yourself. First.

The manager had an office on the far end, down the hall. Mac put the cash in a company envelope. When he arrived before the manager's door, the lights were out and there was no answer to the knock. They tended to hold banker's hours (the old days banker's hours), so he dropped the envelope through the slot. As soon as he dropped it, he wondered why he would leave cash wide open, ready to be snaked. Couldn't he write a check?

Disappointed in himself, walking toward his office, the manager walked his way. She had the unworried walk of a family with lots of real estate, which they did. Mac liked her anyway.

As they entered each other's personal space, "Hi, Joy. I just dropped rent in the slot."

"Oh, good. Thanks, Mac," she said and looked at him with concern. "How are you?"

He was beginning to see he really did have good people around him in his life. With a shrug and palms to the sky he said, "Umh."

"As to be expected." She smiled. "You let me know if you need anything."

"Oh, and I left the rent in cash. I can't believe I dropped cash in your mail slot."

She touched his wrist. "Don't worry, Mac. Cash is perfect." Then she patted a goodbye. "Everything will work out."

If only Mac had that confidence. She entered her office; he went his own way.

The minor task out of the way, he ran down the list of items to be completed. Number one: prove his innocence. This would be done by figuring out who was responsible for that ersatz uprising. Sure, Olivera was the guy but there was more behind it. Someone, something else. Motives would expose the perpetrator and if someone else was guilty, Mac was innocent. And he'd seen enough in this business to know bystanders can get sucked into the whirlpool. Item 1-A meant he also needed to deal with Delilah and the brother. She kept Mac close for a reason that reason wasn't readily apparent. Hidden motives made Mac antsy. This all had to do with the EIR and those mines. Payouts and loose deals, Mac needed to get with Zoey to tackle the tangled legal web. Which lead to Frankie's work. The Nike. That boat was an actionable lead from Jack back at the bar. The boat leads to an owner which leads to where the money came from. It's a rule as old as time: follow the money.

He texted Frankie to see if she had any information on the boat. Her answer was typical. *Isn't that what I pay you for?* Always supportive, she was. But she was pleased to hear he had a new lead. Treasure hunts require clues, after all.

No sooner had Mac sat at his desk than, instead of working, he went back in his mind to the riot. He couldn't hold his paperwork in the front of his mind.

Images of the scene flashed like a montage. The rush of the arrival with the barrage of women and men screaming, jostling. The goats baying nervously. Filmore upon the pedestal, disheveled and obstinate. Mac closed his eyes and searched for a detail to reveal the cause and the result. What was the catalyst? The strike of the match that started the fire. The moment. He couldn't see the forest for the trees. How could he zoom out and change his perspective? What could he do?

Clearly, Zoey could add detail, but Mac didn't want another opinion, only a different vantage point. Could there be video of the event still? He hit Facebook and looked up the wife's page, the one he saw taking video early on. Olivera's wife. The videos were gone. The sheriff and D.A. probably put an evidential kibosh on them.

But this was the internet. Nothing that salacious can stay hidden. So, Mac hit YouTube and searched for "Mayor Riot" and the sort. There was a video about a similar situation that occurred in Central America, and an old Spanish story along the lines of a Shakespearean play, *Fuenteovejuna* by Lope de Vega, even a Mussolini bit. Then tucked a dozen videos down was another point of view of Cuyamaca. There it was, a new look that would offer new info. Clues on the never-ending journey of discovery that would save his happy ass.

Mac watched the video through. Then again. And again. Nothing new. No great revelations in any way, shape or form. Maybe he was missing something. He slowed the playback to a quarter speed and let it go. There must be more in one of the frames he was missing. Like doing forensics. Now, Mac would tackle it in minute detail. He found it in the very first whip pan of the video. The phone whipped across the crowd and right there on the periphery was Brad, the citizen journalist.

Of course, Brad was there. There were clicks to be had and he had a Los Angeles tie-in from when Filmore hid out in the Biltmore. However, the last thing Mac wanted, after not wanting to go to jail, was to ask Brad for any favors. Worst of all, to know this favor would mean owing him. Big time.

Perhpas Zoey had an idea. This was a talk they would

have face to face.

When she arrived, Mac's fingers made a pyramid in front of his face, index fingers over his nose, thumbs under the chin and his eyes were unfocused, wandering.

She rolled her eyes and said, "What's the problem?" She plopped her bag in one chair and sat in the other.

Mac moved only his eyes and said through his hands, "Brad might have good info."

"Great! Let's go get it."

He lowered his hands and gripped the chair armrests. "He and I don't like each other. And I don't want to owe him."

"You're serious?" Here, she laughed at him. "You don't want to owe him?"

"No."

"The County of San Diego, even maybe the State of California, are considering you for a murder charge and you're concerned with owing a blogger?"

"You don't understand." Mac got out of his chair and looked out on the street; hands clasped behind his back.

"I understand fine. You're an asshole." Zoey stood, threw her bag strap over her shoulder.

Mac turned and said, "Wait. Zoe don't go. I need your help."

"You're not interested in anyone's help, Macondo. You have quite a vision of your own little world in your head."

"C'mon..." Mac smiled, put his palms to the sky. "I'm asking for your help, right now, aren't I?"

"That might be but you're still going to have to learn to express your needs, Mac." She dropped her bag and eyed him. Squinted. Thinking. "Are you capable of becoming more mature than a fifth grader?"

"What's that, ten or eleven? Easy." Mac sat in his chair again, activated his laptop. "Look at this."

She came around the desk, placed a hand on his shoulder while he played the video with Brad's phantom frame. "See. He was there."

"I never saw him."

"Me, either."

"You know he's got something."

"You know he does."

"Why hasn't he released it?"

"Maybe it's big and he's following up."

"Maybe it's nothing."

"Could be but let's act like he's doing his job. Did you call him?"

"No, I wanted you to."

"Me?"

He nodded.

"You're something else."

"So, I've been told."

Zoey turned his office chair, so Mac had to face her. "He doesn't like you either, I assume."

"Let's call it a stalemate."

"Of course." Zoey went to her seat while she dug around in her bag for her phone. "I'll call him for you and set up a meeting."

"Zoe, you're the best."

"But you have to ask."

"What?"

Zoey walked into the hallway and made the call. It was quick. Mac barely had time to get another ten seconds into the video running at quarter-time.

He looked up, "So?"

Putting her phone in her back pocket, she said, "He's a reporter. He believes in the ethical responsibility of the law and the fourth estate more than his dislike of you, Mac."

"I knew it!"

"You're excited that a guy that hates you as much as you hate him is—"

"—is willing to put his ethics and responsibility before his personal feelings. It gives me hope."

"You are a strange man, Macondo."

Mac just smiled right back. "I would think, as an ethical person yourself, you would understand his decision."

"I understand Brad's decision. I'm confused that a guy

who is comfortable in the gray areas is so enthused about someone else's black and white areas."

"Learn this now. If it helps me, it's good." He slapped his laptop closed. "It's as simple as that." He stood out of his chair. "I'm guessing he's willing to talk now."

"That he is."

"Then, let's go." Mac looked out the window as he closed the blinds. "It's raining. Do you have an umbrella?"

"I'll be fine."

"Nope. It's like the storm last week. Broadway and Third is already a pond." He put on a hiking rain jacket from his corner jacket tree, pulled a full-size umbrella and handed her an overcoat.

"This? I'll look like a man."

"Better than a drowned dog."

"True that," she said as she put it on. "Who knew you'd be so prepared."

"Hope for the best, plan for the worst, Zoe. It's like the boy scout motto of small business."

"Uplifting stuff."

He grinned. "This isn't as easy as it looks."

She laughed and said, "You don't make it look that easy, Mac."

Chapter Thirty-Three

The Brad Scene

To Mac's surprise, Brad's offices were an old bank building over on 5th and Main. In fact, he wasn't all that surprised where they were or what they were. Mac's surprise depended on how nice they were. Granted, with open office culture, it's a bit easier to create a pleasing space. A few cubicles, a sofa and bean bags and people think it's a fun place to work. The truth was the business looked like it did better than Mac previously assumed.

Of course, Brad had his own office, and they were briskly shown in by an assistant type of young lady. She quick knocked and entered.

Behind the swinging door, looking out the window beside a big ash desk was Brad, the citizen journalist.

Mac said, "I was walking by and saw your light on."

"To what do I owe this pleasure, Mac?" It was no pleasure at all. "Tough break on that jail time. I never expected a law-abiding citizen like you to get pinched." Brad sat in his ultra-designed office chair. "They must not honor the medals of other departments."

With the medal, again.

Zoey took a seat in one of the two wooden chairs that faced the desk. Mac stayed standing behind the other.

"I'm working here. What do you want?" Brad. Comfortable with something of a cat playing with yarn in his eyes.

"You know why I'm here, Brad. Are you going to make me ask?"

"It's my only joy. Indulge me."

This guy. At least he knew the set up. Mac wouldn't

have to explain everything. "I saw you in a clip at that riot. Can you help?"

"Help what?"

"Help with a new angle. Bring some new info to the table."

"Oh. Help you?"

"Yes, Brad. Help me. Can you help me?"

"Why didn't you say so? Of course, I'm pleased to help a colleague in need."

Which he was everything but true, in Mac's mind.

"In fact, I've found additional footage of the event," Brad said and brought a diagram up on his screen. "Check this out. I mapped it."

He showed them a 3-D model of the Cuyamaca town square. Clicked. People appeared in the square, moving all around. It was a reenactment of the event that allowed views from every angle. It must have taken him days.

"I know what you're thinking," Brad said. "I have a program that creates this once I sink the videos. It takes longer to sink the videos than it does for the program to spit this out."

"Amazing," Zoey said.

"AI. They mostly use it in court cases, but it draws crazy views when I use it on the right story. They're worth a couple hundred one-offs and occasional subscriptions."

Zoey said, "What's a one-off?"

"People pay what amounts to a couple bucks for access to the site for a day. If they like it enough, they pony up for the full subscription."

"I thought you just did local journalism," Mac said.

"We mostly do. And the customers who care are very loyal. We also explore deeper dives. Long reads. Investigative journalism that deals with concerns of the Western states. Also, art and lit."

"I seriously thought you were a pop-up shop," Mac said shaking his head.

"For an investigator, you aren't very curious, are you? You never even looked."

"I guess I never did."

Getting back to the video, Brad pointed. "Look. The two of you never even show up until Filmore was in a body bag." Brad indicated Mac and Zoey at the very end of the animation. "I don't see how the sheriff could convince a D.A. to prosecute you, let alone a jury to convict. You weren't even there."

"This should help clear me."

Zoey was thoughtful. "Maybe. The gears of justice are not necessarily well oiled."

"That's why I'm sharing this with you. I don't know what it is but there are a lot of powerful interests converging on that town and, Mac, you're the scapegoat."

Mac looked between the two of them. "They have to have come up with a better alternative by now." He knew they wouldn't, but you could trust the courts, right?

"Mac, I have a pup reporter at a news conference down there right now. The D.A. promised new information."

"Oh, great." Zoey sat in Brad's chair.

"C'mon. It's not about me."

The other two looked at each other then looked at Mac. Their eyes said what their mouths didn't. *You can't be serious.*

To prove the point, Mac's phone buzzed. Then buzzed some more. As the research guy, he set up Google alerts for his name and his name was buzzing. The D.A. was going after Mac for the murder of Chester Filmore. A warrant was already cut, and they expected Mac to be in custody presently.

The details didn't matter. They were after him. He needed that lawyer and he needed to stay out of the pokey until he developed a case for himself.

Outside the office, most of the staff had their phones out and they were recording. A few pointed at him and others at the front door.

Fucking Brad set him up, Mac was sure. Brad knew this was going down and he wanted the only footage of Mac taken into custody. In their very own office. As Mac sussed it out, two officers entered the main doors.

"Sorry, Mac," Brad said. "But you escaping may be worth as much as you taken into custody. There's a side door if you move quick. And don't forget this video. It'll be here."

Mac didn't waste his time with a response. He lit out of the office and hit the fire exit. Knocking through a pair of vapers, he ran down the street. A line of mannequins, fully dressed in men's and women's clothes, covered with clear runs of plastic watched as Mac rounded a corner and headed for one of the alleys. Two San Diego Deputies had no chance with Mac in DTLA. The clack of their footsteps on the wet cement betrayed their approach then past the alley.

A ladder hung off a fire escape and Mac ran and leaped to grab it. He did his best monkey bars impression and pulled himself up the ladder then onto the landing. As he placed his feet on the metal grating, the officers came into view and turned down the alley. They looked around the garbage bins and bags, saw no movement then headed for what they imagined were greener pastures.

As he watched the alley entrance for a moment to ensure they didn't return, he wondered if it'd be more expedient to prove his innocence or solve the case somehow. That video would clear him as soon as he convinced the ADA to look at it with a clear head. Pondering the issue, it may serve Mac better for this escape to hit the news. With the sensationalism, Brad's recreation would get more attention, clearing Mac. That was a lot of steps to fall the right way.

Maybe there was another way.

Filmore fell off that pedestal. Not ready to take a similar fall, Mac wasn't getting bumped off.

How exactly do you prove a crowd killed a person? Investigation, like any number of jobs, held as a basic tenet that a definable goal was necessary. It's useless to prosecute the foot soldiers, so to speak. By definition, they were pawns. Who instigated this whole thing and how can Mac indubitably tie him or her to Filmore's capture and death?

The classic move would be to do what they've done in the drug wars all these years. Start with that foot soldier and turn him. Then keep turning them all the way up the ranks until he reached the head. With questionable results and no time for that, Mac needed to start making bets and winning. He needed a target. The right one. And now. Because he was not going away on a trumped-up murder charge by a paid off politician. This ends now.

"Hey!"

It was Zoey standing straight below him. He was concentrating and didn't hear her walking down there.

"Are you coming down or is your plan to hide out on a fire escape?"

"Ya, I'm coming down." He climbed down the ladder and released for the remaining drop, just touching his hands on the ground to cushion the fall. "Are they gone?"

"Looks like it. I didn't think you'd be that spry. You're faster than you look."

He raised an eyebrow, "Like a ninja." He wiped his damp grimy hands down his hips.

"Like a thirty-something desk jockey." She laughed then said, "But not an embarrassing one."

"Embarrassing? What do you care," he said as he spied the alley entrance again. This place stank.

"Well, I can't have my future partner embarrassing, or in jail." She headed down the alley.

"Where are you going?"

"To prove your innocence." She stopped. "Aren't you coming?"

He followed. "I'm thinking I have to see who started the riots. We need the bad guy."

"Same difference," she said as she picked her way through the puddles.

Mac wasn't too sure about that partner thing, but he wasn't going to turn down the help. This shit was a mess.

"We'll go to my place," Zoey said. "They'll be waiting at yours."

"You're up in the valley. I have a better idea." Five empty taxis sped past his flagging hand. "Let's get my car they'll still be looking for me on foot."

Chapter Thirty-Four

The Next Scene

Albie's place. No cars out front and all the curtains drawn. The rain stopped.

Mac and Zoey got out of the car to knock on the door anyway. Mac figured on camping out on the backyard table if no one was home. As he knocked, a voice startled him.

"He's not home, Mac." Standing there was Reyes, bright eyes on them. "My condolences on your father."

With a nod, Mac acknowledged Reyes. "Know where he went?"

"You know the answer to that. He had a dozen tomato sprouts in dixie cups. Too early if you ask me."

"Okay. Thanks, Reyes."

"No problem." Reyes raised his eyebrows then said, "You better get out back then. You're already trending on the socials."

"What?"

"Oh, ya." He looked both ways conspiratorially. He checked the rain as much as for the cops. "I understand you wanting Albie but come by my place if the backyard doesn't cut it."

Zoey jumped in. "That's not a bad idea, Mac. It's wet out here," she said as she peeked over the fence.

Reyes agreed. "C'mon. I'm around the corner and you need to get off the street." He walked away without checking if they followed.

Zoey was right after him and, after watching them for a few steps, Mac relented.

Reyes' place was a similar building to Albies. The original wood frame bungalow. But he had the artist's eye rather than the engineer's. Even though Reyes fought California with all his might, he embraced the style. The home was painted orange and white with cacti, succulents, a lemon tree and an avocado all out front. Rocks instead of grass with the bright red apple flowers of aptenia creeping through and three begonias in pots that hadn't moved since he took up residence.

The inside was eclectic. Saltillo tile floors, white walls, two guitars and funky art and dishes on the walls.

"Make yourself comfortable," Reyes said as he went through the doorway to the kitchen. "I'll get you coffee." He came back to the threshold. "Whose car were you driving?"

"Mine," Mac said.

"Here's what we'll do," Reyes carried two cups of coffee and a sugar contraption. "My milk's bad. The girl and I will move your car into the garage and you two can use my car."

"I'm not going to get you in trouble for aiding and abetting," Mac said.

"What?" Reyes went to one of those key hangers people have by the door. "Fuck those guys. C'mon." He threw the keys to Zoey. "You move my car onto the street, and I'll go grab yours."

Reyes walked out the front door expecting Zoey to follow, which she did. Reyes was one of those guys you just did what he told you, no questions.

Mac pulled his phone out and as he typed his name in the browser to search, he stopped. What was he doing? He turned the thing off. Not sure how badly they wanted to catch him, he wasn't going to let them track him with his phone. Three TV remotes sat on the table, he picked each up and hit the power button. If they were all on, they would do something.

The machines went through their startups and Mac planned how to straighten this situation out. Initially, the thought of Frankie rescuing him popped up, but the reality was she wouldn't, couldn't, interfere with local police. She and her department mostly didn't officially exist. Like he just did with Reyes, Mac had to depend on other people to help him out. He didn't have his dad. That put a pang in his chest and even more worry in his mind. Well, next best ally with the cops was Blinkman. He may not be able to help, but he'll have an idea how to fix this. Somebody had to have an idea.

"We have to find the actual perpetrator," Zoey said as she walked in the front door.

Didn't seem to be any mention of Mac on the local news stations. He turned off the TV. "The real culprit."

Reyes entered the house, Albie in tow.

Albie said, "Ya. You need the real bad guy. 'Innocent until proven guilty' and all that but the longer you're tied to the case, the worse it gets." Reyes got himself and Albie each a cup of coffee. They turned around chairs from his dining set to face Mac and Zoey. "I've been thinking. You should call the lady at that government acronym to get you out of this."

"No, she'll stay a mile away from this. I'm just an asset that lost its value if I'm a suspect."

Zoey said, "You underestimate your value, Mac."

"You overestimate people giving a shit." Mac paced with his hands behind his back like he was a professor in front of a class. "But what does all of this say about what is happening with this case?"

Albie put his cup down. "That this charge is bogus."

"Okay, besides that." Mac acknowledged the additional vote of confidence, though. "This grandstanding ADA wants to get me but who is she protecting?"

"Or what is she protecting?"

Reyes piped up. "They are using you to release the pressure."

"They want the public's eye somewhere else, is what they want," said Albie.

"If they have a suspect and charge them, most of the

people's attention and the media's eyes go elsewhere." It was Reyes.

"No more drama," Zoey said. "Cut and dry case. Nobody cares. Justice is served."

"In everybody's eyes but the wrongly accused." Reyes was getting into this.

"Expediency and PR." Albie stood up. "This all ticks me off. I'm taking a piss!"

"It has to be the mine," Mac said.

"We were there. That deal is dead," Zoey said.

"What mine?" Reyes said, leaned back and assessed. He seemed to time the engagement.

"There's a mine down in Cuyamaca. Filmore wanted to turn it into a nuclear waste facility."

"Like in Nevada?" Reyes had his wheels turning. "Did you know they are offering sixteen million bucks for towns to even think about holding nuclear waste?"

"What d'you mean?" Mac hadn't heard this.

Reyes continued. "I don't just write rock puff pieces. I also do investigative stuff and I've been working on a piece for High Country News about what to do with industrial waste. Whoever takes on the nuclear stuff is looking at billions of dollars flooding in."

"For the construction?" Zoey looked between Mac and Reyes.

"Plus, more for holding it on a rotating basis."

"That's a pretty big boon to the community," Albie said. He was back.

"It's also a consolidation that could affect an entire region, not just a small town." Mac was beginning to see he was at the hub of a massive windfall. He stood between someone and billions of dollars.

Zoey was thinking the same thing. "We have very motivated people against you, Mac."

"And, if we're being honest, another entire group of people more than happy to let you take the fall for this," Reyes said as he finished up the pot of coffee between all the cups. "I won't pretend to know that group's motivations, but I do know people like to avoid punishment."

"I just don't think you can prosecute a mob. You're easy pickin's, Mac." Albie looked at all of them, a big thought rolling around in his prodigious mind.

"What is it, Albie?" Mac sat on the sofa, again.

Albie rose to his feet and said, "You don't like the idea of it, but you have to tap into your big government client."

"No. That leads nowhere," Mac said as he shook his head.

"You're talking federal money for federal issues dealing with federal laws." Albie clapped his hands like he was Pappy from The Treasure of Sierra Madre and said, "You wouldn't only be going to the right place, you're doing them a favor."

"Are you bullying me into reaching out to my client?" Mac was feeling a little cramped.

"You're going to have to do uncomfortable things, or it'll get much worse." Zoey had the corner of her mouth pinned.

"Enough talking about doing things," Reyes said and stood. "Providence favors the bold."

"I already said it, I'm not dragging all of you into this," Mac said looking into the eyes of three people who didn't give a lick what he wanted.

After a breath of semi-respect, Reyes continued. "I'll reach out to my contacts on this radioactive waste site."

"I have friends in DoD that might know what's going on," Albie said.

"Defense?" Mac was really getting worried.

"Those submarines create leftovers. Not a lot but it's gotta go somewhere and San Diego is as tight with DoD as anywhere in the country."

"And you, young man," Reyes said, of course, pointing to Mac. "You are going to use your super-secret decoder ring hook-up to help save your own ass instead of someone else's."

Zoey gathered herself. "Let's go. You can drop me

around the corner from your place so I can get my car."

Mac considered how he would get in touch with Frankie. He wouldn't activate his phone. He couldn't get to his laptop. The only answer was to visit her office. If nothing else, maybe they could tie him into a call.

Out the front door and parked directly in front of the house was a souped-up Cal-bug. Reyes' car was a tricked out light blue Beetle, lowered front end, alloy wheels and a black racing stripe over the running boards. Mac must've been worried earlier because he didn't even hear the glass-packs rumble when they started the car before but sitting inside, there was no mistaking the rumble of the custom exhaust. This wasn't his car, but he wasn't going to sneak around. This car meant hiding in plain sight.

Chapter Thirty-Five

The Escape Scene

The sun broke through the darkness in that bright crystalline way after a rain, sparkling in the sky and off the ground. The clouds had parted.

People hustled down the sidewalks of Broadway as Mac made his way past the old movie palaces, eateries and converted electronics stores. He turned down 5th and spotted Zoey's car.

Half-seated, leaning on her quarter-panel was a man in jeans, sweatshirt and rain shell. He looked ready for a hike. It was Blinkman.

They pulled just past and parked, blocking a parking structure entrance.

Mac exited the car with his hands out in a question.

"You're not the only one who knows how to research," Blinkman said. He gave Mac a hug. "Nice car, by the way."

Mac pushed back and said, "You can't be here. You'll get yourself in trouble."

"Shit. Don't you worry about me." Blinkman raised his hand in a wave. "Hey, Zoey."

She smiled. This was her kind of guy. "You really shouldn't be here."

"He just lost his dad," Blinkman said with a head tilt to Mac. "And I'm not going to let his pride put him in jail."

Zoey couldn't agree more. "See?"

"Great. Maybe you can all join me in the cell next

door." Mac scanned the street. "Are they staked out at my place."

"Claro."

"Look," Mac said, he needed both their attention. "I can't tell you what to do but my next step I have to do alone. There are no visitors at the client's place."

Zoey grimaced. "So, am I supposed to just sit around and wait."

"No. You're coming with me," Blinkman said. "I have an idea that you'll be perfectly suited for."

"And what is that?" Zoey said, perhaps even curious.

Blinkman slapped Mac on the shoulder. "Let's get him on his way."

"Before you go," Zoey said. "Give me your phone."

"Why?"

"Are you sure they can't track you when it's off."

"C'mon. That's some James Bond stuff."

"So. Think about it. Are you positive all those secret apps and VPN you're using from the government—are you sure they can't keep an eye on you?"

"We don't live in 1984."

"Does your phone show ads related to your last conversation?"

"Siri doesn't listen."

"Are you willing to bet your freedom on that?"

Mac handed over the phone. It didn't do him any good dead and pocketed, anyway.

It wasn't a long drive over. Mac still spent more time looking in his rear-view mirror than where he was going, as if the police were more likely to be behind him than in front.

Within the building, the smooth walls and cold floor echoed as he followed the guard with the uncanny ability to stay in step and time with Mac. The amount of silence that allowed the syncopated echoes made the space feel empty though Mac was sure there were people working away diligently throughout the place, hidden behind the walls.

After two rights and a left, they arrived at an assistant

next to a desk controlling any traffic. She had a blonde bob, crisp white shirt and a black skirt with fashionable but understated flats. How much did they pay these people? Mac wasn't billing enough. Her clothes were top notch.

The guard walked directly past and opened the door that well-dressed attendant protected.

The room was empty save for a conference table with chairs for a dozen participants and a technical box in the middle.

Before Mac even decided which chair to inhabit, the box vroomed, and a hologram of a miniature Frankie appeared. "Sorry I couldn't be here in person."

"I'm not sure I truly expected to be able to meet you at all." Mac sat at a chair at one o'clock on the conference table. Being too close to the holo invaded his personal space. The edge chair provided distance.

"You're in a bit of a pickle."

"I am."

"And you're looking for help."

"I am."

"You do realize the nature of our relationship makes that difficult for me."

"I do." This wasn't going to go the way Mac wanted it to, of that he was becoming sure. "I—"

"Look, Mac. You shouldn't even be here."

"Where else would I go? Besides, you don't answer to local law enforcement."

"We are all accountable to the law." She held the silence earnestly.

Then they both laughed. She continued. "I had to try. It's practically in my employment contract. Those yahoos don't have a legal leg to stand on. Don't you worry about it."

"They want to put me in jail."

"Back in jail."

"Exactly. One of my life's goals is not to become a statistic."

From her body language, she turned to look out her

window, but the hologram just showed her rotate her body. "We are all statistics. Don't be fooled into thinking you are different from anybody else."

"Great." Mac was a little restless. "I appreciate both the civics and the philosophy lessons but what I really need is an assurance that you can help me."

Frankie faced the camera, again. "I can investigate it for you but no promises. The web around this is vast. On first blush, I can see the Department of Defense and the EPA fingerprints."

"Platitudes."

"I have bosses and underlings to worry about, too, Mac."

"So, as far as you're concerned, I'm fucked."

"I wouldn't put it that way."

"Not in polite company."

"You'll work it out."

"Will you at least dig on this mine for me? There must be information I can't find by myself."

"Mac. It would be the type of information I hire you to find."

"Oh, for fuck's sake."

"Keep me posted, Mac." End transmission.

This wasn't going to be easy. There are no shortcuts. Mac got himself caught in a loop in his mind that he would receive help. And they may to an extent, but he knew it. In his bones the truth was always there. If you want something done, you had to do it yourself.

"This case needs to be blown wide open," he said to no one. Mac pushed the chair to the wall as he rose and headed out the door. Frankie might help, but Mac's tail was on the line. Mac would have to save himself.

He forgot he had the bug until he got out to the street. Mac needed a better car. He needed to get down to Cuyamaca and talk to Olivera. Mac was sure the only person who really knew what was going on in that stinking little town was Olivera. Not Delilah. Not the sheriff. Not the city council or anyone else. Filmore knew. And Olivera knew.

Filmore was dead.

Olivera was the last man standing.

It was time to hear it straight from the horse's mouth.

He hoped Albie's bug could make it. The car didn't have air conditioning but, as a bug, it did have a heater and an abundance of gas vapors. Mac had to crack the window a few inches and blast the heater to make up for the cold wind. The people's car must've also meant freeze balls in German.

Of course, by the time Mac reached Camp Pendleton, about halfway there, the rain began to fall. If you hadn't noticed, even the windshield wiper technology improved over the years. Especially the windshield wiper technology. And the defrost. It wasn't freezing. Just in the fifties. But rain and cold made the car fog up and Mac's new car knew how to blow air on the windows in a way the Cal bug did not. Just like this case, Mac couldn't see his way clear from the rain on the outside and the condensation on the inside.

The roll into Cuyamaca was accompanied with a wet arm and a lot of empty parking spots. It seemed, no one ventured into this rain. Mac pulled in front of the cafe. A warm cup of coffee and a piece of that pie awaited him. He had business but energy beyond anger would serve him best.

He thought better of this parking. He pulled out of the street spot and drove past around back by where he interviewed the cook, then found a spot on the residential street half a block up. Know your exits. He walked down around the joint and walked in the front.

"Hi, hon."

He was greeted by the waitress as he entered the door. She followed him to a booth with cup, coffee carafe and a menu. In the hopes of hiding his face, he sat with his back to the door.

"I'll be back in a jiffy."

The place was empty except the four old guys in the corner table by the kitchen door. The type that argues everything over coffee and eggs every morning.

They were into a deep discussion at the moment. Mac, feeling self-conscious, exposed and wanted by the law, couldn't remember if they were already talking when he walked in or started when he did. Soon enough, when each in turn caught Mac looking them over, they stopped. The entire place was silent.

Mac felt the extra wetness in the air from rain, jackets and boots. Smelled it. The moment almost crackled.

He shouldn't be here. Barely a stone's throw from the police station, for chrissake.

The bell on the door rang.

Mac reconsidered his back to the door idea. Might be better to see who's coming in rather than hide.

The footfall was confident, but Mac didn't hear the jangle of a utility belt, at least.

They brushed past him and there sitting across from Mac was Olivera.

"I was coming to see you," Mac said.

"Well, this works out then." Olivera signaled for a coffee from the waitress.

The silence dissipated but the crackle didn't. The old guys chattered. About them or whatever else, it didn't matter.

"You've got to know something about all this." Mac said it and tried to look straight into the old guy's machinations. "What the hell is going on?"

Olivera waited as the waitress came with a cuppa and left. He squinted then focused. "There is more in heaven and—"

"—Don't!" Mac cut him off. "Seriously. You trot out Shakespeare? What kind of a town is this?"

He grinned and said, "I'm not kidding. There's more than you know."

"Enlighten me," Mac said as the waitress returned, a question in her eyes. "I'll have a burger and fries."

"No milk, right? Allergies?" she said.

He was stunned. "Right." It wasn't often someone

remembered his allergies.

Olivera jumped in. "Don't be too impressed. You were a prisoner down the road."

The waitress wanted nothing to do with this conversation. "I'll get that right up." She looked at Olivera who shook his head no.

"How about we start with this prisoner thing?" Mac leaned onto the table with his elbows. "I need you to get the sheriff off my back."

"We don't even know each other, Mac." Olivera shifted his weight. "You know the sheriff can't imagine his town committing a terrible act like that. Only an outsider could commit such a heinous crime. Anyway, it's in the District Attorney Office's hands now."

"Then, what are all these things you're telling me I don't know about?"

"There are so many layers, son. I could never catch you up."

"Like about your wife - and your daughter?"

"Fuck you." That woke him up. "But even that is water under the bridge. We have bigger issues of land and generations of heritage."

"The mine."

"That fucking mine has been at the middle of every problem this mountain town has ever had."

"It created the town, didn't it?"

"The town, sure. But people lived here long before the Spaniards and before the rest who came for the gold."

"Killing Filmore doesn't stop it."

"Nobody wanted to kill him. The corruption was finally too much. It's nobody's fault he had a bad temper and worse balance."

"It seems some people think it was *somebody's* fault."

"That's really why I'm here."

"What d'you mean?"

"I'm not going to lie. I'm meeting you because it benefits me. I'm going to help get you off and then you are going to help stop this mine."

Mac said, "I appreciate the offer but I can't help you."

"Yes, you can."

"Viejo. I think you want me in this mess deeper not to get me out."

"I just had a phone call with a spirited environmental group."

"Like the Sierra Club?"

"Like eco-terrorists."

They both sat in silence as the truth of the situation hung in the air.

Olivera continued. "They tell me you are connected with high-end government stuff."

"Not that it's helped."

"You don't understand. It seems the eco group received new mine information regarding that will aid stopping the storage facility siting acid runoff into the water table."

"Well, good for you."

"Catch up, Mac. These small-timer needed you to take the fall so they could keep the mine. If they can't flip the mine for cash, they don't need you as a scape goat."

Silence.

"You still don't get it," Olivera said. "If this info gets out, you're off the hook."

"You have a lot of faith. I might have gotten help from on-high but there are many miles to go. Somebody just staked their career on nailing me. That bull dog ADA doesn't care about the puppet master's motivations. She's been sent after me. She won't stop until she gets me."

Mac felt a tingle in the back of his mind push to the fore. The old guys stopped talking. They were focused outside. Olivera glanced over Mac's shoulder, too.

Mac didn't even look, just bolted straight for the kitchen. The bell was ringing by the time he slammed through the kitchen door then three strides later through the back exit. Mac rotated the dumpster in front of the door.

This was not going to plan. Whatever the plan was. On the run from the cops was just a continuation but not the plan. He looked left. Then right. Then left, again.

Gonna have to move. His car was around the corner.

Mac lit off to the right behind the buildings remaining on Main when he heard the rev of an engine. Did he underestimate the speed of the cops coming after him?

An old, white bronco stopped in front of him with Blinkman behind the wheel. "Get in."

Mac answered as he ran up to the driver's window. "Are you sure?"

"Let's go! We can discuss the reasons later."

Blinkman hit the gas before Mac had even sat. The lurch of the truck closed the door. They sped past two streets, took a left and a right then onto a dirt track road.

Mac turned to search behind them for the police cruisers that must be following and found Zoey in the back seat.

"Won't they expect us to take this? They'll see the tracks in the mud."

"Don't worry. Those weren't local guys. They were marshals." Blinkman did a thorough check behind them.

"Besides, I told them you went the opposite direction." Zoey's eyes were peeled behind them, as well. Then she looked at Mac. "I saw them as they ran out of the restaurant."

"What if I had gone that way?"

"I took a chance."

With a decision to go with the flow for the moment, Mac said, "So, where're we going?"

"Away from them. There's a web of these tracks in these hills. I can work us over towards the highway." He offered a big smile. "Don't worry."

Zoey jumped in. "We figured out why they are doing this."

Blinkman picked up the thread. "If you are charged, the town is out of the papers. Forgotten. The story is over."

"So?" Mac didn't know where they were going with this.

Zoey leaned over the front seat between the two and

said, "Who do you think is doing all this?"

Mac turned to her face right next to his. "If I knew, don't you think I'd have gotten out of this already?"

Blinkman swerved through a mud puddle, spun his tail and scraped a line of bushes along the side of the Bronco. "You're too close."

Mac realized he was falling for the same shiny keys everyone else had fallen for. "The companies behind the mine."

"And who do you think is leading them?" Zoey couldn't wait for him to figure this out.

"I thought it was Olivera, to be honest."

Blinkman, eyes steeled on the dirt road, glanced at Mac now and said, "Pendejo. It's Filmore."

"Why would she do that?" They had lost Mac again.

"You think because you had a little slap and tickle you were in the clear?"

"What?"

"Kid, it isn't Delilah."

"Oh, shit. It's Junior."

Zoey clapped her hands and cackled.

"Bingo," Blinkman said as proud as a poppa of his kindergartner getting a base hit in t-ball.

"I wrote him off."

Back to his usual tone, Blinkman said, "Because he's an idiot."

Unable to stay out of it any longer, Zoey said, "But Junior has no control. Delilah blew the deal because she's wants to go green."

"And Junior wants the cash." Starting to really see their line of reasoning, Mac said, "And if I go down, Junior can tie Delilah to me and drag her down..."

"And move forward with the deal and the mine and the Billion." Delilah and Blinkman actually said this together.

Mac couldn't help but approve of this plan. "So, we're going to Filmore Ranch."

Blinkman agreed, adding, "And dragging the cops along with us."

"Is this going to become a locked room mystery?" Zoey said from between their heads.

"Well, we'll be solving the case with cops at the door," Mac said, eyes in the distance, trying to imagine what was over the horizon.

Then Mac decided, he didn't know what or how, but this would work out. "When we get there, see if one of you can sneak away up to that office. There must be contracts for the deals. The paper trail will solidify Junior's involvement outside of Delilah's influence."

"It won't hold up in court to get him prosecuted," Blinkman chewed on the idea aloud. "But it could spring you from suspicion."

That was all Mac needed: to be free of their clutches. The wheels of justice weren't his concern, but his freedom surely was. "We have more than this theory, though. Right?"

"We do." Zoey laughed now. She held up Mac's phone. "When we turn this on, we'll have a homing device for half the black and whites in the county."

Blinkman whooped and banged the roof. "Shit's about to get interesting!"

"Shall I?" Zoey held her finger over the button.

A deep breath. Mac was about to play Russian Roulette. On second thought, not completely. He had an advantage he'd never really counted into his calculations. Help rode in this cab right along with him.

"There's no time like the present," he said.

Zoey turned the phone on and a plethora of bings, blangs and bongs emanated from the machine. "You know you can turn off the notifications on your device," she said and handed it to him.

There was a slew of news and social media updates that had nothing to do with Mac. He was relieved the media had ignored his story for the moment but deep down, he hoped Frankie might have sent him more info to help him out. No dice.

They banged up and down on the fire road along a

ridge for a few miles through tight spots, but it was graded and maintained to some extent. The state of California is a place where fires have to be taken seriously and the ability to traverse the terrain allows those occurrences to be addressed. This one also allowed our group of marauders to ride a short cut to Filmore's.

It was a good thing Blinkman had the all-terrain tires, there was just enough of a layer of mud to make going up and down a little more interesting than they needed right now. After wending down the hill, they approached Filmore's place from the opposite way as previously and turned left into the house. Coming to a stop, Mac heard a hovering helicopter above.

Blinkman scrunched his neck to look up and out the windshield. "Looks like air support is here. TV choppers can't be far behind."

"And you thought nobody cared," Zoey said as she closed the Bronco's door.

"Could be rain, though," Blinkman said as a gust of wind helped him slam his own door.

All three walked toward the entrance to the house. Mac slowed his gait and said, "Now, you don't have to come in here with me."

"In for a dollar in for dime," Blinkman said.

Zoey simply kept walking and knocked on the door.

Mac supposed that was answer enough.

Delilah herself opened the door. She took in all three then smiled at Mac, "Fancy meeting you here."

All Mac could think was, "this girl picks the strangest times to flirt." Then he said, "Can we talk?"

"Come in." Delilah opened the door completely to allow them entry.

Zoey asked as she passed, "Junior here?"

"Junior! We have guests."

Feeling like Delilah wasn't taking this whole situation very seriously, Mac didn't have a lock on what was happening. Mac couldn't tell if his nerves were frayed from this chase-and-hide he'd been on all day, or something really wasn't connecting.

As Blinkman passed, Delilah said, "I haven't met our third guest."

"I'm his protection," Blinkman said.

"He doesn't need any protection here," Delilah said. "He's amongst friends."

"Oh, he might need some." Junior was at the top of the stairs, taking it all in. "Bold move coming here, Macondo. I heard the copter; the units can't be far behind."

"I'm counting on it." Mac continued past the seating area and took a seat at one end of the dining table. A clear invitation for discussion. Zoey and Blinkman walked around Delilah and sat on either side of Mac.

By this time, Junior was down the stairs. He walked past Delilah and took a seat at the other end of the long dining table, not an ounce of question in his actions. He said, "We're just going to wait until the police arrive. Then they can handle the man responsible for my father's death."

Delilah was standing, her hands on the back of one of the dining chairs. "Junior?!" Her gears were grinding, probably a few teeth broke off.

"Shut up, Delilah. Don't be such a child." Junior said with real hate in his eyes. "How could you defend this monster?"

"I am not defending him. He needs no defense. Mac is not responsible for our father's death."

"That's not what the ADA thinks." It seemed Junior was up for the fight today.

"She is full of shit." Delilah, too. "I would not be surprised if she was bought and paid for."

Junior studied her. "At least you have some instincts left."

The conversation continued as if Mac and the others weren't even there. Mac wondered if they were accustomed to people around while they had private conversations. At the very least, it was poor strategy to have this particular conversation in front of Mac.

But he wasn't about to interrupt.

Back to the siblings. Delilah snuffed and said, "Thank God you were not appointed executor."

"That, too, will change."

"As if you have the nerve."

"It's very simple, dear sister. You are already in cahoots with our father's murderer. Jail time will fix this for me."

"Fuck you."

"Mr. Macondo already did that. As a matter of fact, your carnal adventures are what gave me the idea."

Mac was a little shocked and it must have showed on his face because Junior said, "Did you think you're the only one she gets athletic with, Macondo? My sister is quite the lady about town."

"That was unnecessary." Delilah remained still but she flushed. "What do you care who I fuck?" Now, she surveyed the room, testing the temperature on all the faces.

Mac wondered if this was all a show, somehow. Normal people don't act this way. He needed to take over and direct this argument because what he needed was the information to take Junior down not the details of their pathetic family.

Mac came out of his seat and leaned on the table with both hands towards Junior. "You're not getting the company and you're not getting me."

"I don't need to. Listen," Junior said. The roar of sirens echoed up the valley. "The police and ADA will take care of you. Then the media will set the table for my sister's demise. It's not rocket science."

"Taking me to jail again doesn't do anything." Mac sat, placed his hands in a triangle, working his plan. "I'll beat this." Then he took a gamble and lay his cards out. "My lawyers already sent footage proving I arrived at the scene long after your father's demise. Your money and lies can't put me away."

Junior and Delilah shared a laugh. Mac didn't get what was so funny. He just proved he wouldn't take the fall for them and the last thing he needed was for those two to be on the same side of anything.

The siblings had something else between them. There was a tug of war between affection and disdain. Mac couldn't decide if they would unite and destroy him or obliterate each other.

The roar of the sirens swelled like a wave crashing into a jetty then halted. Soon behind was a rapid rap on the door. "Police."

Mac covered the distance to the door in what felt like a single step. He locked the door then backed away from the danger. "We aren't opening up." Outside the bay window a light rain blanketed the surrounding trees which reflected the blue and red flashing lights.

An exasperated sigh made it through the door, "You're only making it worse with all of this run around, Macondo."

Mac didn't need someone negotiating who had no power anywhere. "The sheriff out there?"

The sound of the cop's utility belt shifting came through the door before he said, "He's on his way."

"Then go make yourself comfortable. I'll talk when the sheriff's here, not before."

Zoey was by his side. "Do you know what you're doing?"

Blinkman was behind her shoulder. He said nothing but his eyes had the same question.

Perhaps more concerning, Junior and Delilah were seated at the table. Junior, his hands crossed on the table. Delilah leaned back with her legs crossed at the knees. No phones, no concern. Simply spectators.

The yin and yang of these two made sense. Siblings, family in general, tended to stick together if not for blood, out of habit. Mac had seen too many spouses return to their cheating partner to only be back in his office again a year later after another bout of affairs. Habit and a drive to prove yourself right are strong motivators. Any scientist will tell you about research bias. How experimenters will go to great lengths, both ethical and unethical, to prove a theory correct.

What he needed was a split between these two. Mac still didn't believe Delilah was the one who framed him. And not because of the sex. She didn't have any reason to. However, Junior had everything to gain. Motive was how you solved cases. If the husband died: look at the wife, and vice versa. If getting rid of the old ball 'n chain wasn't enough, the insurance money probably was.

Junior needed to prove he was right in his assumptions. If Mac could get him to expose his thinking, then they could prove the son was at the heart of the father's death.

Mac also couldn't shake the feeling that somehow Olivera was wrapped up in all of this, even if he was an unwitting pawn. Unsure whether it mattered, Mac figured that if you pay attention those side pieces do change the outcome of the game.

"Are you creating a hostage situation here, Macondo?" Junior hadn't moved but held that pompous chin right out to Mac.

What a glorious answer it would be to put a rabbit punch right on that target. Mac knew it. The idiot knew it. The entire room knew it. And, yet that would only help Junior's cause while feeding Mac's less useful instincts.

Mac had to dig deeper. Investigate this issue and stop getting pulled in other people's agendas and directions. What created the issue from the very beginning?

"Delilah, why did you hire me? How did you get my information?"

Delilah spoke. She didn't even move her line of sight. "I saw that medal you got from the L.A.P.D. and figured you'd be as good as any."

Blinkman piped up. "I told you those things brought nothing but the wrong kind of attention."

"I'm glad to see you've joined the chat." Blinkman saluted in jest. Mac sat at the table again as he said, "I can't help but think if the sheriff and Olivera were here, I'd have the whole group to blame for my predicament in this ratty little town."

"This ratty little town is our home," Junior said. "And

you have disrupted the natural order of things."

At that moment, a downpour ensued with a flash and the close rumble of thunder.

Knock. Knock. Knock.

"Okay, Mac. I'm here! Let's get my guys out of the rain and you go ahead and surrender." It was the sheriff.

Mac went and leaned on the door. "I need Olivera here, too." Mac was putting the pieces of the puzzle together.

"I'm here." It was Olivera.

Was he a set up all along at the diner with a bunch of small-town pricks in cahoots the entire time?

The sheriff spoke up, "You're just trying to buy time."

"Nope." Mac rubbed his chin. Ran a hand through his hair. "Both of you come in. But I need you to leave the gun behind, sheriff."

"You know I'm not doing that. Jesus, Mac."

"Both of you come in and we'll settle this all fair and square. If you aren't satisfied, I'll surrender nice and easy. You have my word."

"Mine, too!" It was Blinkman.

"What good is the word of an unattached voice through a door?"

"Twenty years on L.A.P.D. enough for you?"

"That'll do. I just have to report to dispatch. Lemme go call in."

Mac jumped right in. "No. Drop your gun on the porch and you two can come on in out of the cold."

As soon as they were in the door, the sheriff gave Junior the evil eye, who offered a raised eyebrow. Olivera was distant and avoidant.

"Now, you have two helpers?" The sheriff indicated Blinkman. "Aren't you the lawyer?"

Blinkman held steady. "I was a cop."

The sheriff worked past them into the room. "Well, in any case, even through the door her voice doesn't look that deep."

"Hello, sheriff," Zoey said and offered her hand. "I'm—"

The sheriff interrupted her, "I know who you are. I remember our little exchange."

Mac indicated the dining table offering a seat to the two new guests as he took his seat at the head of the table. "I'm glad we could all get together."

This collection of characters, right here, would decide the trajectory of Mac's life. Blinkman already had. He was as close to a tío as Mac had and with his dad gone, there was no blood left. Zoey, God bless her, wasn't going away.

Most importantly, this collection of small-town big fish had decided that he would pay the price of their greed and hubris. One of the people in this room knew the truth and Mac would shake it out of them.

Mac prepared to pull his very best Miss Marple, Monsieur Poirot.

"I have brought you all here to settle this once and for all," Mac said taking the temperature of the room.

The sheriff sprang straight up. "Oh, for Pete's sake. You're coming with me."

"Sit. Down. Sheriff." Mac would control this room. "I already have enough to get you in hot water with the feds. You might want to ride out the storm for a bit longer."

Olivera, sitting next to the sheriff, put a hand on the sheriff's forearm, who sat and settled.

The siblings still hadn't moved from their poses; however, the expressions had changed. Delilah was bemused and, perhaps, a bit horny.

Junior was pissed and a bit scared. He said, "So, you have finally decided to play a little detective, have you? What is it you were doing on my dime all this time?"

"I believe I was on your sister's dime. And I was hired to clear your father of wrongdoing not to find his murderer. That requirement has become mine alone, through sheer self-preservation."

"For now, I'll sit and listen because your demise is certain, Macondo," Junior said. "Nothing you can do now will save you."

Mac smiled without a hint of it in his eyes. "Junior,

there's a saying among the sailors. Avoid a drowning man, he'll just pull you down." He threw his hands out as if to say, that's me.

He pulled out his phone, which, of course, was now on and pushed, swiped a few times. "I'll record this." He placed the phone on the table, face down. "For posterity."

He continued, "As I was saying: seated around this table are the prime suspects in this murder. Zoey, where should we start?"

Zoey did a circle with her eyes to all the faces around her. "Olivera. He's both the furthest and most likely to want the son of a bitch dead."

"Agreed," Mac said. "I'll admit, I was thrown off by this meeting today, Olivera."

"Mac—"

"No need to apologize. I can see now the set up was, to you, for good reason. A large chunk of this land is still in Filmore's name. I just received the deed information from the county on the way over."

Zoey nodded. "Sometimes it takes a few days for them to dig it up."

"This documentation when connected to the truth about your daughter created an interesting scenario."

"What truth about his daughter?" Delilah leaned in.

"Ah, I see you already guessed it. You must have wondered why your father took such a sudden interest in the high school cheerleading star but didn't want to think too hard about it. Unlike the rumors, he wasn't having an affair with that girl."

"What is he talking about?" Junior looked between Delilah and Olivera.

"I am talking about your half-sister. From the looks of it, Olivera over here knew and also knew the land wasn't in a trust. Since it was still in the father's name, Miranda had as much right to the land as you two."

Olivera didn't budge, but said, "I didn't kill him."

"I don't think you killed him. I think you wanted the land for the girl you raised as your own and the sooner the mess was cleared, the sooner you get the land."

"Who understands what the hell they are talking about?" Junior said as he surveyed the table.

Mac said, "It goes like this: back when they were kids, Filmore and Olivera fought over the same girl."

"Frida," Zoey said.

Mac continued. "Yes. But when Filmore went off to college he forgot all about Frida."

"But she still carried the torch."

"Right. But Olivera stayed around and proximity breeds love, too. Eventually, they got married and played house."

"But the children never came. It's biology. People fire blanks."

"Then eighteen years ago, when Frida and Filmore were both on city council a few sparks flew, one thing led to another, and a baby was on the way."

"It seems they decided to keep it. They loved each other and had a chance at a family," Delilah said.

Blinkman piped in, "They didn't like each other but old friendships die hard."

And Mac kept going. "They worked out an agreement. The land would stay in Filmore's name, and the girl would get a slice of the land when Filmore died. Filmore didn't want anything to do with raising another kid."

"He didn't like the ones he had," Blinkman said.

"So, with the silence came a pay off."

"He was never a good man but did a good thing. He gave me my daughter," Olivera said.

"And a couple hundred acres."

"That, too," Olivera said.

"But you didn't kill him."

"Why would I? I've got my own land, and the rest would go to the girl when she was older. No need to rush." Olivera, again.

"Quite the love triangle."

"Love comes in many shapes and sizes," Olivera said.

"You knew?" Delilah almost forgot where she was.

"Yes, I knew. We didn't like each other but I didn't

want my kid to be from somebody we never knew. As you get older… well, love can require many sacrifices."

"And Filmore's ego couldn't resist the chance to have more of his genes running around." Mac wanted to throw a little gas on the fire.

"That's unfair. No, he never held that over me. Filmore kept his distance. We disagreed on a lot but we both loved Frida. He did it for her. I never would have killed the idiot."

"So, what's the connection?"

"The land was the key piece in the puzzle." Mac cogitated for a moment. "The more I thought about and researched the land, the more it became apparent."

"Is this land the land with the mine on it?" Sheriff said.

"No. But thinking about the land opened up the other possibilities."

"Which brings us to the sheriff." Delilah wasn't going to let him get off track.

"Which brings us to the sheriff." The room was in Mac's hands at this point. The mix between the revelation of someone else's secrets and worry that their own would be revealed put a crackle in the air.

A flash bang whacked the room. Lightning struck an oak in the clearing just below the house with such force the trunk rent, and the wave of energy transmitted right through the group. Despite the scene they had sprung as one to survey the destruction.

Perhaps due to the rain, there was no fire. The split wood, however, was black from where the bolt discharged. The window glowed with the cold and the rain rolled like tears down the panes each choosing their path joining then separating from the others.

The initial jolt surprised Mac but he quickly changed gears to assessing each person, the better to be prepared for what was to come. When Mac got to the sheriff, he was doing the same thing. If the sheriff was questioning motives around the room maybe shining light on that secret helped more than he allowed himself to hope.

The sheriff might already be an ally at this point. Mac planned to beat the sheriff up on his ridiculous pursuit of Mac's guilt, but could he be just doing his job?

How did Mac get into this predicament? He did not belong here. He did not deserve this. It didn't matter, Mac was going to win. It still required a deft touch and patience. Like setting the trap in chess, each move must be taken at the proper time. Moving the wrong piece too early only alerts your opponent to your plan allowing them to build a defense. This game had more dire consequences than a chess match. Time for the next move.

"Sheriff, how did you come to the conclusion that I was your suspect?"

"I'm not discussing my process with you, Mac. You know better than that." The sheriff harrumphed his way back to his chair. That may have been a dismissal, but he was still in the game and encouraged the continuation by setting the dining table as the stage again. "Besides, it couldn't have been anyone from my town. We're good people here." He crossed his arms over his chest and reconsidered. "Mostly."

The rest of the group followed suit and dutifully sat in their seats like students in a classroom. Zoey gave a push, "As you were saying..."

With her interjection, Mac could fork to a different direction, or he could keep after the sheriff. Of course, he kept after the sheriff.

"There's footage all over the internet that proves I arrived after Filmore's—accident."

"Clearly the ADA sees it differently." Sheriff wasn't having it.

"Don't you have an independent bone in your body?"

"I'm just the messenger."

Blinkman jumped in. "That's a bunk, weak-ass excuse. I'd think you have more pride in that badge."

"Don't you question my commitment to the law."

That seemed to have raised the sheriff's cackles. Mac needed the sheriff a little rattled. Unless he was off his game, he wouldn't offer more than the party line we've heard all along.

Zoey picked up the can for a shake. "I just wonder who that law protects and who it's used against."

"My people have been in these parts as long as those other two, don't you come down here and question my honor. It may not be the South, but enough of those confederates came here to make it hard on my family. You saw that statue they finally took down."

The sheriff had enough of the parlor game. He pushed himself up, hands on the table and said, "We're going to the police station."

Blinkman pulled a service .38 from his waistband and laid it on the table. He said, "Just sit down. We are going to play this out."

"Is that a threat?"

"It was uncomfortable in my waistband. Now was as good a time as any to pull it out."

Amused by the dance, the sheriff said, "Okay, okay. I don't know why but, as the curious type, I'm going to keep on listening." He shuffled his hands. "Let's just get this story moving. I'm not your culprit, everybody knows that. Move on."

It was Mac's turn to be amused. This guy really wanted to see what Mac was up to.

So did Mac. The inkling shaking around at the back of his head was that Junior was the guy. It all pointed in his direction, but he still hadn't had that moment of inspiration that brought it all together. That single piece of evidence. The last piece of the puzzle. Junior would clearly let anyone take the fall. Mac needed to coax him out of the bushes.

The man was clearly his father's son. He didn't care about anyone or anything but himself and money.

"This locked room doesn't seem to have any mystery," Junior said. He stood but remained nonchalant and disinterested.

Nobody took Mac seriously but, then again, nobody left. Although Blinkman's piece might be helping on that front.

The cops outside, all these people inside. The helicopters buzzing above. The walls were closing in on Mac and he didn't have an answer. He'd been framed and justice was a concept not a reality. Things were not going to end well.

Mac imagined springing up and running across the table with a leap then pummeling Junior. In his head, the idea of violence felt good. Gave Mac a jolt of hope. Maybe he should do it. Maybe he should stop spinning in circles and solve the case.

Finally, Mac said, "You're absolutely correct. There is no mystery."

Zoey and Blinkman nodded along.

Might as well go ahead and say it, "Because you're the one responsible for your father's murder."

Feeling desperate, Mac pulled out his phone. "Look at this." He pulled up the footage proving Mac arrived late. "I show up after Filmore is dead. You have manipulated the business and the trust to screw your sister. You're the only one with motive. Sheriff, you should be arresting Junior."

Junior sat, nary a movement.

"We've looked into him," the sheriff said. "He didn't do this."

"Then who did it?"

"Fuenteovejuna did it. It was Cuyamaca." Olivera was still but his back was straight.

"I don't believe the people would do this." Sheriff always sticking up for the town.

"They didn't. In the end, it was the land. It was the ancestors."

"Ghosts?" Delilah sounded like she found a plot twist for her podcast.

"Sure. Did he push himself over? Did the ancestors do it?" Olivera was serious. "Junior, you better watch out. If you want to do the same thing, the land will do the same to you."

"You're crazy, viejo," Junior said.

"It wasn't me and it wasn't you. The spirits rose and

took him. The pendejo had to have the mine. 'Easy money,' Filmore said. It was Cuyamaca. Cuyamaca took Filmore and Cuyamaca will take you, Junior."

"That's voodoo."

"No. It is truth. It has begun."

"That's some haunted shit." Junior still hadn't moved from his spot.

"You are damn right," Olivera said with more verve than he'd mustered during the whole affair. "The ancestors will protect the future if we will not."

A rumbling traveled down the hill and an earthquake rumbled the guests. The chandelier swayed ceiling to ceiling and the bookshelves cleared. Then the house trembled, and mud exploded through the front door and windows crashed. Earth, rocks and water flowed. The house filled with debris and the sheriff ran to check on his men.

With the opening Mac considered hoofing it again.

Junior and Delilah investigated the damage to the house inside and out. Olivera went with the sheriff.

Mac would face his fate. It was going down now.

Where were Zoey and Blinkman? Mac panicked. He ran to look behind the house. Maybe they were taken away in the flow. As the mud breached the home, the first thing that occurred to Mac was that they were in danger.

"Zoey! Blink!" Mac searched the backyard. They were nowhere to be found. Not in the pool. Not down the valley by the split oak. They weren't around the side of the house. It was still raining, and visibility wasn't great, but the mud hadn't even reached that far.

He entered the back of the house, working through the ankle high mud. He looked under the table. No one.

As he entered the living room, it was Zoey's voice. "Mac!"

He looked up and on the top landing was Zoey, smiling and holding up a document. "We've got it!"

Then a shout from the office direction, "There's more, Mac." Blinkman.

Junior charged through the broken bay window as

Mac's foot landed on the bottom step. Junior took three charging strides through the mud and tackled Mac.

Mac scrambled but Junior put a flat-handed right cross on his ear. It knocked Mac dizzy and his ear screamed and rattled with a high-pitched tone.

"You little fuckers will not keep this from me," Junior said. He grabbed Mac's hair and Mac donkey kicked before Junior could slam his face in the stair.

Mac twisted and rabbit punched Junior in the nose. Tears sprung from Junior's eyes as he swung uselessly against Mac's upraised, blocking arms.

"How in the holy hell did we get to this?" The sheriff watched from the bay window, hands on his hips, exasperated. He threw a hand at the two squabblers indicating to his deputies to separate the two, who were dragged apart.

The mud splattered fighters panted as the sheriff held the countenance of contemplation when he finally said, "Junior, I do believe these fisticuffs are a tell."

Delilah returned oblivious to the row and announced from the front yard while wiping her hands, "The horses are fine. A little spooked but the mud flow missed the stable completely." She came up next to the sheriff and stopped at the sight of Junior and Mac huffing, puffing and muddy. "It is true."

This landslide knocked loose more than debris. These Filmores had lost their veneer of perfection. The filter was stripped, if for the moment.

Junior looked around for someone to take his side. "I had nothing to do with Dad's murder. I was tired of this PI and his friends. I had to do something about it."

"Like have a fight?"

"It's as good a way as any."

Delilah was unimpressed. "You are an idiot."

Junior had no answer to that. At least, he felt no need to continue this line of conversation.

Blinkman and Zoey came walking down the stairs.

"What were you doing up there?"

"Running from the mud," Blinkman said as a matter of fact. Zoey nodded along. Neither offered anything more, they stopped at the mid-landing of the stairs. Blinkman shook his head at the muddy pair below with what might have been a bit of pride. Zoey, too, was impressed but less so.

"Let's cuff up Macondo. I've had enough of this."

Looking between them all, Mac said, "What about Junior?"

The sheriff looked like he was answering a third grader, "He didn't kill his father, he just wants a business deal same as his dad."

The sheriff's phone blinged with a text which he read, then said without looking at any of them, "See you at the station." The sheriff turned and walked to his cruiser. It was in mud up to nearly the rims of the tires, but he looked confident he was moving on. Which proved to be true when he backed right out, practically did a j-turn at the fire road and gunned it toward the highway.

Zoey watched as the two deputies loaded Mac into their cruiser. Blinkman already sat in the Bronco, engine idling.

Delilah considered Mac in the back of the squad car and looked inexplicably horny.

Olivera broke her revelry, if that's what you want to call it. "I'm not going into town. Can I borrow a horse?"

Without a beat, Delilah passed Zoey and headed toward the stables saying, "Yes, I'll help you saddle her."

"Don't you want to know how this ends up?" Zoey said to their backs.

Barely turning around to answer, Olivera siad, "I already know. The trees live on, and the mountains don't care about our squabbles." Then he disappeared into the barn.

The cruiser bounced slowly toward the highway.

"You really think I did this?" Mac said to the two cops up front.

"Doesn't matter, Macondo. We're doing our jobs." The driver.

The passenger raised an eyebrow, nodded and sucked his teeth.

"Man, you guys are couple of Oreos. Brown on the outside and white on the inside." Mac didn't usually play it like that, but things were getting a little desperate. After that last night in the jail, he didn't think he'd make it through this one. He took a chance. The guy driving looked Latino, and the tooth sucker was a black guy. The tooth sucker laughed silently.

"Do you think we are rookies?" the driver said with a glance in the rear-view mirror. "We show up, do our ten. Pick up overtime if we can and get the fuck out. This. Right here. This is justice. Two brown brothers making good money busting heads. We don't write the rules, Macondo. We do what we're told, collect a paycheck then collect our pensions."

"Work the clock," shotgun said.

"Work the clock," the driver said. "Now shut the fuck up."

Mac didn't get anywhere with them. If the system was full of a bunch of people like these two, who don't ask questions, he was going down the river. He could see it. Corruption wasn't one big event; it was a million tiny instances that rot the framework. Looking the other way. Ignoring what was right for what was convenient.

Swerving through the hills along the highway Mac picked up the Bronco following them, appearing and disappearing like a specter. They were no illusion, those two. They'd be there just like the oaks and pignons out in that forest.

The patrol car hit the straight away leading into town and Mac knew why the sheriff got out ahead of them, each side of the highway had a handful of satellite news vans. That's when he recognized a chop and hum of helicopters again. He hadn't clocked them earlier and Mac wasn't sure if that was because he was caught up in his thoughts or, at home, the ghetto birds were simply a constant.

As they pulled up to the station, there was a scrum of

reporters and cameras jostling to improve their position. The chase gave them time to prepare for the inevitable capture and return of the vaunted criminal, Edward Macondo.

This time was different. There was no surprise to cloud Mac's perception. Clear eyed, the road was rocky. No easy exits. It started here. Again. The deputies parked in the front to facilitate a perp walk. Perception is reality. As they escorted Mac, as that perp, from the plastic back seat of the police cruiser, the frenzy for information, for a bite, escalated.

Making matters worse, the press had now done their homework.

Macondo, what would your father say about this? — Are the allegations true? — Has the LAPD rescinded your award? — Was your escape a plan to harm Filmore's children, as well?

He remained stoic and walked with a straight back, high chin and solid gait. Mac would make his family proud. He wouldn't embarrass them with complaints and pleas of innocence. Words were for the courts, and he would save his voice for when it mattered most.

Zoey wasn't so proud. Later, Mac even admitted, she was a little brave to face those sharks. She confessed to quick thumb work on her phone setting up socials for a new business.

She exited the Bronco while Blinkman slowed to a stop and held up a fistful of papers. "This is a set up. We have the documents to prove it."

Mac was thinking maybe a little help now and then wasn't a bad thing.

"There will be a link to the entire treasure trove shortly on our socials: Helping Hands Detective Agency."

Blinkman came around the end of the Bronco to join Zoey. He clasped his hands in front of himself and said, "More importantly, we have video posted proving Mac arrived after the incident." He looked over at Zoey, who nodded.

"These documents will detail cause, opportunity and

motive for Junior Filmore. However, we also have proof the ADA is on the payroll and pursuing this case against Edward Macondo strictly out of self-interest."

"Are you alleging she's been paid off?" a young reporter said.

"I am."

"Why would she do that? The judge will throw out the case." Another reporter wasn't so sure.

"They simply need attention elsewhere while they complete the real business."

"Which is?" No reporter was going to take this easily.

Now the sheriff jumped in. "There's more to come. Rest assured; we will keep you apprised of the situation."

He corralled Mac, the officers, Zoey and Blink straight into the station.

Once the doors were securely closed, he turned and said, "Take the cuffs off of him."

As the driver took off Mac's hand cuffs, the sheriff took a seat on a corner of one of the old metal desks that filled the room and said, "You sure stirred up some shit, Macondo."

"It's what I do."

"Did you know about all this radioactive stuff all along?"

"We'd been sniffing around it but didn't know for sure until we found the proof at the house," Blink said.

"It probably won't be admissible in court."

"The information just needs to be out. The people around here will stop it. That's why he didn't want it getting out." The sheriff stood. "Probably get me a bunch of tree hugger activists around here now."

"Better than glowing waste," Zoey said.

"What are you going to do about the Assistant District Attorney?"

"That one will take a fair amount of due process, but she'll be done chasing you. Count on it."

"That's exactly what I'm counting on."

"Obviously, I won't be seeking charges in all of this

against you, Macondo, but I recommend you get out of town and stay the hell out."

"Don't have to tell us twice," Blinkman said.

Zoey agreed with a, "Let's go."

The driver unlocked and opened the door. Mac followed his friends through the door and said, "Let's drop in the diner for a piece of that pie first."

Chapter Thirty-Six

The Helping Hands Scene

A new article came out regarding the DDT, and it only got worse. Not only were they dropping drums indiscriminately, but they were also unloading the stuff straight into the water, thousands of gallons at a time. Along with the poison, there was radioactive waste, explosives and all sorts of other stuff dumped off the coast including three million metric tons of petroleum waste. This story wasn't going away anytime soon.

The Assistant District Attorney was in the midst of a Grand Jury investigation on corruption charges and Junior's underground storage facility was going through proper channels. Surprisingly, there was a group of Cuyamaca citizens who were staunch supporters of the idea. They wanted the influx of cash. Of course, others fought just as hard to stop it. Just as a democracy should function.

Delilah hadn't reached out, but something told Mac it wasn't the last he'd see of her. She was just cooling her jets.

Onto the scene at hand, Mac was behind his desk, feet up on the windowsill contemplating the street outside and attempting to ignore his cohorts who currently occupied the rest of the little space in his office.

"I'm thinking," said Zoey. "We should take the office adjacent and knock a door into the wall."

Mac swung his attention back inside. "That's Knack's office."

"He's semi-retired anyway." Zoey knocked on the walls looking for the studs. "Probably lathe and plaster." She smoothed her palm along the wall then swung her hands in a rectangle. "The door could go right about here." She looked over her shoulder beaming.

Blink watched the interplay and said, “I don’t need a desk. I’m the field guy. Besides, I’m semi-retired, too.”

Mac had some figuring to do.

The Helping Hands Detective Agency meant he had two partners to fit into the mix.

ACKNOWLEDGMENTS

Thank you, dear reader, for investing your time and imagination on Mac and crew. More to come!

Tina, thank you for sharing your life and your laughs with me.

Joe and Mike, you've heard all of these, but remember, they can't stop you if you don't quit.

Many people read, commented, and improved this book: Thank you.

See you next time!

About the Author

If Jeffrey Messineo isn't hunkered down writing his latest thriller, he is probably reading one. His love of blind curves and unexpected twists expands beyond the page to the local hiking trails where he invents many of his story concepts. Having read *Bumped Off*, try *California Hustle* or *Reaping Independence*, both thrillers. He is working on a new novel.

Sign up for Jeffrey's Newsletter

at

JeffreyMessineo.com

And I'll send you a short story.

You can also follow

On Twitter: @jeffmessineo

On Facebook: https://facebook.com/JeffreyMessineo

If you enjoyed *Bumped Off*, please tell a friend!

Or, if you're of the persuasion, take a moment to star or write a review of this book on Amazon and/or Goodreads.

www.ingramcontent.com/pod-product-compliance
Lightning Source LLC
Chambersburg PA
CBHW020633260626
47157CB00008B/2718